Run With Wolves

Bailey Rickett

Contents

Running with the wolves.

W ith the grass fresh and green, new life was appearing all around and not just from the earth. Birds fluttered around their nests, the need to feed their newly hatched young programmed into their instincts as much as the ability to breath. Streams and rivers flowed unbothered by the winters frozen hold and beneath the surface there was as much going on in the water as on land.

Yet with all this beauty going on, the scene at the forest edge was anything but.

It had been a long hard winter for the wolves who stuck around to brave the worst of it and the survivors were only just starting to get some condition back to their coats. Most were still matted with the last of their winter fur coming free to reveal a renewed glossy covering and bones that had been come close to the skin started to disappear. That was with thanks to meals like the one they were currently gorging themselves on became more abundant.

The deer hadn't stood a chance, heavily pregnant, she had no way of outrunning the starved creatures and it was not one life that was taken with this kill, but two. It didn't matter to the wolves who all ripped and tore at her still warm flesh.

Licking the blood and stray bits of meat from my chest, I understood the balance of life. Some must die for others to live, there was no point in getting sentimental over it. After all it was the reason why I lived amongst the wolves.

The human side of me had to 'die' for another to live.

Sitting on the warm rock by the stream in the mid-morning sun, the sounds of their frenzied feeding began to lessen and I continued to groom myself, not needed to wonder what kind of monster I would look like. My reflection was clear in the still water below me as if I had been looking into a mirror. White fur was tainted pink, in parts I couldn't reach, red, while that sly grin all wolves possessed was smiling back at me.

My wolf was happy here, she belonged and had a place; a purpose.

The scrape of a nail against stone had me turning around to see our leader, our Alpha, coming over to be with me. I was a guest in their pack and my tail wagged slowly as my ears flattened so as she rubbed herself alongside me I submissively licked her chin.

I lived as one of them despite the fact they knew I wasn't.

The least I could do to thank them for this hospitality was show the dominant ones the respect they deserved and I know they appreciate it. I have proved myself to them as they have proved themselves to me, we are pack, family and she flopped down beside me as if using me for a cushion. I playfully mouthed her leg as her year old pup came to join us and spying my invitation to play jumped on the pair of us. He tugs on her ear a little to roughly, the growl a warning and he settled down squeezing between us.

The afternoon would be much the same.

Contrary to what you may think, this is not a story simply about the wolves of this land. My name is Bianca Lovett and while I appear to be one of them, I am so much more.

I am a wolf-shifter. A werewolf; call it what you will.

A human hidden in wolfs clothing.

Five years ago on my sixteenth birthday, I was due to undergo my first shift. Sixteen is a coming of age for shifters, and mine was bigger than most.

I met my mate.

A mate is the one person destiny has chosen for you; a soul mate. In the fairy tales I grew up with, this person is supposed to love you, protect you - but instead he rejected me and I was left for dead.

That was his first mistake.

One.

S miles, balloons, a steady flow of 'Happy Birthday', the feeling of love and shared happiness; all these things surround me. To an outsider it could be overwhelming but I'm used to it now. Sixteen years of celebrating nearly every birthday like it's a wedding reception will shake off anyone's fear of being the center of attention and don't think I'm complaining.

I love it.

I love everyone here.

They are my pack, my family, so how could they not all be invited to celebrate my birthday? Besides, for anyone's sixteenth, we as wolf-shifters make it a big deal. It is a coming of age when we can fully connect to our inner beast and have the ability to shift for the first time. The irony of it all is after what is generally the best birthday you will ever have; there is a chance of dying. It rarely happens and never has in our pack but that fear is always there.

Sometimes you just can't connect to your wolf.

You're either not mentally or physically strong enough to handle the first shift and as my parents are the current alpha couple I was born with an advantage. One day, maybe, I will follow in their footsteps, but until then I am happy just being their daughter. Besides, before I reach the maturity to even challenge for the position, the reality is my parents would have probably been replaced. I don't mean killed or anything horrible, rules are in place to stop that from happening although it still does from to time. An Alpha knows when their time is up and who will be the one taking the position without the bloodshed having to occur.

"Bianca you look gorgeous!" Leanna my best friend, cousin and partner in crime came running over, finally here. Two hours late is actually pretty good timing as far as she is concerned. "That white dress makes you look like a goddess and is that a real diamond on your neck?"

Self consciously I touched the jewel, it was a 3ct masterpiece and little did she know come her own sixteenth in a three months time, she'd be getting a ruby. Mum had picked up a similar piece for her deciding to go with our birthstones for gifts this year.

"Thanks and yes it is. It's all Mum" I twirled slightly, the Grecian style gown was complimented with the curly up-do of my dark brown hair and thanks to the light tanning of my skin, I could finally wear white without looking like I was dressing up as a ghost. It was somehting that bothered my paler cousin no end and if her lack of a tan is her only issue, she's doing well.

"Wish some of the fashion gene got passed into my Mum. She wanted me to wear something from her wardrobe. I don't do floral or knee length" She rolled her eyes as I knew she would have done to Aunt Alice's suggestions at the time.

"I've noticed. Did you forget your pants with that?" I teased raising my eyebrow as I observed the red mini dress that barely covered her ass cheeks. Somehow she managed to keep it looking classy rather than trashy.

"God you sound like her" Leanna poked me in the arm a little hard yet both laughing we meet up with our friends by the dance floor ready to get the party started.

-

"Are you having a good time darling?" Dad is a little drunk as he takes me away from my friends to a slightly less populated area of the dance floor and despite the base heavy remix of Britney Spears's hit, he dances with me more traditionally. Once the DJ spots him in the crowd, something more appropriate for his style takes over and I have to giggle as around us everyone groans.

"The best Daddy" From where we swayed, he kissed my forehead smiling and had I been some kind of cat shifting species, I'd be purring.

"I'm glad princess. Just be ready as in two days the biggest test of your life will be happening" My smile disappeared for a second, was I really ready for this? "And you will be a strong, proud shifter. Do not doubt yourself"

Spying Mum with Aunt Alice nearby he let me go back to my friends while he grabbed her and the pair acting like teenagers themselves, did a bad impersonation of the tango past us. That's my parents for you and I think it was why they were so successful leading us as a pack.

The packs interests were always first, never their own and it was not always about business. They could relax amongst us if their title did not matter and Dad always told me it didn't.

"We're a pack, a unit. To think any of us are different or special will only fuel jealously and hatred, leaving us to fall apart. An equal pack is a strong pack."

They kept us all in line, leading as Alpha's were intended. We were well respected within the shifter community because of how they ran things and it was how it had always been here. Little had changed since the days of the first Alpha's and it was expected his great great grandson would be the one to take over from my Dad when he matured.

-

It was nearly dawn by the time the last person left and bed had never felt so good, even if Leanna already took up the majority of it.

"Hey Bee?'

"Yeah Anna?"

"Are you scared for the shifting?"

Changed into our pajama's, I rolled to face her. The shadows of the room made her pale skin almost glow while her eyes were dark hollows. Already spooked by her question, I closed my eyes.

"Yeah but I'm kind of excited too"

She sighed; resting her arm over her forehead I could feel her fear.

"Well once you get through it, you have to be there for me ok? I just have this feeling that something bad is going to happen, like I'm going to die"

"Stop being so dramatic" Yet as we fell asleep I couldn't help share her worries.

-

Standing out in the forest just outside our town, we all gathered waiting as the dusk turned to night and as the last lazy rays of the sun disappeared on the horizon, the first star appeared in the sky.

This was it; I was finally going to be a shifter.

"Ready sweet heart?" Dad hugged me briefly, smiling at Mum as she rubbed my back in that soothing way only Mothers can do.

"No" Throwing up was something I was ready for, this? No.

"Of course you are" Mum squeezed my shoulders and Leanna took her place as she leapt towards me, nearly tackling me to the ground. Her doubts from the night of the party had clearly gone yet they were all I could think about.

"Our lil Binky is all grown up" She fake sobbed, and I only glared at her in response. I hated being called Binky, when we were little she could never say Bianca so it kind of stuck as a nickname now.

"You won't be teasing me when I can shift" I warned, smirking as her face fell for a second.

"Of course I will, I've been saving my flea jokes for you" Dam she was quick and before I could respond Dad coughed to get our attention. Two wolves emerged from the forest and nodding at them, he glanced up to the sky before moving to shift too. When he returned as the large brown and white wolf, it was the first time I've ever been scared seeing him.

"You'll be fine" Mum whispered in my ear, kissing my temple the chorus of my immediate family sounded through the night from all around us, calling to my own wolf to come out. The howl sent a shiver up my spine and looking at Leanne she finally appeared to be as nervous as I felt, but still managed to discreetly give me the thumbs up as pins and needles started to tingle in my abdomen, up my chest and spread through my body like a virus.

The stabs got sharper and falling to my knees Mum still stood by me, comforting the human while my Dad called to the wolf. The clearing seemed to sizzle with the anticipation of what was about to happen and as the pain got to much I couldn't stop screaming. I dropped to all fours, my hands digging into the earth as I threw my head up to the sky where the moon was just rising over the treetops and looking back to the dirt, I saw her.

We all take pride of our wolf form, the magic gift of shifting something we know to appreciate and seeing her for the first time, I understood it.

She was beautiful and all mine.

Her fur was almost cream, a dark dusting of black and grey along her back, neck and tail yet her chest and face was completely white. The pattern was stunning and my pain left me as her dark brown eyes stared into my own; judging me.

Was I worthy to have such a proud wolf?

Everyone seemed to disappear from around us as she hesitantly came forward; her caution was clear, never coming straight to me instead weaving left and right. Dad told me this would happen and finally she stopped before me. Her head lowered with that predatory assessment I had seen so many times before amongst the wolves.

I knew what to do, I had to connect to her and as I managed to get some awareness of my own body back I started to reach for her until my Mums screams ruined the peace that settled between us. My wolf looked just as alarmed as I did, her head shooting up startled. The wolf's ears danced on top of her head, looking around as if waiting for something to jump out and grab us. Even worse was worried she'd reject me and I'd be left to deal with the pain alone. Leanna had almost been right, if my wolf left - I'd be fighting for my life.

"They're not connected, we can't stop! It could kill her!" Mum yelled desperately and in that second I became aware something was seriously wrong.

"We have to, the pack is under attack. We are vulnerable out here and need to get back to them" Another voice yelled.

It was like they were speaking a new language I hadn't learnt and my wolf leapt at me causing a new pain to rip through my chest as every bone in my body seemed to crack, moving to find a new positions as my skin was on fire and my heart began to beat to a new pace.

"Alphas, they're here"

Who is here?

I wanted to move, to wake up but something felt different and the new voice in my head told me to stay. Every instinct I had told me to listen to it and so I didn't move a muscle. I wasn't even sure that I could, pain vibrated through me like electrical shocks while yelps echoed through the night. Alongside the savage growls of wolves fighting there were the screams of humans. The stench of blood and fear came next.

These things the new part of me found exciting, tempting, but still she did nothing.

Wait. He's coming.

I had no idea who he was, more worried that she was going for self preservation than helpig her pack. Afterall, if her vessel died she died. My instinct was to go and help, fight - only she had control of my body. Maybe she didn't know what to do with it, maybe something went wrong with our connection. I was certain Leanna's fear be true now, only I'm the one dying.

Something changed in her mind, the calm and certainty that had been present vanished and soon after so did she. Finally I was able to open my eyes and I wished I hadn't. I was quick to identify my pack, Leanna and finally my father where he was still fighting, but it was three on one.

With a groan I stood, surprised to find myself still human. I was meant to shift when we connect, my Alpha was meant to guide me back into control of my body to learn how to turn back human.

Why wasn't I changed? Did I die? Was I imagining all of this? Did I imagine her?

"D-dad?" I croaked, my voice was hoarse as my throat still felt misplaced. He didn't hear me, how could he over the noise of the fight and taking a step I fell back down just as the black wolf got the deadliest grip of all causing the fight to end.

Dad fell to the ground, his paw twitching slightly before there was nothing and gasping I struggled to get to his side, practically crawling on all fours through the dirt to get to him.

Run.

She was back there in my mind, her order clear. I didn't understand how this was happening if I hadn't actually shifted yet or how could she be so cruel. I coulnd't leave my Dad.

Run.

Again the voice demanded that I run but I didn't care; getting to my Dad was more important.

"Grab the girl!" I just made it to his wolf and grabbing onto his fur I couldn't keep silent, my cries coming out in screaming gasps and her voice was blocked out from my mind.

He couldn't be dead.

Looking around I saw the wolf form of my Mum by Leanna who just as still on the dew covered grassed beside her. This was a joke, a horrible cruel joke.

It had to be.

"No, no no no!" I couldn't stop shaking and rough hands grabbed my waist, pulling my away from Dad which only sent me into complete hysteria.

"Shut up!" He growled, the hard impact of his fist on my cheek sent me back into the ground with a thud, but I couldn't stop crying even if I tried after that.

He's here.

She spoke up again, the hollow feeling in my chest that I was already learning to associate with her, returning as she seemed to come and go within me. Her words were cold, scared even and I had no idea what was going on.

Did she know something I didn't?

"Did she shift?" The mans voice wasn't as cruel as the others, if anything it offered some kind of comfort to me in all this madness, but my wolf didn't agree. If I could see her she would be shrinking down low ready to defend herself and I felt myself tensing as her mood connected to mine.

We're trapped.

"No Sir, we stopped them before it could happen," Opening my eyes, it was the one who hit me speaking up and seeing me move, he grabbed my hair and yanked me back to my feet, sniffing the air around me as he did so. "There is nothing wolf about her."

"Good. We got here in time then." He emerged from the shadows as if he had been apart of them and as he walked towards us he was rubbing the back of his neck awkwardly. There was a certain presence that followed him meaning only one thing.

He was an Alpha.

Unlike my father whose position seemed to add to his natural charm, this mans aura was dark, troubled and it scared me more than anything else that had just gone on. Distracted the wolf took over, assessing each of them that surrounded us, avoiding their leader and as if sensing my confusion, she filled me in.

Mate.

She watched his movements as if he were a piece of art to be studied, taking over my mind which left me feeling suffocated as every scent around us was locked into her memory, especially his and then she left me to deal with it alone.

Why wasn't she happy to see him? Surely he was here to help us?

"Yes Alpha, nothing more than a human."

He stopped in front of me and grabbing my chin, his fingers moved my face up to look at him properly yet he didn't actually hurt me as I was expecting. I dont know why I would think that, mates don't hurt mates. "Bianca I presume?"

"Answer when he talks to you" The hand that had hit me before did so again and I dropped down to my knees from the pressure, crying out in the process. My body was trembling with fear and pain, longing for my Mum to get up unharmed and hold me or for Leanna to try convincing me this was a dream.

Better yet for my mate to help me, but no relief or assistance came.

"Why? Why are you doing this?" I almost begged through gritted teeth as the pain throbbed in time to my heartbeat sending me into another round of panic attacks.

"Do you recognize what I am to you, that I'm your mate?"

Lie.

Following her instructions I shook my head.

"Still human so I guess you wouldn't be able to tell yet and that will actually make this easier for you" He muttered bitterly with a hint of regret on his words. "Would you like to know the one destined to love you would do this?"

I wasn't sure if I should answer with the sarcasm in his tone and I was left with a sense of dread that took over my fear and heartache for my family. Squatting in front of me, his dark eyes looked troubled as he seemed to be looking for something in my own, yet the part of me that was my wolf seemed to shrink back even further and I only nodded in response.

My wolf didn't want to be found, she didn't want him knowing she was with me.

The sadness turned to determination, a haunting look that proved he was void of any true emotion and that his heart was as dark as his soul.

How did the fates match me to him? What did I do to deserve this?

"Well mate, five years ago just before I was due to shift for the first time a gypsy gave me a warning. My own father would try to kill me by stopping me from completing that first shifting process and she was right. He did try. Only because I was expecting it, he had no chance and as a fresh wolf, I killed him and the Alpha, my Uncle, which left me as the pack leader."

Something was bothering him, I could tell by his agitated movements that were soon became an obvious need to touch me. I couldn't protest as he held me against his chest, as if we both knew it would be the first and last time for such contact.

My wolf only buried deeper, but her presence was more prominent in my mind rather than body like she knew what was happening already and didn't want to miss out on the contact while we had it. None of this was making sense, she should want to be with her mate and he should want to be with me.

"After I killed them, I went back to the gypsy and you know what she told me next? Have a guess mate"

"I don't know" I stuttered, his grip increasing as I was practically being crushed against him. There was nothing affectionate about it, it was only desperate and clingy. What ever was going on in his twisted mind was finding release in the way he held me yet as he went to speak, anger and betrayal filled his voice. It only broke my heart more, especially once I heard what he had to say.

"My mate, that being you Bianca, would be the one to kill me on the day we first met and I just can't let that happen."

Everything became clear in that moment and I finally understood what was happening.

He was going to kill me.

>> Bianca's picture.

Two.

I couldn't breathe, I couldn't move and releasing me I was then passed to one of the others who gripped my arms so tightly I was certain the bone was going to start cracking.

"Kill you?" I hated how dumb I sounded; like they were the first words I'd ever learned to speak. It wasn't just my body that wanted to shut down, but my mind too. Why would I have ever want to kill him? Sure I didn't know him, but he was mine. What ever he was missing, I'd make up for - he was my other half.

Mates don't kill mates.

"After managing to work out who actually were, I made sure there would be no way for you or your pack to succeed. You don't wait for the predator to hunt you down. You make them the prey!"

Regret seemed to appear on his face as he hesitated, this wasn't right and he knew it. My eyes couldn't leave him as he came closer, the pull he had over me threatened to take over what was left of my senses and as awkward as it would be, I wanted to be held by him again.

Just for a moment.

So did my wolf and I recognise that was where this feeling was coming from. If we never connected, how was this even possible? She shouldn't be able to influence me like this, she shouldn't be there at all. I wanted my Dad back to explain it to me, I needed someone to explain this part to me, but clearly it wasn't going to happen anytime soon. The more obsessed I became thinking about her, the more she turned away and I was left fending for myself.

"No hard feelings mate, but I'd rather you than me." He snapped, turning to leave.

"Please, please don't leave me. We can sort this out!" There wasn't a second of hesitation and instead he laughed at my misery as he walked away - leaving me with his men.

He couldn't kill his mate, but his pack could.

Coward.

My wolf was back, her hatred for him now spreading through me in the same way a vine can take over a wall. Her determination was almost admirable, but I just didn't possess the ability to process it all. Maybe that was why she had managed to take control of me so easily?

"Such a shame, pretty little thing aren't you?" Something was slipped over my head, blocking the four men out of sight as my senses tried to work out what was going on around me. With no hope of that happening, fear and panic took over and instinctively I started to kick out to try and get free of the iron like grip holding me in place.

It was no use and once the first punch landed, the kicks soon followed and my body was beaten like a punching bag, tossed without mercy around in the dirt. By the end I was going in and out of consciousness. Even my wolf deserted me, or maybe she was still there; I couldn't tell.

The bag over my head was cotton, making it hard to breath with each forced gasp that my lungs weren't willing to process and a mixture of sweat and blood covered my face and filled my mouth.

I doubt there was a part of me not broken.

"Throw her over the ledge. If anyone finds her body at least the damage can be blamed on the fall." One commanded.

"Let the wild animals out there have at her, maybe an eagle or something will finish ripping her apart and destroy the evidence." They all liked that comment, their murms of agreement surronding me. In my mind I wanted to roll over, try and release the ache in my side only that was impossible. I was paralysed.

"She's barely breathing as it is, the fall will finish her off. Let's go clean up the mess of the others." They all joked around, soon talking about getting back home and wanting to forget this.

If only I had the luxury to do the same.

I will save us.

I wish I knew just how she planned on doing that as right now it only seemed impossible. There was something about hearing her again that soothed me and as the bag was removed off my head, I couldn't even manage to enjoy the fresh air. or spit out the grit in my mouth. Then feeling of the earth beneath me seemed to disappear and was instead replaced with the feeling of floating, of flying.

The peace that came with it was short lived as instead every fibre of my body felt as if it was on fire, being shredded by an invisible force and I couldn't even cry out as my voice was gone. I never even got the chance to feel the impact of hitting the ground or maybe I did and it just never compared to the agony I was already in.

None of that mattered though as I slipped into the darkness of my mind, and it was there I caught a fleeting glimpse of my wolf greeting me. Even that didn't help me hold on until there was just nothing.

-

The first time I regained consciousness my wolf had already moved us from the remains of my family. I dont know how I managed to shift, I couldn't remember any of it apart from the pain of being beaten. She was in control and with no guidance from my Dad or any Alpha figure I had no hope in getting it back.

I didn't really want it anyway.

I know as a wolf we heal faster, whatever magic that lets us exists is magnified as the beast, but even that left room for questioning as we'd clearly gone some distance. I also knew she wouldn't be able to heal all of my aches, the majority were not physical and I was certain my heart was beating at a new, broken pace.

My family.

My mate.

I felt hazy with the pain all over again.

I will look after us.

With those words I let go, happy in the nothingness that waited for me. The second time I woke, she was resting by a river, the water was still like a glass - peaceful. The longer I had control of my mind the darker my thoughts got, like how I wanted to die.

No.

If I die, she dies and my wolf wasn't wanting another second of those thoughts in our mind and she took over, pushing me out of our being by force. One thing you can't really learn was how to share one body when two souls inhabited it. We get told what to expect, we see our family living at peace with theirs and it's all part of the process of becoming a new shifter.

There was no one here to guide me now, and I was at her mercy.

The third time it was on her conditions and she finally permitted me to have some say in our movements. I had no idea where we actually were or what to do so it was easier for both of us if I merely went along for the ride. She was happy with this, it suited her plans better.

Along the way she spoke to me, trying to comfort me as I struggled with the loss left behind. It helped she was hurting too. She understood the meaning of mates more than I ever could and the longer I let her control us, the better for my human form as she explained to me the injuries inflicted were not passed onto the wolf.

She had been able to anticipate the attack and she held off from completing the ritual for that very reason.

She was smart, a survivor. I had wondered if I was worthy of a wolf like her and I now knew I wasn't.

-

Her instincts were to seek out her own kind, not shifters as I thought, but actual wolves. She didn't trust my kind; she didn't trust humans. The animals were all that was left and it felt like days before we had gone far enough to locate them. Imagine being in your body, but unable to control your movements. Looking out into the world like you were watching a movie in real time, unable to speak or communicate with those around you as you have no voice. Her mind was set on survival and as the first wolf spotted her, spotted us, she froze in her tracks.

One turned into three, who turned in seven. The line of wolves were intimidating, shifters rarely interacted with their animal counterparts. Typically they were scared of us; their senses told them of danger and to be cautious.

Being human, what reason did we have to take the time to mess around with these wild animals? It wasn't like we were suddenly Doctor Doolittle and could talk to them; understand their language any better than our own. Sure we understood body language, but even when we ran as a pack it was all rather - human.

Civilised.

I had only watched my pack together, not being a shifter yet I wasn't able to run with them though I know it wasn't anything like what I was about to experience. This could turn nasty, wolves were territorial and we were as Leanna would say, 'all up in their grill' right now.

The world disappeared as she closed her eyes, her muzzle pointed to the sky she called out to them. Her howl was hypnotic, beautiful and looking back, they hadn't moved.They just stood there, staring with that curious judging look all wolves managed to perfect.

And then they all came sprinting towards us.

The growls and whines met our ears when they were still a few meters away and the closer the got the more nervous I became. I wanted to run the other way, then I realised they did too. They could sense it now; her smell was different to what they would have known.

The second my confidence began to grow, that maybe we could do this the brown wolf charged, the snapping of her jaws mostly in show and my wolf wasn't intimidated at the display of dominance. My Dad once told me, you born to be an alpha or you were born to be one of the pack; it was born not learnt. This wolf in front of us would have been more dominant than her litter mates, not necassarily meaner, but she would know how to throw her weight around and the weaker ones would have followed her like they do now.

The one identified as Alpha stood side by side againt my wolf, curious more than alarmed. Her tail was curled in dominance as her bulk seemed to grow in size as she laid down the law. We offered her no physical challenge, instead a weird aura of calm seemed to be generated from us, setting the others at ease. It was more commanding than any of the others were capable of, so not understanding it - they submitted to it.

Despite the effect it had on her pack, the Alpha's stance never altered and planning her next move carefully, my wolf lowered her ears against her skull as her tag wagged low against the dirt, licking around the muzzles of the most dominant, almost begging.

Not begging, submitting.

They didn't treat us like the others who all seemed to accept us instantly now the initial threat was over. A few warning growls and another warning snap of those powerful jaws had us practically crawling in the dirt until finally they licked us back, returning to normal. They took off back in the direction we found them in and sure enough, we ran with them.

We are safe here.

I wanted to believe her.

Would he, whoever he even was, know I was still alive? Wasn't that part of the mate bonding process? Only we never bonded, he didn't even know I had the ability to shift. The more I thought of him the more worried I became. Hiding in the wildness was not how I planned my life and for just how long we would be out here was a mystery. My wolf hadn't been trained in the ways of the human world, as we lived they bonded to us - understanding the human way while their own was forgotten. Humans were the dominant species in the shifters, not the animals we could become. They came to us as wolves and the wilderness was worn out of them.

I'd never heard of a shifter letting their creature have control like this, some had rituals of staying changed under a full moon, while others had their own theories on how to better their wolves or weaken them like the vegatarians. I was certain it would have happened before; it was just never spoken of or known about.

Instantly I looked at each of the wolves around me, looking for some sign they were not what they appeared to be while my wolf scolded me for being stupid. If there were other shifters - she would know.

-

For days we ran with them, her fitness improving. We once lagged behind them, but now kept up with eldest and after their first kill my wolf didn't hesitate in ripping apart the deer alongside them, ignoring how somewhere I still felt like I wanted to hurl.

I lost track of days, weeks, months. I had no idea how long I had been out of it for and tried to work out where the wolves even roamed near my home. The truth was, they didn't. Where she had taken us was a complete mystery and I even wondered if I had been found, left in a hospital as an unknown in a coma. At night I would listen for sounds to give this theory some reality, a distant voice of a kind old nurse talking to me to keep my company.

It never came.

My wolf didn't help; she had no reason to keep track of time. She knew night and day with no concept of human time and after three nights I found myself the same way. I had no way of checking a calendar, the only thing that could help me was the moon.

It was a full moon when it happened and I counted forty nine, or maybe it was fifty nights before I saw another one. It had to be over a month since my birthday then and I wish I hadn't known just how long it had been.

Did my parents get a funeral?

Did people look for me?

What happened to our pack?

Did Leanna really die?

I was pushed out of the front seat when I started sinking in that kind of depression, my wolf taking over and all the others sensed my pain making them all wary and stay away. Those thoughts led to why me?

It only got worse from there.

The next full moon my wolf let me shift back to me. I was curious to inspect the damage, oddly struggling to remember what walking upright on two legs felt like. My legs ached and my bones didn't adjust to the shift well at all in their weakened state, but her voice was ever present in my mind in a bid to sooth me.

Things had changed, apart from the aches - I was healed.

And I had muscles where before my arms had been thin, typical of a girl my age. Just because we're shifters, doesn't mean we are blessed with instamuscle or good looks. You want to be muscular? You work out. We were after all human.

Free to do what I wanted, I sat down naked on the grass while the wolves all eyed me up suspiciously, unsure of what they saw - only knowing that there was now a human amongst them. Their nose quivered with curiousity, I smelt like the wolf. My screams of agony as I shifted had spooked them, yet being a predator - drew them back in too.

I didn't care what they did. They were not a threat to me.

The first thing I did after discovering I was in one piece was cry. Then I screamed, ripping up chunks of the grass and threw it around me - totally loosing control until exhausted, I curled up into a ball sobbing.

I'd lost my family, my parents and my best friend.

Despite being alive, I lost my life.

I didn't want to be here, I didn't want to be alive if they weren't.

So I gave into my wolf, retreating into that furthest corner of her mind as she had done to me that night when she didn't want to be found, because that was exactly what I wanted to happen to me.

I wanted to disappear.

--

Ok, so a bit of a dull chapter, not a lot happening but I wanted a clear break between the night and the future so from now on, things will be getting more interesting! Well, I hope you think so :)

Pic is of her mate. >>>>

Three.

The morning started out much the same. The pack wandered with little reason other than to patrol their territory; a region I knew as well as I had once known my own home.

Home; even now thinking about it hurt. I missed summers by the pool, hot showers, the smell of my Mums perfume drifting from their bedroom and the leather of the furniture in my father's office.

There was no point in dwelling on the past.

We had fed well yesterday and wouldn't need to do so again for a few days and as they all carried on their way, I walked as a human through the forest. My body that had once been well looked after and slightly plump was now thin with muscle. The wolf diet wasn't as nurturing to my human like it was to the creature I let roam free and the miles I travelled alongside them had left me fit and able to endure as much as the animals.

I had no clothing, the items from years ago lost. Out here in the wilderness I didn't need them anyway. If anyone should ever come by, they would only see me covered in fur. Not that I'd even seen a person, human or shifter since that night - and I didn't want to.

My hair that had once been spoiled with salon treatments hung dry and feral around my waist. The ends were in ruins from where I had tried to hack at it with an old blade I found left at a campsite.

Thankfully spring was bringing warmer weather and I could wander as a human longer than in the winter, when the cold would snap at my skin and turn my toes red. The pack stopped by a river, a few deciding to chase the fish that teased them just under the surface while others wrestled in the grass or like me, lay in the sun. The tan I once had used to make Leanna jealous, and now even this early in the season it had already come back to me.

If she was here, I knew she'd still be jealous.

Thinking about her hurt more than thinking of home.

I wanted to hear her flea jokes and not for the first time, I wondered what would her wolf have been like? Having raced with the yearling pups earlier for no other reason than we could, would I have been faster than her? Would she have been lucky enough to find her mate young? Would he have loved her like they were supposed to?

I sat up as the familiar brown wolf came over to my side and I gently rubbed behind her ears, treating her like I did the others. To me they were each like a pet, while I lived amongst them, i was not one of them. It wouldn't be long before the Alpha was due to have her pups and I knew where we were going the second they started to head north.

She returned to the same rocky outcrop every year to give birth them and I lazily opened my eyes to watch her for a moment. Her mate was never far from her side; despite her being the more dominant one he didn't seem to mind. He would lick at her muzzle and always lay at her side, a companionship my own wolf envied.

I could feel her even now refusing to acknowledge the sight.

We talked about own mate every now and then, the darkness of his hair and eyes. How nice it had been to be held, his scent. The conversation that night was as burnt into our mind, absorbing as much detail from it as we could. My wolf blamed the gypsy, I blamed him. She thought he was a coward for not being able to kill us, and tried to convince me it was all human emotions that got in the way. It was his wolf that warned her of what was going to happen, and he alone that influenced his pack to leave rather than kill me completely.

The new information didn't help ease my mind. He killed my family and ruined my life. While the years allow wounds heal, it didn't let you forget them.

Revenge played on our minds.

Despite the help from her mate, my wolf still saw them as weak and mates are not chosen on those kinds of traits. The wolves in front of us had proved to their pack they were fit to lead, they knew when to travel to lower lands in pursuit of food for the winter and when it would be safe to head to higher ground in the summer. In some ways they reminded me of my parents, firm but fair. If discipline was needed, they'd step up and they made we all pulled our own weight while making sure the young ones were able to grow into adulthood and the elderly were not left behind.

The Alpha pair laid together, watching two of the yearlings wrestle nearby. He put his head on her back as she rolled onto her side and together they sighed content with their life.

As long as we were out here, we'd never have that peace or satisfaction. My family was dead, my mate – gone. Going back to civilisation was never going to bring them back or miraculously cure his fears of me killing him. My father had been right in saying I'd be a strong and proud shifter. I had the perfect wolf for it; it was as the human who lacked those things.

Thinking like that angered her; I don't know how she thought I had potential for much more than this. A human trapped in a wolfs body. Even free in my human form I knew she was in control and sometimes I think she didn't like it. It went against the natural order of human dominance and yet I couldn't be bothered fighting her. She was waiting for the day I would, and I knew then I'd win.

I just didn't see the point.

The pack set of after an hour or so and we followed. My feet were hardened from the brutal terrain and giving in I shifted back to one of them.

With her keener senses, it took seconds for me to smell it.

It was sweet, heavenly and saliva began to drip from my mouth without a second thought. Ignoring the pack, they kept going without me and the breeze that came down the path lured me on.

Stop.

I was in control now and my wolf wasn't impressed with my timing as we carried along the well-worn path that was barely wide enough for us. The sounds of the pack became silent behind us, being a part of them for so long; she wasn't comfortable leaving the safety it provided.

Stop. Now!

Stopping – it wasn't because she told me to, but so I could sniff the air again. I'd never been more attracted to anything in my life. It was like sugar and something in the back of mind starting to reappear, a part of me that used to be happy and care free, sitting on our kitchen bench with Leanna while Mum hummed 'You are my sunshine' and made us hot chocolates.

Chocolate; I could smell chocolate.

Then I heard the footsteps. Unlike mine they were heavy and in a set of two, crunching over the fallen leaves and small bushes that covered me.

Well done.

So not only was my wolf clever, strong and a survivor; she was sarcastic.

I froze, wondering if I should make a run for it back to the pack or stay hiding. If I ran, would they see me or follow me and if follow - would that put them in danger?

I dropped to the dirt, crawling under the bushes and the scent of chocolate was stronger now and so were a variety of other things.

Sweat, leather, water, plastic, fire.

How did I miss all of these other, stronger smells?

You'll get us killed.

Then I saw them, three men, boys more like it. Their tent was set up in one corner of the clearing and two of them sat by the fire. It was the one walking around near where I hid that caught my attention though; he had the chocolate.

A whole god dam block of it.

"Do you guys feel that?" He asked, his dark brown hair was cut short and flattened against his head. He must've taken off a hat to get it looking like that. He wasn't thin, not like I was at least and from under his sleeves his arms were shaped in the way that hard work helped create. Apart from their manly smell, there was another scent around them. It was a part of everything and I couldn't place it until the fair bellowing of a cow was heard somewhere past them

Cattle; they were farmers.

I had never known them to come this high, or maybe we'd just never stopped so close to the boundary of human lands for us to notice. It had been some time since I had seen another human, and I couldn't bring myself to move away.

"Feel what?" The youngest of the three piped up, looking around they had to be brothers. They all had dark eyes and the longer I stayed still, the more my wolf was screaming at me to leave.

"I dunno, I'm getting some strong messages!" That got them all on edge, the other two standing to look around as if they knew I was there. The youngest one seemed to sniff the air and they all grouped together, narrowing their eyes on the bushes where I hid. Humans wouldn't be able to sense me, their eyesight was limited and their sense of smell was weak.

These weren't just innocent farmers.

Shifters!

My wolf hissed at me, finally letting me in on the secret since I took so long to work it out. I groaned silently, of all the people to run into they were not simply humans – but shifters.

"Me too Jay. It's like there is one of us nearby. What's going on? No one comes up here!"

Run!

I tried to scoot backwards and with a final look at the block of brown heaven in his hand, I took off down the path and the only problem was within a minute I wasn't alone.

They weren't as fast as I was, they didn't know the land as well either and breaking out of the bush land I kept my head low and sprinted across the plain. The sight of some of the pack on the hill in front of me, made my heart soar, and instantly they all got tense seeing the trio in pursuit of me. Their howls and calls soon erupted like a battle cry and the others began to turn back, curious as to what was going on.

Because they were used to me, the shifters didn't bother them like they would have normally. The yearling and I guess you could call him Beta started to trot forward with their tails and hackles up. I bumped heads with the pup and saw the other three coming over, their whines of uncertainty making me anxious. I didn't want them to get hurt.

We gathered as a unit, pacing around as the trio hesitated to come closer. They looked at each other constantly, trying to work out what to do. They'd be able to tell the difference between actual wolves and me, but this would be something new to them completely.

It was when the Alpha arrived I knew things had to end quickly. She was pregnant and the remaining members of our family stuck close by the pair. These three were intruders to our territory and we all stood staring at them, waiting for a sign of them to fight or take flight. Their wolves were not like mine; nervous is the company of the wild animals and slowly walking backwards the air around us changed. They were retreating, but as the dominant pack – we had to make sure they knew it. I leapt forward with them, just like they had done with me we charged and now the table had been turned. They weren't going to hurt them; they were making a show of it. Snapping at their heels, running alongside them growling – the trio were defeated and didn't deny it.

Only as I followed behind the one who still had the lingering hint of chocolate about him, he stopped and before one of the others did go to attack, he shifted. The duo with him paused, another staring match starting as we all eyed each other up. Picking a target, the human would be the weakest.

"Shift, why hide behind your wolf clothing!" He demanded and both my wolf and I snorted, amused at his attempt at taking control.

Don't do it.

I had no intention of listening to his orders, dropping my head slightly as behind us, the Alpha's howled and the rest of the pack joined in. It only excited those around me more, and they all bounced against each other playfully, the adrenaline only growing as they carried on.

And then one of the shifters lunged for my pack mate.

I had knocked him down before he could take hold of the wolf, the yearling yelping in fright at the sudden attack. It was a weak move, and as a stronger wolf – I defended him. We had fought another pack some time ago; it hadn't been much of a fight, as animals knew their laws. The yelp only stirred them all up more and two others ran to my side, nipping at the shifter on the ground as the wolf refused to accept his place.

These humans would play dirty with little respect for how it should be done.

I let him up, my hackles up my skin was tingling with the anticipation of a fight. Spit dripped of my fangs as my lips curled back, daring him to try something again. He didn't back down, jumping up I met him mid-air and we started to box, our chests slamming against each other as we fought to get a grip on each other. A nip on the cheek, a tug around the neck, but my paw hit his eye and with that second of distraction, I got the grip I had wanted on his neck.

Using my full weight, my wolf loved the chance to fight and knocked him to the ground, not letting him up. Fighting to the death wasn't common practice, as soon as dominance is established – it ends.

This idiot thought he stood a chance and wouldn't give up. He fought like a human, not a wolf.

"Let him up! He will stop!"

I forgot one had shifted back to human, the pack circling him and the other who was smart enough to lay in submission. With a final shake of his scruff I stepped back and this time, he didn't chase after me.

The bark like sounds called the pack back to me and we ran off together back to our alpha, like a bunch of happy dogs who had just become best friends at a dog park. We all congratulated each other on our success, the pack won and we all crowded around the Alpha, a new song breaking out amongst us.

"Wait! Who are you?"

I didn't even stop to look back as we all took off through our territory, the intruders had been defeated and we had other things to worry about now.

-

Two days later, my wolf followed the yearling girl to the river. The heard of deer scattered the second they saw us and we watched interested as they fled. We had no need to hunt, a chase would be fun, but feeling lazy we wet our paws and lingered on the banks.

Shifters.

We looked around, the wolf with us completely unaware of the danger and sure enough, the three shifter wolves charged out from the tree line, circling us.

She wasn't a weak wolf, definitely her mother's daughter, but the young wolf kept close to my side. While the shifters would recognise her stance of dominance, they wouldn't care for the animal and my wolf kicked into protective mode, snapping at the one to get to close to her.

We were willing to stoop to their level, death may be the warning they needed to back off and leave us alone. The pack was nearby, and deciding to give them what they wanted, closing my eyes I shifted.

My pack mate got nervous then, slinking around my legs like a cat.

"Let me send her back."

The largest of the trio nodded, their snarling stopping as I ran my hands down her back and pushed her in the direction of the pack, urging her to go I felt my wolf's influence spreading over her and surprisingly she did what we wanted and ran back to the others.

While my hair covered my chest, the rest of me was dirty and remembering nakedness in front of other people I blushed slightly and tried to cover other areas.

"Do I need to shift and settle this physically or will you speak to me?"

Talking was unusual. In human form I would talk out loud to my wolf. Even though she was in my mind, I needed conversation from time to time. Now I could get actual responses, I didn't want them.

Sure enough the trio all shifted, the younger pair trying to retain some modesty covered themselves too while the eldest, the one who had the chocolate didn't bother.

"Who are you?" He demanded.

"Who are you?" I retorted.

"I asked you first."

"I have a pack of wolves meters away that will not hesitate in making a mess of your pretty human bodies."

It wasn't a complete lie. I could provoke them into attacking, I just didn't particularly want to.

"I'm Jay, that's my brother Connor and my cousin Adam. Now you."

Lie.

"Daisy."

Following my wolf's guidance, I couldn't help getting nervous. Instantly memories of that night started to flash back to me; being held against my will, the feeling of each punch and as my heart started to race I got dizzy. The feeling of my arm being held had my screaming and I leapt away, shifting as I did so.

"Daisy calm down. Are you ok?" All three were frozen in place as I snarled at them; the youngest, Connor looked like he might cry.

"She has rabies. Shoot her before she infects the forest!" Adam declared, glaring at me.

My wolf didn't like that, tensing to lunge towards him.

"She doesn't have rabies. Daisy, we're not going to hurt you. We're just, curious. No one comes out here."

We moved away from them, putting a good amount of distance between us and reluctantly I shifted back.

"If no one comes out here, why are you three here?"

"We're farmers from south of here, some of our cattle broke through the fencing and we're just rounding them up before the wolves get them." He explained, taking a slow step towards me.

"Then go away, back to your cows."

"Why are you here first? You're alone aren't you?" He spoke to me like a child; soft and patronizing I had enough social interaction to last me however long.

Lie.

"No. They're just hiding."

'With the wolves? We've watched you all for a day, there are no other shifters around here."

"What year is it?" I blurted out, not really thinking it over.

"What year do you think it is?"

Adam snickered and nudged Connor amused. They thought I was crazy.

Maybe I am?

"That's not what I asked."

"Two thousand and eleven."

Five years; for five years I'd been living with the wolves. I felt dizzy again, sinking down onto my knees that familiar numbness took over stopping my tears and the ache in my heart.

Not now, don't appear weak!

I nodded, looking back to the shifters who had come closer in the time it took me to space out. At least now I knew.

"Are you alone out here? Where is your pack?" Jay asked again, slowly walking towards me.

"My pack are back there, leave us alone or next time you will see what wolves are really capable of." The venom in my tone even made me shudder and Connor and Adam swallowed nervously. Even Jay was put off and my confidence grew.

They were not dominant wolves.

"We could tell our pack, have shifters running all over these mountains looking for you." He threatened.

Idiot.

He may have been taller, but I knew I was stronger and my wolf was angry, giving me her strength. It didn't matter we were naked; it didn't matter for the time being I was out numbered – he didn't threaten us. My hand clamped around his neck as I jumped up, knocking him to the dirt with a thud, his breath was knocked out of him upon impact and straddling his chest, my hands tightened.

"Do not threaten me shifter."

The other two were in shock, before snapping out of it and they came running over to try and grab me. His hands clawed at my arms and with a grunt he managed to roll slightly and to balance myself I had to let go. Jay's throat was red; the imprint of my hands making a pattern over his skin and the other two grabbed an arm each to drag me off him.

No, I was not being held captive again.

I went dead weight and they came in closer to try and lift me back up. My foot kicked straight to where I knew it would hurt most between the legs and Adam fell to the ground, groaning. Connor dropped my arm in fear, while Jay was still gasping for air beside him.

"Final warning; forget you ever saw me!" I demanded, shifting and running back to my pack.

I was welcomed back in as if I had been gone for months, not minutes and we took off to higher ground. I hoped I had scared them enough to back off, to follow me now would only be signing their death certificates and even if other shifters came to find them, they would die too.

For every time I had considered returning to the human society, I mentally slapped myself. I couldn't go back; I couldn't live amongst them anymore. My mate had sealed my destiny that night when his pack left me to die. I wasn't one of them now, I was wolf and this was where I, where we – belonged.

-

The next few nights went by much the same. We made it the whelping den and being back in the most familiar region of our territory had the pack in good spirit. The change was easy to see and with plentiful in these parts so we never went hungry.

It was on the tenth night that the pups were born and with the new arrivals, we were all on high alert. It would be a few more days until we were permitted to meet them, their tiny cries were strong and with no problems there were four pups this year compared with the two of last.

It was a full moon and leaving the pack I shifted, enjoying the fresh grass against my skin and wandered through the world that was nearly as bright as day. It all made me smile. Pups could do that to a person, no matter how damaged they were.

Lost in my own world even my wolf felt content, relaxed even and maybe it was because of this fact, we realised too late and couldn't do anything to defend ourself as a lasso tightened over my shoulders and I was pulled to the ground.

I couldn't shift, the rope would hurt her too and every time I tried to stand, I was pulled back down.

Shifters!

Pointing out the obvious, their scents were becoming too familiar to me now and the growl that erupted was completely wolf. She was so close to the surface all I needed to do was get free and she would have free reign to rid us of the pest this trio had become.

"Let me go!"

They didn't answer and seeing them circling me cautiously had my rage reaching an unknown level.

"Let me go now and I won't hurt you."

Adam had the courage to laugh at that.

He dies first.

At least my wolf and I were finally agreeing on something. The more I struggled the more the rope tightened and rubbed against my skin.

"Settle down, we just want to talk." Jay spoke with calmness that the situation didn't really have room for.

"Fine, talk." I stopped struggling and moved to sit crossed leg, refusing to look at them as they regrouped rather than circle me.

"Who are you Daisy, you're running around here like a wild animal. Shifters don't do that."

"Maybe they should and they'd have more manners than keeping people tied up with rope like a criminal!"

"You'll just run or attack us, we're not stupid."

"Yeah you are, do you forget my last warning? What makes you think, this rope will stop me?" I made eye contact with him then and sure enough his gaze diverted quickly.

Weak.

"Stop making this into a fight. How old are you? You're like what, twenty? Eighteen maybe?"

"I'm well, what month is it?"

"March."

"I'm twenty."

They all looked at each other for a second, and sighing I tried to bend my arm enough to start pushing at the rope.

"You asked me what year and now what month it is. How long have you been out here?"

"Five years."

"What?" They all spoke in unison and I only rolled my eyes.

"Did you lose control at your first shift?" Connor spoke up and I was surprised he even managed it. My gaze turned to him and I could see him squirming.

"You could say that."

I shuddered at the thought, not willing to go down memory lane again.

"Where is your pack?" Adam asked, for as brave as he tried to act, his voice was trembling.

"Dead."

I felt the rope tighten as they all stepped back and I realised they thought I did it. I guess in some ways I did, he was my mate after all.

"Now let me go or you'll be able to say hello to them for me."

Again I growled and I saw them think it over.

I heard the panting first, a faint whine and knew my pack was looking for me.

"Well you can't say I didn't warn you!"

I got their attention back and opening my mouth I called to my wolves. Jay dropped the rope, giving me a chance to start losing it from around me as the first wolf appeared, followed by the others as they ran towards us. They quickly stripped off their clothing, shifting into their wolves as if that would help them and the second I got free, my own was taking over, going for Adam like we had discussed.

The shifters didn't stand a chance, the wolves remembered them from last time and as I was out for blood, so were they. The trio grouped together, unwilling to separate and as each wolf advanced on them, they'd chase it back. I stalked around them as they had just done to me, almost pitying Connor who was already laying in the dirt, whining – his fear only excited the pack.

If anyone saw us now, it would be the strangest thing to witness.

Wolves don't act this way.

I lunged forward, set on taking down Adam when the gun shot rang out, spooking us all and looking over in the direction it came from, I realised I wasn't the only one with a cavalry and theirs had guns.

--

Jay >>

Four.

My wolf pushed the pack away, urging them to leave while we didn't loosen our grip on Adam. He didn't know how much danger he was actually in as he squirmed underneath me and the wolves began to retreat like we told them to. The dirt bike came flying over to us, and finally I dropped the useless being in my jaws, glad he didn't try to fight back and only whined, not moving.

Squaring off against the bike – the gun didn't deter me.

"What the fuck?" The man leapt of the bike, and I say man because even though Jay and the others had to be around my own age, he was pushing thirty and it wasn't just hard farm work that defined his arms. Leanna and I used to drool over men like him, in magazines and movies. His blue eyes were set on challenging my own and an unfamiliar feeling of disappointment came over me seeing the pretty redheaded girl that had sat behind him with the gun.

"Do we shoot it?" She asked, slipping off the vehicle she kept close to his side and the trio all shifted to speak to him.

"Don't Taylor, she's a shifter. Her name is Daisy." Jay spoke up, the scents of his blood made me want to look and inspect the damage, but I wasn't going to give this new guy the satisfaction of breaking his gaze.

One of us was going to have to give in and it wasn't going to be me.

"A shifter?" I could see his nose flare as he inhaled my scent, a tiny smirk appearing on the corner of his lips. "I'll ask again, what the fuck?"

"Cody, we found her a few days ago and followed her. We got the cattle back in the paddock and came back out, she's alone." Connor spoke this time and I knew who top dog was around here.

"Shift!"

His command was useless, instead my ears went flat and I revealed my teeth while my body was vibrating with the rumble of growls.

"I said SHIFT!"

The four shifters all stepped back from Cody and behind the pack weren't impressed with the distance I had forced between us. I had no idea how my wolf was doing that and I'd have to wait until later to find out.

"Fine, you want to do this the old fashioned way?" He pulled off his sweater, and jeans, turning to the girl he handed her his stuff before shifting into a rather large black wolf. His own snarl quickly appeared as he snapped his jaws towards me.

My wolf was furious, the challenge clearly received and we began to circle each other, our tails high and proud behind us as we eyed each other up. He was strong, fit and there was little weakness to be found.

In all, it would be a fair fight.

"Cody, I don't think that this is a good idea." Jay went to stand in front of the girl and she glued herself to his side while the other two kept close to them. Was that his mate?

Mate.

The thought had my wolf seeing red and she made the first move, charging towards Cody - we went in for the tackle. He slipped up slightly, not expecting me to be as heavy as I was and my teeth snapped down on his leg.

I wasn't going to fight like a wolf, they had no right to experience my mercy and I was out for blood.

On we wrestled; neither of us getting a clear advantage or lead and the sounds of our growls filled the night. My pack cried out for me and I couldn't answer, not giving into the distraction they provided and things got brutal. As we began to tire our bites got nastier, he was as frustrated as I was from the lack of submission. He may have been built well, but he wasn't in my league of fitness. Hours of wrestling with the pack and spending days stalking the herds gave me better concentration, my stamina able to endure more than his and as the four shifters saw me starting to come out the victor, the bitch shot me.

I fell backwards, whining and that was all the pack needed. Ignoring my will for them to stay back they charged and Cody leapt forward to pin me down. It was like my leg was on fire. My wolf's pain threshold was higher than mine and even she was struggling with it, especially as we had numerous wounds all over our body and fatigue was starting to set in.

With me weakened, his confidence grew and as he came up and got that oh so vital hold, I grabbed his chest - biting down hard to take the force of my pain and he yelped in response. My good back leg came under his belly and as I wriggled, trying to get him off me I felt my nail against that soft flesh of his belly and focused on that.

It got him off me as my pack arrived, no longer playing or faking their aggression. The redhead took aim with the rifle and I was surprised to see Connor knock it up to the sky as she fired again.

Cody shifted; panting heavily his muscular abdomen was cut and bleeding like his chest with numerous bites and scratches all over him.

"At least show your face." He demanded, his eyes were troubled and he slouched holding his wounds. Jay went over to help him only to be pushed away.

He wasn't used to losing and he knew he would have if the bitch hadn't shot me.

I was surrounded by a mass of snarling, howling angry beasts and with the gun out of action; I decided I'd be safe to shift. I really wished I hadn't as the pain was all new and my leg buckled from underneath me.

The yearling girl stood beside me, and I leant against her to stand again.

"Leave us alone." My voice was croaky and dark, trying to mask the agony I was in was and so far I was failing.

"You fight well."

"You're a cheat." Still leaning against the wolf, I turned knowing if they tried to follow there were ten wolves for them to get through before me.

It was time to go.

"You won't heal if the bullet is still in there."

I groaned, why did he even care?

Not willing to appear weak I stopped, clearing a path so we were in direct view of each other I closed my eyes and holding back my scream, felt for the intruder in my leg and pulled it out. Gasping I threw the bullet to the ground and that was when the human part of me had enough and I fell to the ground before my wolf could take over.

-

I'd never slept so well. The soft bed underneath me seemed to lure me back to sleep yet the voice in my mind was constantly repeating wake up.

"I don't want to go to school," I groaned, rolling over I pulled the blanket up high over my head as if to make the noise go away. It didn't work and the more conscious I became, the louder it got.

And so did the smell of bacon.

Mum must be making breakfast down stairs and I stretched out, avoiding the cold spot on the bed before lazily opening my eyes.

Wake up!

Wake up!

Wake up!

"Leanna?" No one except her could be that annoying and focusing I looked around my room.

This wasn't my room.

I quickly sat up, the blankets and pillows being knocked off the bed as I sat against the bedhead and looked around. Pale blue walls surrounded me and the tiny windows in the top corner of the left side of the room were covered with metal bars. The floor was white vinyl like a hospital and the aroma of bacon filled the air.

"Where the hell am I?" I asked no one, closing my eyes the fight and fainting came back to me and looking down at my leg it had been neatly bandaged. The thin white hospital style dress gave me some modesty, but just wearing something felt constricting after being naked for so long.

We need to get out.

"Clearly."

I ripped off the bandage to find a faint pink scar where the bullet had struck and my rage instantly began to swell. I needed a door. Looking around the walls I finally saw it, painted the same color as the walls it blended it well and running over to it, I growled at finding it locked.

So I did what anyone would do in my position.

I banged the crap out of that door, the metal not even denting as my hand began to get streaked with blood.

"Sedate her!" I knew that voice.

Adam.

My wolf instantly bristled and we stepped back from the door, pressing against the wall like we could be blend into it. We weren't in the forest now; there was no way to hide in here. A tiny panel appeared in the top of the door and sure enough a tip of a gun appeared.

"She isn't there."

"She has to be, there is no way out!"

Somewhere memories of a million action movies I used to watch with my Dad came back to me and holding my breath, I grabbed the tip pulling it forward into the room before ramming it backwards. The feeling of something solid wearing the force of the hit pleased me and the commotion behind the door told me I'd got one of them.

Idiots.

The panel closed and the creaking grind of metal had me covering my ears. My wolf urged me to move behind the door so I did, moving with it as it slowly swung open.

Wait.

The squeak of shoes against the vinyl filled the room and the first man appeared inside and he quickly checked each corner only before he turned to where I was, the second one entered and I sprang into action. I punched the back of his head sending him stumbling backwards and grabbing the second ones gun I rammed it hard up under his chin. I had no idea what to do with the gun now I had it so dropped it on top of him and shifted.

I worked better this way.

I was expecting something as clinical as the room but instead it was more like a cellar with old wooden floorboards and weak fluro lighting and I saw Adam as he saw me.

"Oh shit! CODY!"

As much as I wanted to see Cody again and finish our fight, I had no idea where I actually was and needed to get outside. Sniffing the air the bacon showed me the stairs and I ran up them. Paws don't open doors and luckily I didn't need to shift as I saw the green button with Exit above it.

The door groaned open and cautiously I stepped out into the bright lights of a kitchen where the girl who had the gun stood with that oh so tempting meat in a frying pan, sizzling away as if it was just any other morning and they didn't have someone captive in whatever that dungeon was.

We looked at each other for barely a second, her fear obvious as she screamed and Adam found some courage to chase me up the stairs. The kitchen door was flung open and Cody and Jay came running in and seeing me, Cody didn't care about his clothes this time and jumped forward, shifting.

I ducked under him as he landed as his black wolf, running past Jay who was knocked over as I bolted past and finding freedom I was in some kind of ranch house. The back yard was fenced off with perfect white panels and to the left I saw a pool.

In a leap I was over the fence, running down the gravel drive I could hear them all coming behind me and I kept running to the tree line in the distance.

Jumping another fence I saw the horses in the corner rear and start pacing around nervously and not bothering with them I kept running, hating how many fences was in this stupid set up. The heavy breathing of Cody was even more annoying as he managed to come along side me and at the next fence, he didn't aim to jump it and instead caught my back legs as I leapt up to the top panel and pushed me down.

I was quick to roll away, growling we stalked around each other again and this time I kept an ear out for any sounds of a gun being loaded.

To my surprise, he shifted.

His chest was heaving as he tried to catch his breath, holding his hands up in surrender a quick look around told me it was still just us.

"We don't want to hurt you. Please shift so we can talk."

I shook my head, looking up at the fence beside us I couldn't jump it from this angle and with no run up.

"We want to help you."

I didn't need help; I needed to get away from them.

"Daisy, we are no threat."

He just kept talking, his breathing finally coming back under his control and for whatever reason; my wolf wanted me to listen.

So I shifted.

He looked too triumph at my decision and I had punched him before I realized what I was doing. I was only surprised again as he didn't fight back, yet I could see him getting tense.

"You are welcome to stay here, we won't bother you."

"Why?"

"Why what?"

"Why let me stay?"

He was silent for a few moments, rubbing his jaw where I had hit him.

"Because you clearly need help. Look at you! You can't run around with feral wolves, it's not right."

I punched him again.

"Stop!" He growled, standing I didn't back down as he tried to intimidate me.

"Where are we?"

"What do you mean?"

"Are you stupid?" I cocked my head to the side, wondering how hard I had hit him so he had trouble understanding my question.

"No. We're on my ranch, ah just outside of Montana. Why?"

That was a good few states away from my old home and I realized I had no idea where my mate had even come from. He said he been looking for me, so maybe not nearby.

"What other shifters are around here?"

He hated the way I was demanding things of him, but to his credit – he obliged.

"There is a family group like ours about five properties over, a bigger pack heading towards California. Two groups merged a few years back south from here so they pretty much dominate the region. Are you hiding or on the run?"

I only glared which told him more than words could.

"Look, come inside. Have a shower, have some breakfast and we can work out the rest from there?"

He is no threat.

"Do not tell anyone I am here."

"I won't. Promise."

We shifted and made our way back to the house. I was more comfortable being in my wolf form and considering he was naked and we had a few paddocks to go through he shifted too. The others all stood on the front porch waiting and I could sense their relief that Cody came back unharmed. The two guys that were dressed like guards stood at either end of the veranda as lookouts and I was curious as to why there were even here.

Cody didn't acknowledge any them as he carried on walking through the house and I hesitated before following him. Snarling I glared at all of them before following him up the stairs and keeping an ear out made sure no one was following or planning anything from behind. He stopping at the end of the corridor and I nudged the door open before returning back to my human form.

"I'll get Taylor to bring you some clothes in; they might be too big, but better than nothing." He called from the other side of the door. I waited for his footsteps to disappear and listening in, could hear the others downstairs arguing now.

Adam wanted me left in the cell, Taylor didn't want to share her clothes, Connor was silent and Jay only asked Cody what happened.

Ignoring them I locked the door and stepping into the tub, it took me a few minutes to work the taps, nearly falling backwards as the water came out colder than the mountain river. It then turned boiling and once I got the water right I nearly cried at how nice the water felt.

Using the washcloth, the smell of the coconut hair products had me practically purring in delight and I wasn't shy with the conditioner or the tropical body washes. It took me a few goes with the razor I found in the cupboard to shave my legs and finding scissors tried to neaten the edge to my hair. I may as well make the most of these things while I had them.

"Ah Daisy, are you ok in there? It's been an hour?" Jay called out.

I muttered yes and heard Taylor pipe up about how much I needed to bathe and she hoped I didn't use all her shampoo. I felt like pouring it out to spite her, but decided not to be rude. Feeling better I got out, the soft towel was even better than waking up in a bed and I didn't want to dry myself, preferring to cuddle it instead.

"There are clothes out here for you." Taylor was clearly unimpressed and the wolf in me wanted to teach her some respect, but I held her back.

People weren't wolves; even the shifters. As much as I wanted to get her back for shooting me, I had to at least try and remember how to act civilised.

Peeking out the doorway, I looked at the pile in front of me. I would never have worn things like that before; clothing had become so unimportant it was weird to have to try wearing it again. The underwear had tags on, and her reluctance made a little more sense now and going for the maxi-skirt I pulled it up under my arms like a dress, tying it tightly. Nothing else fitted me, even the underwear was loose and looking at myself in the mirror, my bones were more visible than I expected them to be around my shoulders yet the muscle in my arms was undeniable.

Spying the hair tie on the sink, I tied up my hair, something else I had not been able to do properly for some time and stepping out of the bathroom, I felt vulnerable. My wolf was with me every step of the way, listening to the now hushed voices below; there was no one else in the house. Each scent I could identify and my hands were trembling as I walked down the stairs.

The house was well kept, nothing elaborate like my old home. This wasn't a pack house; they were farmers so clearly their wealth was not like what I had left behind. Cody seemed take the position of Alpha around here and so far he was the only one I had an inch of respect for. He said there were another family unit a few properties over, so clearly this was it for them.

I looked at the front door, I could make my escape now and if those guards were still out there I'd take care of them easily. Getting out of that cell had been easy.

Too easy.

I needed to get out while I could.

Stay.

I was surprised to hear her voice telling me not to go back to our pack, to our life and I was annoyed to find her moving towards the kitchen. My heart instantly started to race, I couldn't go in there. I was defenceless, this wasn't right.

No fear.

'Easy for you to say', I thought back taking a deep breath they went quiet as I appeared in the doorway.

"Hungry?" Jay spoke first and all eyes turned to him.

"No."

Remembering my manners I tried to smile.

"No, thank you."

"You're really skinny." Taylor pointed out and Connor nodded beside her. She pushed her chair back slightly and instantly I stepped back, glaring at her movements.

"And you're lucky I haven't killed you yet."

Her mouth dropped open and all of them got tense. Every movement they made had me flinching, desperate to run away only my wolf wouldn't let me.

"So why have you been running around as a wolf for the last five years? Clearly you're a winner at making friends."

Adam was already walking a thin line and my glare moved to him. He grabbed a piece of toast from the table, and I tensed as he picked up the knife to spread butter all over it. Butter. My mouth began to water at the prospect of human food. Cody said nothing, watching me as I watched each of Adams actions. I wasn't sure if I was in fact watching Adam now or the food in his hands and as he dropped the knife it clinked against the plate and unwillingly I jumped, stepping back against the doorframe.

"We still have a ranch to run, go." Cody's command was clear and Jay was the only one to hesitate, but even he caved under both our gazes. Once we were alone, he sat back in the chair clearly comfortable within his own surroundings and motioned to the table. "Hungry?"

"No."

Liar.

'Shut up!' I snapped back at her, finding it weird not talking out loud to her now like I usually do. I didn't want them knowing what was going on in my mind.

"What's the deal with you guys?" I asked instead, slowly walking around the table so we were on opposite sides.

The food on the table was interesting only to me, like the chocolate Jay had earlier and I scanned it hungrily. Giving in, I curiously picked up a piece of the crispy bacon, almost moaning at how good it tasted.

"Born and raised out here, my Uncle owned the property next door and when he died my Father took over. Some travellers came through while we were out with the herd and we're all that's left. I have Brett and his brother, Kane on payroll as security for the property. Backup in case anyone should come on by again."

Cody spoke with little emotion in his tone, feelings were a weakness and I thought back to how I had cried and begged the night my mate left me. I would never appear that weak again.

"I-I'm sorry for your losses." That's what you say to people who have loved ones taken from them. I used to tell that to myself every time I saw my reflection and I hated how I could feel the tears starting behind my eyes. Where was my wolf blocking off my emotions now?

"And I'm sorry for yours."

I grabbed the knife from the table, holding it in front of me defensively.

"What do you know?" I practically screamed at him, moving back around the table so I was closer to the way out.

Had I just walked into a trap?

"Nothing – you look like you're about to cry so I guessed!" He held his hands up in innocence again, watching me with curiosity rather than fear.

I told you he is no threat.

I lowered my hand and dropped the knife.

"I need to go. Thank you for the shower."

For whatever reason, only one half of me was willing to disappear again.

"We all know what it's like to lose someone Daisy."

He's right.

'Shut up.' I snapped back at her and stopped by the front door to look back at him. He leant against the door frame completely at ease, which now only made me feel worse. I was out of my depth socially, emotionally and curling up in that bed was more appealing than chocolate right now.

"Here me out, one night. Then you can leave back to those animals."

"Why do you want me to stay?"

He seemed strangely eager and they were all too friendly causing my paranoia to grow. Maybe my wolf had lost her mind as she was willing to accept the offer.

"No one has ever beaten me in a fight before and, you look as broken as I feel. Someone needs to give you a chance."

"I don't need a chance. I need to be left alone!"

"That's what I used to think too."

And then he turned and walked out the back door leaving me alone. Cautiously I walked back into the kitchen, watching as he headed to the bike he had arrived at the fight on and took off down towards the paddocks.

One night.

"Fine. One night." I muttered back to the voice in my head.

—

Cody >>

Five.

One night had turned into six and on the seventh I left back 'home'.

Staying in the house was exhausting. Every sound was new and distracting, so I'd spend the nights awake in case anyone came into my room and I'd sleep during the day while they were out doing their work.

We rarely spoke to one another.

I didn't like Taylor or Adam, the urge to rip them apart was mutual between my wolf and I, so it was just easier to avoid them. Jay was persistent, constantly asking if I needed anything and willing to wait me out, presuming soon I'd break and we'd end up as best friends or something just as stupid.

Connor was the only one I spoke to. He'd be the first home for lunch and in the afternoon. He was also the first one up in the morning and it was while everyone slept we'd talk. Maybe because he had only just turned eighteen or because of his quiet and calm nature, I found something in him I could trust.

That said, I never told him much about myself while he was happy to pour out his life story. It helped me understand Cody a little more too. I understood what he meant when he said he felt broken; it wasn't just their parents that had been killed but his mate as well.

I didn't ask anything else after that, and I couldn't look at him the same way either.

Connor also filled me in on what was popular now in music, even lending me an iPod to listen to while I was alone. The more he told me about movies, celebrity gossip and world events the more I felt like an alien. Everything was foreign to me and he'd stop if he thought I was becoming overwhelmed.

Eating their food had made me sick for the first few days, and on the day I left it was the first time I hadn't had to throw up or wait for it to painfully go through my system. My wolf thought this was a good sign, that I was adapting and maybe I was.

"I've been talking to her Cody, she doesn't say much about where she comes from, but I think she trusts me."

"That's good Connor, be careful though. She clearly has a past and I've seen the way she watches Adam and Tay. Don't go anywhere alone with her, if she thinks like a wolf she might be waiting for us to seperate to take us down."

"I don't think she will hurt us, Taylor shot her and Adam was a dickhead — I wouldn't like them very much either."

Cody sighed, getting up from the dining table.

"I'm going to go downstairs for a bit, I'll leave the door open so if anything happens just yell."

"Ok, I'm going to check the missing person's database and see if I can match anything to her. There aren't any Daisy's and I think that was a fake name."

"Careful with all that hacking computer stuff Connor."

"It's totally untraceable, don't worry!"

Cody left him and I headed into the kitchen where he sat with a laptop in front of him. He jumped, unaware I had walked in and I looked at him suspiciously.

"You need to wear a bell, you're too quiet." He scolded, slamming down the screen.

"Maybe you need to learn how to use your senses better." I snapped, feeling guilty as he looked hurt at my harsh tone. That was saved for the others, not him.

"What's your name?"

"Daisy."

"I'm using my senses now and I know that's a lie." He challenged and I had to smile a little. His fear of me was starting to weaken, but I didn't mind. I don't want people to fear me, just the ones who should.

"Senses? Using your computer is a sense?"

"You heard?"

"Good hearing is one of our senses." I sat down beside him, listening to the other three in the living room and the grunts and thuds from downstairs where Cody was taking out his frustrations on a punching bag. I couldn't stop being on constant alert, it was hard to turn off. In the wild anything or anyone may sneak up on you and that happened to me once before. I'm not going to make the same mistakes again.

"What are you hiding?"

"I'm not hiding anything." Except myself, I thought staring him down.

"Then what's your name. How about I try and guess it? Will you tell me then?"

Bianca wasn't a common name and I liked my chances so nodded, sitting back in the chair I was looking forward to this.

"Hannah?"

I shook my head, unable to stop from looking amused.

"Sarah?"

And so his list of names started, opening up his laptop he went onto a name site and while I declared that was cheating, he started reading out the most popular names of the year I was born.

"You could be here a while." I teased, but he didn't give up.

"Jessica, Emily, Stephanie, Chloe, Amy, Ruby, Alice...."

"You're reading a list. Let me look and I'll see if it's there." He moved it over and after I remembered how to use the flat mouse, I smiled victoriously. "It's not."

"Well cuts out 100 names."

"Loser."

He grinned, and I had a feeling he wasn't as cut out for this farm work as the others. He carried on saying names, so much so that I tuned out and listened to whatever was on the TV. I didn't know the show they were watching, but they all seemed to like it.

Maybe I would be like them if things hadn't happened, in fact by now I would have finished college and be starting my life.

"Leah, Leanne, Leanna..."

I gave away too much and my head snapped up to look at him. He grinned yet the look on my face had him stopping.

"Leanna? Is that your name?"

"No. She was just someone important to me."

Again he proved my decision about liking him a wise one and he dropped it, daring to reach out and touch my hand, ignoring how I cringed at the contact. I didn't like people touching me, but there was something comforting about it too and I didn't pull away.

"Ok, did you want to see a cat getting a bath?"

Confused I didn't give myself time to dwell on my past and nodded. Sure enough you tube appeared on his screen and we were both in tears from laughing from what we saw. I hadn't laughed like that in a long time and decided I really did like Connor.

By eleven everyone was in bed, or so I thought and as I restlessly moved around the house. I stopped at the top of the stairs as I heard voices from the living room. Creeping closer my wolf was getting anxious and it didn't help my own nerves.

"I got the name Leanna so I tapped into the police database and did a search for anything in 2006 with that name and I found this." Connor went quiet and I wondered what he had found.

"Shit. I remember this, the police kept it quiet because they're all shifters. Some random attack wiped out half the pack. That must be where she's from!" Cody practically yelled and quickly went quiet again. "Are there pictures of them? Of her?"

Pictures?

I moved through the shadows of the lower level, pausing by the doorway to see the pair of them sitting on the sofa with the laptop between them. A few clicks had a picture of my old house on the screen and worse, to the side in the picture finder crime scene photos.

"Does it mention a Daisy?" Cody asked softly, back to whispering.

"No. The daughter of one of the deceased was never found, though there were signs of a struggle nearby in the forest."

Sure enough pictures of blood on the grass and sand came up on the screen and I knew exactly where that spot was. That path had been the one my mate had walked down when he left me to die, behind me my parents and family laid dead already and the small cliff drop had been marked with a yellow flag where more blood had been found.

"What happened there?" Cody asked, pointing.

"In the report it was suspected her body was dropped down the ravine, only police searches found nothing."

I looked again and a picture of me from school appeared on the screen along with the missing persons report.

"Do you think that's her?"

Connor nodded, "It has to be, she's younger there though."

"Does it have her name?"

"Bianca."

That was all I needed to hear and in seconds I was out the front door, shifted and running back into a place where it didn't matter who I was.

The pack welcomed me back as if no time had passed and I was treated to a sneak peak at the pups that were nothing more than fat little balls of perfection. A day later I blocked out my time in civilization and instead focused on the hunt. My wolf wasn't talking to me like she normally did, everything we did in her body was at my control and if I didn't know better — I'd say she was sulking.

It had been her idea to come out here, to live as one of them and now she only offered me memories of a shower and pancakes. Considering I was staring down the furry hide of a rather large, old stag — maple syrup and strawberries didn't exactly pump up my appetite for the raw bloody mess I was working on making into dinner.

A few of the pack kept in sight of the herd, acting like they didn't care they were all there while the fawns and mothers kept knitted together and the defenders lingered around them. The rest of us spread out, ready to get them running and break him away from the safety in numbers routine.

It was basic and obvious, yet these animals never saw it coming. They knew to stay together, but never saw beyond that. I crouched down low, waiting for him to come a little too close to the bushes when the piercing howl shattered the otherwise peaceful dusk and the herd stampeded before we were ready for them.

The pack gave chase only I didn't move with them, knowing all too well that howl was not from one of them and as the wolves regrouped unsuccessful, it was new kind of blood I wanted.

Breaking away from my pack, I headed south and it didn't take me long to find them. The five wolves didn't walk with the same care as their wild cousins, feeling superior to nature. I had my anger at a failed hunt to get rid of so I was curious to see how long their air of invincibility would last. Connor stuck close to Cody, the black wolf walking in front of the others while Taylor, Adam and Jay mucked around behind them.

Cody stopped; growling and the trio split up and kept walking.

My packs calls soon sounded, sharing the disappointment although I knew they'd try again. These things could take days and it wasn't like they needed the kill desperately. The five shifters stopped and carried on, Adam falling behind as the sounds of the wild ones got them nervous.

Just like I had stalked the stag, Adam was now in my sights.

He knew he was being watched, constantly looking around unnerved and as he started to trot to catch up, I pounced. He yelped in shock, and I leant over his body, careful of his claws as he squirmed beneath me and gripping onto his neck, his lack of fight should have told me to back off, that I'd won and he had submitted.

I wasn't in the mood for being nice.

He yelped and whined again, if he was human he'd probably be peeing his pants in fear and maybe from that smell, it wasn't just something he'd do in human form. I went to make the final shake, aching to feel the tear of his flesh beneath my jaws when instead I was knocked backwards.

Cody was snarling over his cousin, and the other three ran to stand behind them. Taylor shifted and ran over to her brother, crying as I realized he had passed out — she thought he was dead.

"I told you we should've killed her!"

This had a whole new wave of anger flowing through me, and Cody lunged towards me. I readied myself, set on taking him on again with no fear of the red headed bitch cheating only he never reached me as Connor took the force of his hit.

The smaller and weaker wolf yelped as Cody landed on him, releasing him instantly. Part of me wanted to make sure Connor was ok, protect him while another part was glad to see them falling apart. Connor had used something I'd told him in trust, to look for information behind my back and remembering that I turned and ran back to my pack.

We moved on after the herd, and in the early hours of the morning we nested. It was nice to be back amongst them, the sounds of the forest more familiar to me now than that of the house. The snores, whines and growls from dreams were like a lullaby and I decided the shifters would have gone back to their home.

"Just leave her out here to die!" Taylor hissed. Her whisper was barely audible over the sleeping pack, but my wolf wanted me to hear them. The stupid creature wanted me to go back with them.

"She's been through a lot Tay, she needs help!" Connor defended.

"I don't know why we have to be the ones to do it. She nearly killed me, again!" Adam whined.

I left the pack, walking down towards the water were they sat on the rocks and Adam was washing his cuts before they healed.

"Why are you here?" All of them jumped and Connor fell backwards into the water with a loud splash. Adam helped him up and the inched closer to together like the deer herd when they knew there was danger.

"To bring you back, we know what happened and you can't hide out here anymore." Jay spoke first while Cody and I entered another staring match.

"You know what happened?" I laughed; a bitter twisted sound I didn't know I was capable of. "Enlighten me Jay."

"Your pack was attacked, like ours and you were lucky enough to get away."

It sounded so simple and clapping I walked closer.

"Yes, just like you."

"No need to be a bitch about it." Taylor snapped and growling she cowered down by her brother.

"Tell us what really happened then, we know there was an attack and you clearly got away." Connor stepped forward, not scared like the others.

"No, the wolf got away. Bianca died with her family."

They didn't know what to say to that and shifting I went back to where I belonged.

Only Cody did the same, following after me so I ran faster; so did he. We ran for miles until I had no choice other than stopping as my legs were shaking with exhaustion and my tongue rolled out the side of my mouth. He was in worse shape than I was; the second I stopped he collapsed. His panting was like a tractor; mine the same and a fell down a little distance from him.

It took some time before we could get the energy to shift; still spread out on the grass of the meadow we had pushed ourselves to hard.

"Seriously, stop running!" He gasped, and I managed to sit up thankful that in that week I hadn't lost too much of my fitness.

"Stop following!"

"Tell me what happened that night." He was using his alpha voice, the same one my Dad always threatened Leanna and me with when we were in deep trouble.

"Why? Why do you want to know?" I growled back.

Groaning he managed to sit up, the sweat was pouring off him and I saw him look at me confused. I wasn't looking as much of a wreck as he was.

"It helps to talk, you've got it bottled up inside you and you need to get it out. It helps, a bit."

"But you know the story. Pack attacked, pack killed — I survived."

"How?"

"They thought I was dead and they threw me over the cliff."

"Who are they?"

"The pack that attacked us."

I could see him getting frustrated, I wasn't giving him anything.

"We have as long as it takes. I sent the others home." He fell back onto the grass, his chest still frantically moving up and down.

Three days he followed me, the pack wary of the new wolf and the majority picked on him a lot. He held his ground though and none of us let him near the den.

Tell him.

Staying out here with us made my wolf trust him and I hated how quickly she was willing to let them in. We'd been on our own for her whole existence and it confused me no end.

I headed down the river with the yearling girl, one of my favorites of the pack. Maybe because I had always favored her our bond was closer, like normal humans do with their dogs.

Not willing to stay on his own, Cody followed us and even joined in our play as we headed down there. He watched curiously as I shifted, with the warm night I headed into the water and the yearling ran in after me. She didn't stay in long, running back to the shore she instead climbed up onto the rocks and after shaking her coat, laid down yawning.

"Do you have names for them?" I turned around to see Cody walking into the water, looking away to give him some kind of privacy and as he sunk lower into the water I couldn't help turn around to admire his chest.

"No, they're wild animals not pets."

He said nothing, swimming out near me with long graceful strokes and instinctively a made sure to put a little more distance between us.

"The attack happened on the night of my first shift."

He stopped swimming, moving so he was floating and those blue eyes seemed to glow under the moonlight, distracting me.

"You were lucky to get out alive."

"I don't know if luck had much to do with it. We were attacked by my mate."

I ducked under the water and let the darkness consume me. Despite the moon light outside, it didn't penetrate the water's surface and movement in front of me had me going back to the surface to find Cody much, much to close.

"I don't understand, your mate was the one who attacked your pack? Had you not shifted yet? Did he not know who you were?"

The truth hurt, even now. My wolfs anger stopped the tears, but not the pain inside. I left the water and in seconds the yearling was back at my side before sounds of the pack had her running back.

"Where is she off to?"

"Dinner. Hungry?"

"Starving, but I'll wait till I can go home."

I smiled, ignoring the look of pity that had taken over his features.

"Bianca, did he know who you were when he attacked?"

With no help from my wolf, I was left open and weak. Tears ran down my face as I managed to nod and everything I had kept locked away was out on display. Cody came to my side; pulling me against him I couldn't fight his touch. To be held with care had me completely sobbing and my tears mixed with the fresh river water already covering his body.

After I finally managed to calm down, I looked around and realized we weren't standing anymore. We sat on the rock where the yearling had been earlier and I was still being cradled in his arms. He didn't have to ask any more questions, I poured it all now.

My birthday party, my parents, the shifting or lack of and everything up until I was lured to his brothers campsite because of something as stupid as chocolate.

"Thank you for telling me."

He was wrong though, I didn't feel better getting it all out. Instead my eyes hurt and I felt like I had just been torn apart inside all over again.

"He can't know I'm alive."

"I agree. You'll be safe with us."

"You can't make promises like that. It's better that I stay out here."

He shook his head, wiping the wet strands of my hair away from my face.

"It's not. You're human, not wolf. Despite the last few years — you need to be amongst your own kind."

He's right.

'Traitor.' I snapped back at her, not sure how I could actually live with them all again.

"You have all the time in the world to adjust, we've all lost people we love Bianca. You're strong, a survivor. Don't let this be the end of your story; we can help you." I couldn't help but lean against him, hearing his heart beat under my ear — things the wolf and the human enjoyed.

If I could have stayed in this moment forever, I would have.

"Are we friends?" I finally asked as we stood up.

"If you want to be?"

I nodded and we started walking towards his home.

"I could do with a friend."

We shifted then and before we started the journey home, I sent my pack a message that I was going and just maybe, one day I'd be back. Their chorus erupted behind us, and I knew they were saying goodbye.

-

I was welcomed back into the human world with fake smiles and caution. Despite the fact Cody knew the truth, the next morning the routine was much the same as it had been before we'd left.

"Bianca, come with me." Cody headed downstairs like he did every night and I lingered at the top, not willing to let myself be trapped down there again. "Trust me."

Two words; two impossible words.

Connor sat on his laptop in the living room, Jay was watching TV beside him and the other two had gone out into the small town nearby to meet up with some friends. Reluctantly I started down the stairs, pausing half way and demanding he stand where I could see him.

He obliged, the dynamics between us had changed now. While we still sought to challenge each other, the respect towards the other had finally been established.

"I'm not going to hurt you, I promise."

I came down, still keeping distance between us.

"When I'm mad, or get the urge to just run away — I come down here." He moved down past the room I had been kept in and into another on the opposite side. Curiously I followed and found him in a gym. I never worked out in my old life, Leanna and I used to avoid them like a plague and the scent of sweat wasn't inviting.

"You're strong, but you do better with endurance. How are you're one on one skills?"

"Lets find out?"

He grinned, clearly liking my answer.

He threw me some gloves and I slipped them on, moving to the red mat we began to circle each other. He started prattling on about defense being important, but I had already tuned out.

"Ok, well let's see what you got."

I fake charged, my wolf coming to the front as she was keen to learn more. He stepped back and I kept my distance. He went to mirror my actions, only I didn't step back like he did and took a swing. Everything was by memory, movies, tv and school yard rumbles, my wolf invaded my mind trying to work out what she should do. Sure it was based on fiction, but it was practically the same thing.

I kept my hands up, defending my face and as I swung, he went for my stomach. Instead I kicked at his side and he bent down to dodge it, forgetting his own attack.

"Enough playing hey?" Our competitive streaks, otherwise known as wolves came to play and it was now a matter of trying to out maneuver each other. We punched, dodged, kicked and in the end, I was pinned underneath him, furious.

"Let me up!" I snapped.

"Admit I won."

"No."

"It's training, fun. Just admit it."

"I know you wouldn't, let me up!"

He applied further pressure on my arms, and no matter how I struggled I couldn't get up. Oddly, my wolf loved it.

"Fine, you won this training."

He let me up, rocking back so he was kneeling and as I got up I kicked out and knocked him backwards, leaping over and now I was pinning him.

"Say I win."

"Really?" He muttered, not impressed before he grabbed my waist and stood up, holding me against him.

"That is cheating!"

"No its not, it's called knowing your opponents weaknesses." He looked triumphant and the fact he was double my size didn't help.

"Put me down." I growled, ready to rip his eyes out if he didn't let me go.

"You're holding onto me she-wolf."

His words took a second to register and sure enough his hands left my waist, appearing either side of his head as he wiggled his fingers looking more than happy with himself. Rather than fall on my back as he stood, I had my legs gripping his waist and my arms were around his neck. Only now he was standing, I still held on.

I let go and stumbled backwards, glaring though it lacked conviction as my wolf was just as amused as Cody. Some help she was!

"Now, shall we get into some training?" He mocked, heading over to the punching bag he stood behind it and waved me over.

Furious I went and stood where he instructed and I don't think that bag had ever been hit that hard.

—-

Adam, Taylor, Connor >>>>>

(left to right)

—

Six.

Being human again was hard. I had to shower daily, dress and be civil. Meal times were hardest because I had to remember manners. I had only been feeding in wolf form, hence the neglected state of my body so having to chew - not rip and swallow as well as use cutlery, cook – apply condiments and salad dressings, was hard.

Two weeks after my return, I still couldn't stand being around Taylor or Adam. Adam's fear radiated off him like death on a corpse and while she was not a strong enough shifter to do so, I could feel Taylor's resentment and desire to fight.

Jay was constantly trying to make peace, trying to find topics Taylor and I could share an interest in, like shopping and pink sparkly items – those kind of things that had become so irrelevant to my life. I admired him for trying, but until we had at each other nothing was going to ease the tension.

Connor was my biggest ally, I forgave him for his computer searches and rather than wait for Cody to tell him my story, I did it myself. In return, on those late night and early mornings we spent together, I taught him things like he had been doing for me, only rather than catching up on politics and the economy, latest computer software and advances in mobile phones; I taught him to fight.

Oddly he didn't like being in his wolf form, beneath the skin the animal was more controlling than the human and it scared him. Considering how quickly he had been to submit when we had met in the wild, it confused me. I guess the wolf saw his weakness and used it to his own advantages.

Determined to help him, I was always making him shift and be in wolf form. I had him practicing using his senses by setting scent trails for him to follow and practicing how to listen so when I snuck up on him, he might stand a chance at hearing me. The sooner he and his wolf learnt to work together, the better for them both.

When I wasn't with Connor, I was with Cody.

Our workouts weren't easy on either of us. We'd both walk away on shaking limbs and bleeding with bruises, although I think he liked it. None of the others here could go into combat with him; the guards he hired did occasionally, but they were happy to keep to themselves and patrol alone.

My pack had yet to move on to higher grounds, so most nights I still left the house and called out to them. I'd still get their replies, checking on their missing friend – just hearing their howls was like getting a hug and helped settle my nerves from being at the house. Even if I wanted to, my wolf never let me run away again.

It was going into the third week when I had another nightmare about my shifting night. My mates words about making the predator the prey haunting me as I woke, covered in sweat and screaming. It wasn't the first time it had happened since being in the house, but because they were all out and doing their own thing they never knew. This time Cody happened to be coming in early and heard it all so came to check on me.

I shifted instantly as someone appeared in my room, still pumped up from the dream it took me a few moments to realize whom it was and seeing Cody, I was glad no one else witnessed it. I refused to shift back and so, he shifted too; laying beside me in wolf form as he waited for me to calm down.

He didn't mention it that night when we had dinner.

As usual I sat back from the table, staying out of conversation and guarding my plate. I refused to eat in front of them, struggling to stop myself from simply shoving food into my mouth like it was my last meal. Connor tried to encourage me to eat with them, so did Jay.

Taylor and Adam still ignored me.

My nightmare played on my mind, and as everyone went their separate ways to sleep I waited for my alone time with Connor. Cody continuously hovered and I'm not sure if it was because my episode this afternoon had him worried about me or his family should I flip out again.

"Connor, the pack that took over my old one after my parents death – do you know much about them?"

He shrugged and I followed him up to his room, well aware Cody was taking his time in the bathroom so he'd be closer should he be needed.

"I know a little, but I could probably find out more. Why?"

I paused, listening as Cody finally went to his own bedroom down the hall.

"I need to know if it's him leading them. Can you get a photo?"

Connor nodded, smirking slightly.

"This is so Mission Impossible, of course I can. I can get more than that!"

Now he had my interest.

"Don't tell anyone, but as much information that you can get would be great."

I left him alone, not sure if he was going to go sleep now he had his 'mission' and went downstairs. The amount of remotes they had was confusing and I managed to get the television turned on and silenced. I started watching news programs; curious to see what was going on and by dawn I resorted to watching infomercials.

"So buy one get one free deals are what keep you sleeping during the day?" For the first time ever, Cody was the first up – not Connor.

"I can't resist, good thing I don't have my credit card handy."

"Remind me to hide mine then."

My first instinct was to poke my tongue out like a child, so I did and he grinned in return. Day by day things I used to do, tiny bits of who I used to be started to come out and that was one them. It was mature I know and my mind drifted to all the times Leanna and I would beg our parents to go shopping or like now, order random impulse buys from the TV. The screen started flashing and we both got distracted, watching the free offer on the pan set if we rung up and ordered now.

"Why are you up so early?" I turned back to Cody; this wasn't part of my routine.

"I'm always awake first Bianca, who do you think turns on the coffee?"

He had a point.

I'd often fallen asleep out here and woke because of the aroma of the coffee machine taking over the house and it was the first thing I noticed when I left my room. I couldn't drink it yet; it was disgusting to me now and yet the year I turned sixteen, Leanna and I had just starting drinking it like it was going out of fashion. The four sugars and carton of milk added to it may have helped us like it, but now I'd rather drink blood.

Leaving me I turned and watched him go to the kitchen, curiously following as he played away with the one appliance I hadn't worked out how to use yet. Leaving it on he made himself a cup, winking at me as he passed and went up to his room.

So much for always being alert.

-

"Bianca!" Connor called in a shouting whisper from Cody's office at the side of the living room. He was engrossed on the computer when I appeared and glancing towards the printer he saw me and jumped again. "Stop sneaking up!"

"In the wild, you'd be dead."

"I'm not in the wild." He snapped back, getting up he headed over to the printer and grabbed the stack of papers.

"What's this?"

He flicked through the pages and pulled one out from the middle to pass over to me. I dropped it, unable to even hold something with his face on.

"Damon Lyall, Alpha of your old pack. Well after it was merged as one with his. He is a mean mofo too. Did you know he killed his own Father AND his Uncle?" Connor spoke like he was idolizing him and put all the printing in a folder and passed it over.

Was I ready to read this?

"I know, ah, thank you for getting this for me."

"No worries. What are you going to do with it?"

I shrugged; gripping the folder like it had been glued to my hands.

"Curious."

I could hear the others coming in for lunch and quickly ran upstairs while he flicked on the TV. Sitting on the bed, I held my breath and took out the printing, scared at what I would find.

I didn't get far as for at least the next hour I stared at his picture, already knowing every inch of it from my memories.

Coward.

My wolf hissed, and I agreed. The longer we stared the angrier we both got and putting it away, I started to think.

He said a Gypsy told him his future, so who the hell was she?

One of the things Connor had printed out was a Facebook log. I wasn't entirely sure what Facebook was, but it had quotes from Damon as well his relationship status, some pictures and he'd mention places he had been to. Scanning over, nothing really interested me a great deal until I saw a picture he had been tagged in, what ever that meant.

I'd have to ask Connor more about this program and finding the photo on the next page he looked to be at a street festival and the woman was dressed, as you'd expect a gypsy to be. Her maxi skirt was a red velvet and gold bells hung from around her hips and ankle while the white peasant style blouse left little the imagination of what was underneath it. A sign in the background read Esmeralda's Imagination and I wondered if there was something on internet to search for it.

I hadn't been a big computer user in my old life, what I remembered was limited so far everything Connor told me was like another language. Maybe Goggle or what ever he said could help?

In the end I had to wait two days so I could go on the computer without them knowing and it took me all morning to work out how to look for things on it. Not only did I find the stores address, but also a webpage listing her services.

Fortune telling was one of them.

I made a few notes and put it all away, not expecting to walk into Taylor when I left my room.

"Watch where you're going!" She snapped. My growl didn't seem to deter her and without thinking we stepped wide around each other, testing the other.

Just like I had with Cody I moved forward, invading her space and where as he would step back, she flinched – but didn't move.

"What is your problem with me Taylor?"

"Everything. You attack my family, and then just expect us to bend over backwards doing what ever you want. You need to be in a mental hospital or a zoo and leave us the alone!"

I shrugged; maybe I was ready to be committed.

"Feel better?"

She growled, not impressed with my sarcasm and lunging forward I braced myself for her attack. As I fell onto my back flipped her over me and she was quick to shift.

Taylor stalked towards me and I stood, watching her movements closely. The commotion had the guys running in and standing at the base of the stairs, Cody was beyond mad.

"Taylor. Shift back now!"

She ignored him and I held up my hand to silence him, "She's been wanting this fight Cody, let her have it."

"Taylor!" Adam yelled, knowing full well his sister was in trouble if she didn't back down. She lunged at me again and I jumped to the side, the wolf quick to follow I didn't have time to save my clothes and shifted ready to meet her.

Her teeth dug into my shoulder and furious I turned my head to snap at her. She had me on a good angle; if I had been weaker I would submit to her now.

Unlucky for her, I wasn't that kind of wolf.

I put all my energy into standing, throwing her off balance and deciding not to risk making a bloody mess in the house leapt down the stairs and trotted outside. She had no chance in beating me and my lack of taking her seriously stirred her into frenzy.

Taunting her further, I sat on the law in front of the house and as she barged past her family who all begged her to stop, she did – skidding to a stop.

I didn't move, just sat there waiting for her and that didn't help her mood any. She came at me again and I darted out her way. As much as I wanted to rip into her, my wolf was more interesting in playing with her. Had she been more of an opponent, I wouldn't have taken it so lightly and we despite everything – we didn't really want to harm her. Not permanently anyway.

By the end, she was exhausted, and the guys sat on the top panel of the fence watching. Now they knew I wasn't going to hurt her, they calmed down and when she looked like she might drop, I finished it. Taking hold of her neck, I squeezed as I pulled her down – not to kill but enough for her to know how close she came to having me end her life.

I shifted, my hands around her neck and gripping onto her fur she went to move, hopeful that she might stand a chance because I was human again. Problem was she still couldn't move as my strength didn't vary in the hold around her neck..

"Try this again, none of your family will be able to save you."

The wolf only whined and I stood up, hoping she really had learnt her lesson. The fact I could then walk inside proved to me she had, not another growl was heard from her. The others all went to help her up and shifting Taylor was bruised and covered in tiny cuts from where I had nipped at her continuously.

She deserved it.

My wolf was quiet on the whole matter, more interested in what information I might be able to find amongst the print outs of Damon. Later that night when we worked out with Cody she wasn't enjoying it like normal, completely distracted. The downside to that was I had to work over time without her help and after messing with Taylor in the afternoon; I was getting tired.

"Thanks for today, I really thought…"

"You thought what Cody? That I had no control?" Now she was interested, my chest rumbling with a growl.

"Yeah. Sorry, honestly you handled it better than what I would have if the situation was reversed."

We stayed quiet for the rest of our training and I said nothing going back upstairs.

I hesitated outside my room, sensing I wouldn't be alone and opening the door Taylor was sitting on the end of my bed. She had a black eye and moved stiffly, while the worst of her wounds had begun to heal. Most were artificial and would have disappeared with a shower. I had made my point.

"I'm sorry." I walked in and left the door open, not willing to make her feel more uncomfortable.

"Ok."

"Could we start over?" I only stared, not sure what she meant by that exactly. "You know, us girls gotta stick together."

"No I don't know." I answered coldly and her face fell in disappointment. "I guess if we're starting over, you can show me what you mean?"

"Really? I'll do anything to make it up to you!"

I liked the sound of that.

"Good, you can start by teaching me how to drive."

Going cross-country may not be easy in wolf form, especially in areas where wolves aren't typically seen. The world doesn't know about our kind and to change that would be disastrous.

"Drive?"

"In a car, I never got to learn."

"I can do that!" She nodded enthusiastically and I hesitated as she came towards me. "Um, tomorrow then?"

I nodded and closed the door behind her, glad to tick something off my ever growing to do list.

-

True to her word, Sunday was spent teaching me to drive.

Everyone was cautious of my budding new friendship with Taylor, considering not even twenty-four hours ago she'd wanted to kill me and I hadn't been waving the flag for her survival.

The automatic car didn't take long to master and a few hours later we headed back home. We both had slightly sore necks from my constant braking, yet I could ease the car into the garage well enough. Getting out, we left passed the smaller shed at the side of the garage and I eyed up the dirt bikes kept in there.

"The guys will have to help you with those, I don't ride bikes." Taylor got out of the car and I was impressed with her patience. Now she let her walls down, she wasn't that bad to be around. We had a long way to go and the bonding time in the car helped. Her annoying level was similar to Jay, but it was getting more tolerable.

"How did you go?" I knew Jay was only making conversation. The four guys had been watching us since I turned on the ignition and we headed down the road that went around the property.

"Well, as long as we avoid intersections and traffic, she's got the hang of the driving side." Taylor and Jay started towards the house, only after being stuck in the car for seven of the eight hours of the day I was itching for a run.

I missed my wolf. I missed the pack.

She assured me this was how it was supposed to be with the human in control and had things never happened, I'd be like them. Our bond was stronger than most shifters of my age; it was hard for it not to be after what we went through together. Her happiness was felt in my core, and I guess she had been right to convince me to stay here.

"I'm going for a run." I called out and the pair stopped, turning back to look at me. "Ah, did you want to come?"

"No I'm starving and could do with a nice relaxing bath after today!" Taylor kept walking and Jay hesitated before nodding.

"Sure!"

We shifted and started down towards the back of the property. I could tell he was struggling to keep my pace, and I didn't want to slow down for him, I had my own fitness to maintain.

I let my wolf hunt a rabbit, ignoring the disgust from Jay and since we had left his family's property I felt free. It would be so easy to keep running though, find the pack and slip into that routine again. It was like Jay could read my mind, subtly trying to herd me back around towards home.

Instead I shifted.

Night had just taken over the land, turning into a new and completely different world to the one you see in sunlight.

"Can we go back?" If I didn't know better, I'd say Jay was afraid of the dark.

"Jay, why did you come after me? You could have just left me out there, instead you followed me."

He shrugged, smiling slightly.

"Honestly, you had that same broken look about you Cody used to have after the accident. He ran off too, only he went a few towns over to a bar not the forest and he had us to go find him and bring him home. You clearly had no one to find you."

The familiar ache in my chest flared up thinking about my parents.

"You didn't know me; I could have been a killer or completely mad or something?"

"No, you were just hurting. You could have killed us that first time we met, but you didn't."

I reached over and gave him a hug and he was as stiff as a tree at my touch. A few seconds later he relaxed and hugged me back.

"Thank you for finding me."

His smile was worth the human contact, while I wasn't completely comfortable with it, it wasn't so bad.

"Any time."

We kept walking and I could tell he wanted to say something else, the silence making him cave.

"Can we go home now?"

"Ok." He seemed surprised I gave in so easily, yet that disappeared as I kept walking and didn't shift. He said nothing besides the odd curse word as he stepped on a sharp rock or tripped on a branch. Years of living in the dark had helped my eyes see better and like Connor, Jay didn't really use his wolf much to help him in human form.

I wondered if other shifters were like this.

So did my wolf.

In the end we did shift and ran back home. Cody was sitting on the stairs out front and seeing us he stood up instantly.

"Where have you two been?" He demanded, standing he walked out to meet us and Jay quickly shifted. His tone grated against my nerves and instead I sat down, simply staring at him.

"Out for a run?"

Jay was confused; it was like we were in trouble only we hadn't done anything wrong. From inside Taylor and Adam's figures could be seen by the window, the light of the living room making them look like shadows on the curtains and Connor walked out to stand at the top of the stairs were Cody had been sitting.

"You went out at four; it's now close to nine. Did something happen?"

Then I heard it, hidden below his anger it was obvious. He had been worrying about us.

"No, Bianca just had a lot of energy to run off. We didn't go that far from the farm Cody." Jay dropped his gaze and his whole figure seemed to shrink. There was no argument in his tone as he made our run sound like a confession.

"I went looking for you and you weren't close to the property Jay."

"I didn't think we went that far."

Shifting, I had enough.

"What is your problem Cody? I know Adam and Taylor went that far a couple of days ago!"

"Don't worry about it." He growled, turning and storming inside there was no guessing where he was going.

"Sorry Jay, I didn't want to get you in trouble."

I rested my hand on his shoulder and he nodded.

"It's fine Bianca, he just gets like that sometimes after what happened. He's controlling, but it's because he cares."

He headed inside and the look on Connors face stopped me from following.

"What?"

"Been giving yourself computer lessons Bianca?"

"No, I haven't touched it."

Liar.

Connor laughed, as if he could hear my wolf and shook his head.

"There is a thing called search history and you didn't clear it when you were done. What's with the psychic chick?"

I froze, not wanting them to know about that.

"Bianca?"

"It's nothing. I was curious; my future is pretty unclear right now. Maybe they can offer some guidance?"

"Just one psychic Bianca, you searched for the store and the address and used Maps to work out a way to get there by foot." He crossed his arms, clearly not buying my lie. I hated the fact he knew so much about computers.

"I used to see her, in my old life." Still a lie.

"And she didn't give you a heads up on what was coming?" Connors doubt was still clear and I didn't like being interrogated like this.

"She did - a big change that I needed to be preparing for. I know what she meant now, if only she could give me some clue as to what's next."

I let my tears fall, trying my best to appear innocent and finally his bad cop routine started to break.

"You don't need a psychic Bianca; most of them are fakes anyway. Does it mean a lot for you to go and see her?" His family was to kind, Cody was the only with half a brain and I had no problem in taking advantage of it.

"Yeah, it really does. I know not everyone believes in them, but I do."

Liar.

Only now when my wolf spoke to me it wasn't with an amused disappointment and lying to her friends. She was just as eager as I was to see this woman and now it seemed like a possibility, her excitement matched my own.

"There is an end of summer fair down that way in a couple of weeks. I can probably talk everyone into going and while we're there, you could go see her?"

"You'd do that?"

He nodded his smile like Jays and a pang of guilt at lying to him made my stomach churn.

"If it'll help you, yes."

I quickly hugged him, amazed at how this simple gesture seemed to impress them so much. We headed inside and for the first time since my return, I didn't go see Cody. I was scared he'd be able to sense my lie and all I wanted to do was keep reading through the information Connor had already got me.

True to his word, two weeks later we all piled in the car and I was going to find the gypsy who ruined my life.

Seven.

No one could understand why Connor wanted to go to the festival yet as we pulled up in the car park, you'd never had guessed the amount of complaining Taylor had managed to come up with in the last week on why we shouldn't go. She was out of the car quicker than Jay and Adam and the trio disappeared before Cody had turned off the car.

The second I got out, I decided we should have listened to her and glued myself against the side of the car. The sounds of the crowd ahead and the scents of different shifters was too much, and I was on the verge of having a panic attack. Cody got out, and was talking to Connor on the other side of the car. I had no idea what they were saying as the more I panicked, my hearing seemed disappear. The pounding of my heart took over as the only thing I could hear and before I could fall over, Cody had me by the shoulders and was faintly calling my name.

In reality, he was practically screaming it.

"Bianca!"

"What's wrong with her?" Connor was scared, and I had to close my eyes as the daylight turned into a blinding spotlight.

"I don't know."

Relax, breath, I won't let anything happen to us.

It was my wolf's voice I heard first, calling me out from the darkness I was falling into and opening my eyes Cody was looking as scared as I felt. Looking around he had sat me in the back of the car, the door open above us I didn't protest as he hugged me.

"Are you ok? What was that?"

"I can't do it. I can't be here." I muttered, concentrating on my breathing I caught Connors gaze and he tried to smile.

"Why? What's going on Bianca?"

The screams of children from a ride had me flinching back further into the car and he realized what was going on then.

"The crowds. I didn't even think that would be an issue. I'm sorry."

"You're not the only one." I muttered.

How can we find her if you're hiding in here?

'Shut up.' I snapped at her, but she had a point.

"Did you want to go?" Cody offered and taking a deep breath I shook my head.

"No I need to do this."

Good girl.

He extended his hand and helped me out of the car. Before I could freak out again as a car passed us, Connor took my free hand and gave it a squeeze.

"We're here for you Bianca. If it gets too much, just say and we can come back here ok?"

I hated feeling so weak and out of control, so I only nodded not trusting myself to speak as Cody came up behind me and the pair of them guided me towards the blocked off street. I was scared I'd crush Connors hand as we walked through the entry, the scent of other shifters had my wolf on edge and I looked at them all suspiciously yet none of them even glanced in our direction.

"Connor, did you want to go find the others? I can stay with Bianca." Cody offered and it was obvious the youngest one in our group was eager to go and see what was on offer.

"No, it's fine. Maybe later."

The further we went, the more confident I became.

I thought hunting had been intense, the concentration needed to make sure you didn't find yourself face to face with an angry bull with deadly antlers was nothing compared to how alert I was now. An hour later we stopped by a food stand and Cody grabbed us all a drink and something to eat. Now I was a little more relaxed, I had a look around properly and down the end of the street I saw the store I had come here for.

Connor found a spot under a tree and I leant against it before sitting.

"Now it's just us, why did you really want to come here Bianca?"

I didn't answer, curious to know what he did.

"I was looking back over some of that stuff I gave you, is this the reason?"

The picture of Damon and the woman that had to be taken here was once again in front of me and I snatched it out of his hands.

"No, it is a coincidence."

"Bianca, I'm trusting you to tell me the truth. If you've put us in danger coming here, I deserve to know."

I hadn't seen this side of Connor and a part of me felt almost proud at how protective he could be. There was no mistaking the threat in his tone and Cody appeared as I was about to tell him which quickly shut me up.

"Alright, water for the lady, coke for the guys and check out these burgers!"

Considering I'd only been eating home cooked food, the site of the food van burger was tempting and also a little disgusting. The first bite silenced my doubts and the way my stomach churned once I finished it made me regret eating it.

"Cody, can you go see what the lines are like for the rides? I might see if I can get Taylor to go on that dropping thing." Connor smirked evilly, still half way through his burger while Cody and I had finished.

"Sure, you guys ok?"

I nodded and knew Connor was sending his sibling away for one reason only and the second Cody was out of earshot, he pounced.

"Tell me what's going on. Why did you really want to come here?"

"I really want to see the psychic. The only thing I never told you guys is why he wanted to kill me." So I finally told him the whole truth about that night.

"Shit Bianca! This is on the border of their territory, if they know you're alive and here – we're all dead!"

"He's not here. My wolf has been looking. Let me go see her, alone. No one will know I'm with you guys."

"And what are you going to do exactly?"

I shrugged, not entirely sure. I was happy winging it.

"For someone so smart, you're acting stupid."

"Please Connor, we're here. Let me do this." I begged and rolling his eyes he nodded.

"Ten minutes and if you're not back, I'm telling Cody everything."

I knew I made him in ally for a reason and we shook on our deal. We found Cody and walked around for a few more minutes, going into the direction of the shop. Outside a stall had been set up with a girl offering to read tarot cards, although judging by how bored she looked I wasn't sure how accurate her readings would be. There was nothing different about her, she was just human and probably paid to try and lure the real customers inside. Her outfit matched the one the woman had worn in the photo and it was probably just them playing the part.

Looking over, the park at the side of the building had been set up with temporary toilets and I saw my escape from Cody and Connor.

"You guys go ahead, I'm just going to the toilet."

Connor looked over in that direction and nodded.

"Ok, come on Cody, let's go see if we can outsmart the carnies!"

"Are you sure you're ok alone?"

Cody's concern made me feel guilty for lying, but I could worry about that later.

"I'm fine, it was just nerves this morning. I can go to the toilet without an escort." I smiled and Connor nodded.

"See, she's fine. Come on!"

Reluctantly he let Connor lead him away and scanning the crowd for the other three, they were nowhere nearby so I ran over to the store.

No weakness.

I let my wolf take over, instantly feeling more secure and walked through the plastic beads that covered the door. It smelt like a bad mix of herbs and incense, deadly to my sense of smell and I wondered if that had been on purpose. There were a lot of other shifters out there, maybe she did it to weaken us. The sounds of nature that filled the room were clearly artificial and distracting as I tried to hear for voices or anything that made it clear I wasn't alone in here.

Back room.

The store was dimly lit, candles lit up in odd spots around the room and the walls were lined with books and as I neared the counter the jingle of bells came from the back room as my wolf suggested and sure enough two people emerged. The elderly lady was crying, dabbing her eyes with a tissue and the toxic mix of rose perfume didn't help with the stench already present.

"Thank you Esmeralda, it was nice to hear from my Tommy!"

"Please Ms Parks, there is no need to thank me. I share my gift to help people!" She comforted the old woman and rather than wearing the same costume as the girl outside, today she was in pants and a more fitted white blouse that hung off her slim build which was dwarfed further by a rich red coat. Her whole look appeared to be more inspired by a pirate captain than a fortune teller and as she saw me the gentle smile disappeared. The fear in her eyes pleased my wolf and I only smirked in return.

I looked idly at a collection of crystals on the counter while the pair finished up and Esmeralda walked Ms Parks to door. I watched her cautiously as she left the building and strained to hear her tell the other girl she was taking a break. Coming back in the main door was closed and locked, setting me on edge as I became trapped.

"Well she-wolf, I was expecting you sooner. I almost wondered if I got it wrong and he did kill you."

Her voice was like ice, nothing like the soft spoken manner she had addressed her last client with.

"Rather than kill me, how about we make a deal of our own?"

Kill her; was I even capable of that?

Let me do it.

My wolfs anger made her stronger and I was struggling not to shift. While I doubted my own abilities, my wolf was out for blood.

"What kind of deal?"

Surprisingly I spoke as cold as her, the power in my voice felt as she hesitated her approach.

"You want to know the future don't you. I can tell you what you need to know."

"Like you told my mate to kill me?"

She laughed, shaking her head and the way the mane of blonde hair moved made me wonder if it wasn't just her clothing that was part of a costume.

"I never told him to kill you, he decided that. I merely told him the truth – his mate would be the one to kill him on the day they first met."

Her brown eyes looked me up and down making me growl.

"Clearly you're still alive so no harm done."

"No harm done? He killed my family and ruined my life!"

"Did he? Really? What is so ruined about your life? You seem to be doing well for yourself."

Her attitude and lack of empathy pissed me off further and I wondered just how much she knew. Something about the sly smile she had on her face told me it was a lot more than I did.

"Come she-wolf, let me see your future."

It was tempting and cautiously I followed her into the back room. Purple velvet lined the walls with a string of fairy lights around the edges and more candles on the shelves against the wall. The ball in the middle of the table reminded me of a snow globe and I took the seat she pointed out, listening as best I could outside the room in-case of anyone else coming in.

"Hand."

I put my hand as she directed and hovered hers over mine, the surge of electricity that ran up my arm startling me only she didn't seem to notice as she closed her eyes. As I watched the ball began to swirl, a black mist rising from the center so it turned into something resembling a tornado.

"Look into the center, you don't have to tell me what you see."

I did as she said, jumping back as Damon's face filled the funnel.

"Don't be scared, nothing in there can hurt you."

Swallowing I looked again, my wolf growling as she saw him. The man with him was someone I recognized, but I wasn't sure from where and Damon pulled a gun, shooting him straight in the head. Gasping I moved my hand away, and the tornado disappeared.

"What was that?"

"Something you needed to see from the future. There is more, do you want to hear it?"

"Yes."

She sat back in the chair, looking calmer than before.

"Thank you for not killing me, I knew you would accept my deal."

"I haven't done anything yet." I warned.

"You won't. You need me too much, just like he did." She pointed a red fingernail in the direction of the ball, "Do you know him?"

"No, but he looks familiar." I admitted.

"He is from your old pack and once you find him, your true journey will begin."

Oh she was good, I was hooked.

"True journey?"

"Do you ask yourself why the fates would choose a mate like him for you? I know you do, such a strong she-wolf paired with a monster like that, it makes no sense. Wrong. It makes perfect sense. I first saw him before he was a pup. He was angry, set on destroying himself. He was a kid, no one that young should be so angry. I saw his future when I touched him and the potential. I warned him of his Fathers attack." She went quiet, appearing almost sad.

Regret.

My wolf saw it first and I nodded.

"His father saw the potential, but unlike me – he saw the darkness. I should have kept my mouth shut. Ninety years and a fifteen year old wolf shifter fooled me." Esmeralda shook her head with regret and I wondered just what kind of relationship they had.

"Wait, ninety?" She barely looked thirty.

"I am over a hundred now, perhaps I am starting to get wiser with my age. Shifters are not the only magical beings on this earth Bianca." She clicked her fingers and behind her another wall of candles lit up as if to prove a point. "The pup managed to survive, because of me. I guess the fates knew it would happen, so they gave him a mate strong enough to do what was needed."

"How am I supposed to stop him if two strong and older wolves couldn't? He already tried to kill me and why would I want to?"

"Say the first word that comes to mind when I say, mate."

"Coward."

"And that is why you will win. The true why is up to you. Is revenge not enough?"

Revenge? I decided long ago that more killing was not the answer and wondered if she was setting me up for something else. Was she merely acting as puppet master, moving us around how she wanted. She said she had been fooled by Damon once before, was it she who was out for revenge?

She got up and moved the edge of the carpet, lifting a tiny trap door she pulled out a small wooden box and passed it over to me. The lid had the figure of a wolf engraved on the top and as I went to open it, she stopped me.

"I am sorry about your family Bianca, I didn't want to tell him what I saw next – it was you or me and I quite like being alive."

"You say something like that, how can I trust you?"

"Trusting me would not be wise. I have learnt my lesson, now it is time for you to learn yours. The future is unpredictable. Every minute that ticks by has the potential to change it all. Listen to your wolf, your instincts will never prove you wrong."

Kill her to keep her quiet.

"I should kill you to ensure your silence about my visit."

The fear was back in her eyes, she herself had just said the future was unpredictable and clearly she didn't like where it was going now.

"Perhaps. Wouldn't you like to know what is in the box?"

I had forgot about it and glanced down at it curiously.

"Wolfs bane."

My wolf growled, clearly knowing something I didn't.

"What does it do?"

"There may come a time when you need to be human, walk amongst the wolves without them knowing who or what you are. You will need this in your future, I promise you that."

That sounded wrong and an alarm bell went off in my head.

"Human? So I couldn't shift?"

"No matter how you tried. Each leaf will last for twenty four hours and only ever take one at a time otherwise you might find yourself more permanently changed." She warned.

"Why would I trust you with this then? How do I know that all you just told me isn't a lie?"

She smiled standing, her victory obvious.

"Because you are going to leave now and unlike your mate, you do not kill for no reason. I will be here, alive, to greet him when he comes tonight for his yearly reading and I will tell him the same thing I do every year."

"What do you tell him?" I whispered, clutching the box I was scared the wood would splinter.

"That his mate is dead."

"You tell him that, every year? Why?"

She left the room and I followed, my wolf eager to hear her response too.

"Because you are not the only one who doesn't like to be threatened. His charms stopped working on me years ago and I've been waiting for you to come and set things right. Curious, where have you been? I was starting to think it was true."

Lie.

'As if I would tell her.' I snapped back.

"Around. He is coming here tonight?"

"Yes she-wolf so you should leave now. You're not ready to see him yet. Remember the man in your vision." She pushed the door open and the sounds of the festival returned as if we had been in our own little world. My wolf seemed to accept what she said, retreating only I wasn't done yet.

Not expecting it, I easily pushed her against the wooden panel of the now open door and my forearm squeezed against her neck.

"If you have lied to me today, about anything - remember I've come back from the dead once and I will do so again to get my revenge on you."

Her struggles were futile and I only pressed harder as her eyes looked like they might bulge from her head. With a growl I stepped back and she held her throat, gasping as Connor came running through the door.

"I- I promise I haven't."

"Bianca?" He looked between the pair of us, clearly worried and I held up my hand to silence him.

"I didn't hear you."

She looked at Connor and recognition appeared over her face.

"It makes sense now. Good luck Bianca."

She quickly disappeared into the backroom and Connor grabbed my arm, pulling me outside.

"Ten minutes! It's been twenty and you totally disappeared!" He growled, but I didn't care.

"Connor? You found her!"

Cody and Taylor came running over and soon after so did Adam and Jay.

"Sorry, I got offered a free reading and couldn't refuse. I lost track of time."

Connor said he was going to tell Cody the truth if I didn't get back in time and the way they all acted told me he hadn't.

"A reading? Oh a psychic. Anything interesting?" Taylor piped up, glancing inside.

"Not really." Yet I looked at Connor who only narrowed his eyes.

"Ok, well I'm glad you're ok Bianca." Cody turned and stalked away, leaving us all staring after him.

"If I didn't know better, I think my dear old cousin has a thing for you." Taylor piped up and the boys all groaned, following after him. Looking back at me she saw the box. "What's that?"

"A gift, it's nothing really."

I followed after Taylor, not looking back. The rest of the day was spent trying out rides, eating sugary food and by the time the sun started to set, I ignored Esmeraldas warning and made no effort in getting them all to leave. As soon as it was dark the bulk of the crowd headed to the oval a street over and I felt my wolf retreating like she had the night Damon attacked.

He's here.

I looked around, inching closer to Connor and Cody as we searched for him. Now I could shift, the process complete I wondered if he would be able to tell if I was here. Could a wolf really hide from another?

Wolfs bane.

The first time I saw him, I didn't want to be defenseless, yet my wolf was adamant I took it. We found a seat on the oval and I kept the box hidden as I opened it, taking half a leaf I decided I may as well try it. At least if anything happened, I'd be close enough to kill the gypsy. That is, if it didn't kill me.

"What are you doing?"

Connor hadn't given me a second to breathe since we left the store.

"Disappearing."

I whispered back, ignoring my nerves the leaf tingled on my tongue before I swallowed it.

Nothing happened, I didn't feel any different.

"What do you mean you're disappearing?" Connor paused, looking me up and down before sniffing. "What did you do!"

"He's here. I'll tell you more later."

"What are you to whispering about?" Cody looked over, sniffing too. "You ok Bianca?"

"I need some air, could we go for a walk?"

He nodded and Adam watched us without saying a word.

"You're different. Are you sure you're ok?" Cody was confused, that much was obvious and I said nothing as we headed back to the main part of the festival.

"My wolf is hiding." It wasn't a total lie. "Cody, he's here."

"Who? Your mate?"

I nodded, deciding to let him on part of the secret.

"Shit, how does she does that? I can't even smell you. It's like your human!"

"I don't know." Liar.

The fact she was still in my mind was a comfort and clearly it worked if he thought I was human.

"Do you know where he is?" Cody looked around, the bulk of the crowd was gone now and some of the cleaners had started tidying up from the day.

"That psychic store."

"What if he sees you?" He pulled of his cap and sat it on my head, the world's quickest disguise "Did you, did you want to see him?"

"Yes."

I wondered if what Taylor had said was true, the hurt in his eyes obvious as he nodded.

"There is that ferris wheel, we can sit on that and get a look from up high?"

Nodding we headed over, both of us keeping an eye out. Had he already gone inside?

We'd just made it a quarter of the way up when the ride stopped and I looked down on the road, looking over each person who lingered in the street. Behind us the first firework sounded with a giant popping bang, and I jumped not expecting it.

There!

Cody held me, as the fireworks started going off and I almost forgot the reason why we were up there as I met his eyes.

There! You'll miss it!

Swallowing nervously I looked back down, and I was certain my heart stopped when I saw him. Three others trailed behind Damon and as he walked towards the shop, he stopped. He looked around, before looking up at us and I lowered the cap slightly so he couldn't see my eyes.

Not much had changed, and my wolf was growling in my mind. Unable to connect to my body, I sat silent and as the wheel kept turning he went inside.

"That was him?"

"Yeah." A feeling that was completely my own filled my stomach, twisting my gut I clenched my hands on the railing and the flimsy bar bent slightly under the pressure. "I should go down there and kill him."

"No, you're better than that."

"I'm not. I want to rip his throat out, and watch the life leave his eyes and..." I didn't recognize my voice, my eyes not leaving the building. I could wait for this wolfs bane to wear off, shift again and let my wolf have at him. He was a coward, he was weak. His strength came from his pack not his own abilities.

If I take down the pack, I take down the leader.

"Bianca, you're better than him. You're angry, hurt and trust me – revenge isn't as satisfying as you'd think."

"How do you I know?"

Cody sighed, sitting back the chair rocked slightly and now I gripped the bar for completely different reasons.

"The ones that killed my family? Jay found me at a bar, I know he told you that. Did he tell you the part where he found me covered in blood and half beaten from the fight they put up? I killed them all, I hunted them down and killed them."

The darkness in his tone was new, I knew he had his own secrets but I didn't know that.

"It felt good when I found them, the first three died easily and the others took a little more effort. To stand there on the line between life and death..." He went quiet. I recognized that distant look, I had my own place I went to when I looked like that.

"It's after the rush leaves you that regret takes over. You don't need to go through that Bianca."

He was wrong. Seeing Damon gave me a thirst that needed to be quenched, so I did what I was becoming so good at.

I lied.

"I'm sorry you went through that, you're right."

We got off the Ferris Wheel and it was then I caught a familiar scent. Closing my eyes the man who had been the one to put the bag over head came to mind and opening my eyes, he stood on the corner of the building having a cigarette. He didn't look as big as I remembered, nor as strong and I had to close my eyes as my wolf was fighting for control. She couldn't have it, the plant stopped her.

It didn't stop the head ache she was giving me trying.

As we walked past I turned to look at him, and distracted by the phone in his hand he had no idea how he was wasting the last few minutes of his life.

"I need the toilet again, I promise I won't disappear this time."

"He's just in there, I can stay?" Cody offered, looking at the shop nervously.

"It's fine. He won't know I'm even here. I have all the closure I need."

Reluctantly he nodded, and kept going back to the oval where the last few fizzers sparkled up from the ground. Being in human form posed more of a challenge and as I passed him, he whistled – checking me out.

I giggled, turning around shyly and kept walking. Being a predator, he saw a target. I was a weak human girl to him, only unlike last time a few things had changed. I passed the toilets, still hearing his footsteps behind me and certain no one was around stopped to meet him.

"A pretty little thing like you shouldn't be out here all alone." He was older than I remembered, closing my eyes I had only seen part of his face and with the moon the only source of light again, he matched it perfectly.

"Why? Is the big bad wolf going to get me?"

"Are you looking for one? I could help with that!"

"Doubt it, you don't look like a wolf to me."

And then it all became obvious on how I could kill him. I needed to call out the beast.

"Looks can be deceiving."

He got closer and the cigarette stench only got stronger. He had enjoyed that night in the forest, it was his grunts I had heard the most with each hit and as my wolf went through her memories, he had been one of the three who had been fighting my Dad. A new anger filled me and all of these feelings were my own, my wolf couldn't connect and that left little room for doubt in my mind.

He had to die.

"How about you run, and I'll show just how much of a wolf I can be." He growled and I gasped, doing as he said. Sure enough the thud of paws came from behind me and I slowed, waiting. The second his steps lessened I turned, the wolf snarling as it leapt towards me.

Ducking, I rolled as he landed and turned to grab at my arm. Without hesitation I poked him in the eye, his yelp muffled from the steady sound of the music still playing from the now finished fireworks. He shook his head before his paw wiped over his eye and he snarled again, turning to find me. I used the distraction to find a thick branch nearby and as he came running over, I swung out, knocking him over.

Just like I had with Taylor, I jumped onto his body and my hands gripped through the fur around his neck. My knee knelt into his ribs, the sensation of them cracking from the pressure had him gasping and wiggling, but I didn't let go. Just because I couldn't shift and they couldn't sense me, I still had her extra strength plus my own.

Kill him.

"You made a mistake not killing me that night." I growled into his ear, his eyes rolling up to look at me as his fight stopped and he understood my words.

He whined, if he was human he'd be begging and with another growl I snapped his neck.

Getting up I looked at him with disgust before heading back to the toilets and quickly washed my hands, wiping away the dirt on my jeans and fixing my hair. Stepping out of the stall, the group was heading over and seeing me they all visibly relaxed.

"You ok?" Jay asked.

"You said you'd be a sec." Cody reminded me.

"Sorry, I think it was all the fast food today, my stomach is aching."

Liar.

I knew she didn't care, her satisfaction was heavy in my mind as my own flowed through me as easily as my blood. It had been to easy, he had been predictable, weak. My wolf got lost in her thoughts, thoughts she didn't want me to know yet and so I left it behind, focusing on everyone as Connor looked at me so answers he wasn't getting.

I wasn't telling them about what just happened. Ever.

"Come on, let's get you home then. Who would have thought someone liked Jays cooking?" Cody teased, his family laughing with him while Jay look offended. The joke lasted the whole walk back to the car and I knew then Cody was wrong. The only regret I had was not being able to see Damon's reaction when they found his pack mate dead.

It was time to make the predator the prey.

--

Esmeralda >>>

So, what do you think of Bianca now, will she regret her revenge like Cody??

Eight.

"Bianca! There you are, I've been looking everywhere for you!" Leanna grabbed my arm and it took me a few minutes to focus on the details of my room. Nothing had changed, only as I looked down I saw the white gown I wore for my birthday party and touched the diamond around my neck.

"Sorry, I needed the bathroom and thought I'd touch up my lipstick." I answered, only that wasn't what I wanted to tell her. I felt trapped in my body, like when my wolf had taken over and I was only going along for the ride.

"Good idea, there is certain Mr that wants to dance with you," She winked and laughed, "And he isn't your Dad!"

I felt nervous, my heart starting to beat as we made our way back downstairs and into the party.

"I hope when you shift he's your mate. How good would that be? Despite you family taking the pack from his, we know he's going to challenge your Dad and then you can be our Alpha's!" She started filling me on her daydream and the feeling of unease that had unsettled me back then returned.

How could I have forgotten about this?

"I don't think this is a good idea!"

"You're just nervous, oh look there he is!" Leanna quickly fixed up a stray curl and then obviously pushed me in his direction and left me standing alone.

"Bianca, I don't think I've wished you happy birthday yet!" Ethan was quick to take Leanna's place at my side and it was hard to miss the way our parents were all staring curiously.

"It's ok, I think everyone else has made up for it."

"Well, happy birthday." He took my hand and kissed it gently, looking into my eyes as he let it go as if he was searching something.

I knew he wasn't going to be my mate and perfect the fairytale; I had no idea until I went through the shift, but a part of me just knew.

"Would you like to dance?"

Nodding he led me towards the dance floor and just like when Dad came out, a slower song came on meaning we had to stay close to each other.

"They all want us to be mates." He whispered into my ear. I had been close to guys before, I had a bunch of friends only none of them had ever held me like Ethan was or whispered in my ear in a tone like his.

"We're not mates." I answered quickly, hoping he didn't get offended.

"I know. I also know we can't possible know for sure until you shift, but you have that feeling too?"

I laughed, nodding and he spun me elegantly around. I had no idea he could even dance like this. Despite us all being in the same pack, attending the same school – we weren't in the same social groups and my knowledge on him was limited to the fact he was expected to challenge my father when the time came. He wasn't much taller than me, but he was rather solid and fit. I think he was on swim team and the majority of the she-wolves here had a crush on him. With his blonde hair and blue eyes, there wasn't much not to love.

"Well this isn't awkward."

Turns out he was a nice guy too.

"Not at all, hey Ethan – did it hurt to shift?"

I decided to talk to someone who had just gone through it, his birthday was last month and turning serious he held me a little tighter and gave me the truth.

"Yeah, they tell you it'll pass and no one admits it, but even a month later it still hurts afterwards."

We kept dancing and I rested my cheek against his chest, wondering how the hell I was going to get through it.

"Bianca!" He let me go and I turned to find Damon standing in the clearing he had attacked us in and looking around the party had disappeared. Ethan still stood behind me and the silver casing of the gun seemed to glow in the moon light and before I could process what was happening, the bullet was like an arrow gliding through the air and I turned to watch as it found its target and Ethan fell to the ground.

-

"Ethan!" I jumped off the sofa, screaming his name and in my daze I tripped over the coffee table.

"Bianca?" Cody was down the stairs before the others could get out bed and I quickly stood up. I was drenched in sweat and my leg was throbbing where I had hit it.

Ethan had to still be alive for Damon to shoot him; it was vision from the future not the past.

"He is from your old pack and once you find him, your true journey will begin."

Esmeralda's words came back to me, my true journey?

Find him.

"Bianca!" Cody had been yelling my name and as he started shaking my shoulders I blinked out of my daze.

"Sorry, I – I had a nightmare."

"Again?"

"This one was different." I sat down in the chair trying to remember Ethan's last name. I could get Connor to help me find him.

"Want to talk about it?"

I sensed the others hanging outside the room, Cody had obviously kept them back and even if I wanted to shift I couldn't. If half the leaf would equal twelve hours, I still had another five to go.

"No, no it's ok."

I lifted my legs up against my chest and held them close against me, trying to remember every piece of information I could about Ethan.

"Well, if you're ok – you know where I am?"

"Thanks Cody."

I didn't deserve to be around these people, and the second I heard them all get settled back into bed I went to Connor.

"I thought you'd come here." He yawned; sitting up on his bed he patted the space in front of him. "Tell me what happened last night."

So I told him everything the psychic did and about the plant which is why they couldn't sense my wolf. The one thing I left out was the dead wolf, so made up for it by telling him about my dream instead.

"Let me guess, you want me to find that Ethan guy?"

"Could you?"

"Cody hates it when I hack into the police database, but at least then we'll know if he is really alive and will be able to get an address." He sighed, pinching the bridge of his nose before looking at me again. "No more lies?"

"No lies, that's everything."

"Can I go back to sleep now? Unlike you, I don't get to sleep all day and have to get up and do work."

Nodding I gave him a quick hug and left him alone, sitting on the top step I listened to them all sleep. I felt exhausted, like I could sleep for days and most of all I felt lonely.

I missed the pack.

You have a new one.

'It's not the same.' I sighed back and she didn't believe that was true.

Getting up I was going to go back to Connor, but if I was going to sleep when they did and not have the ability to shift I needed to make sure I was going to be protected. In this house, there was only one I trusted like that.

"Cody?" I whispered, if he was asleep he probably wouldn't have heard and I had only just turned to door knob to go in and try again when he was standing in front of me. "Can I, if you don't mind, can I sleep with you?"

He only looked at me confused and there was something else there I didn't understand so I took his silence as a no.

"It's ok, I was just-"

I didn't finish, turning to walk downstairs he grabbed my arm to stop me.

"Come on, you look like you need some sleep."

I didn't realize how weird it was going to be laying beside him until I was in bed. I wanted to touch him, feel someone beside me and the human part of me told me this was more than I should be doing.

"Goodnight Cody."

"Goodnight Bianca."

It didn't take long for his breathing to steady out and with his back facing me I stayed on mine suddenly wide awake. His room was the most basic out of all of them; even the guest room I had taken over had a picture of a sunset on the wall. His clothes were kept away in the closet and the only sign of décor was a rug on the floor.

Waking up the pillow was moving and opening my eyes I froze as I realized it wasn't a pillow underneath me; it was Cody. His skin was warm and smooth under my cheek, I didn't even notice he didn't have a shirt on last night and for the first time I appreciated each perfectly sculpted muscle on his chest.

His arm was around my shoulders, holding me against his side as he head was turned down in my direction and his chin was resting on top of my head. He moved again, rolling onto his side as we laid horizontally against each other rather than me leaning on him. My heart was pounding, this was all new and exciting and terrifying at the same time. I wanted the contact, to know I wasn't alone and I had never expected it to feel this safe and nice.

Yes, it felt nice.

He was bigger than me and for all my strengths the second his other arm came down from his side to hold me I didn't want it to move. I felt tiny, fragile and my wolf was even more relaxed and content than I was. Her emotions had me feeling weak, if we were to fight now – I couldn't even think of trying to hurt him.

Nervously I moved my arm up in the free space to go around his waist and I pushed against him, testing how close we could really become. His scent was like a drug, so masculine and powerful if he asked, I'd submit to him. Closing my eyes, I got lost in the moment, drifting back into a happier sleep and I didn't want to wake up in case that had just been part of the dream.

I don't know how long we got to stay like that, the heavy footsteps down the hall woke us both up and panic was in his eyes as he looked down to mine. Without a word he rolled over and stood, leaving my wolf whining in my head for him to come back while I was frozen in place where he left me.

He opened the door and stepped out, the frantic voices of Jay and Connor pouring into the room.

"Cody, she's gone!" Jay yelled.

"She's always up when I get up and she isn't anywhere down stairs so I tried outside thinking she was waiting for me and..." Connor was silenced as Cody shut his door and I got up to get close enough to hear.

"It's ok; she came in with me last night."

Silence.

"Nothing like that!" He defended and it took me a few minutes to click on to what 'like that' actually was. "Connor, what did you mean she's up when you're up and is waiting for you?"

"We've been training together." Connor admitted.

"Training? I try and get you to train and you won't do it!"

"I know but you remember how I was telling you that I was catching her up on things, she returned the favor and gets me out in wolf form."

I couldn't believe Cody didn't know about that, considering he was the one to turn on the coffee machine. Then again – we were either out then or had already come back in and I thought Connor told him everything.

"Well, no training today. You guys don't even get up this early so if you're up – go get started and I want to bring the herd in from the top pasture too."

Groaning the duo left to wake up Adam and Taylor and I didn't move away from the door fast enough so as Cody came back in, I was mid step back to the bed.

"What are you doing?"

"Getting up?" I turned back to face him, trying to resist the urge to hug him as everything about him seemed different now.

"Were you listening?"

"Yes."

"Thanks for working with Connor then, kid needs all the help he can get."

He moved towards the closet and not knowing what else to do, I ran to my room. In all the time I'd been here, I had never felt more rested or happy and the more logical part of my brain was trying to shut it down.

A few minutes later there was a knock of my door and Cody stepped in.

"If you're up, I think it's about time you started working with us."

"What?"

"Get dressed; you're learning how to herd cattle today!"

-

The good thing about setting out with them was the fact Jay gave me a lesson on how to ride the dirt bike. Taylor took her horse while the guys used bikes and when they stopped for lunch by the herd, he was more than willing to show me what to do.

In the afternoon, he was on behind me and I got in a good few hours of practice. It was harder than the car and it didn't help that my concentration was non-existent as my wolf stalked each and every one of those cows like she would a herd of moose.

Cody's eyes never me, if my wolf wasn't looking at the animals we were bringing down lower – she was staring right back at him. Last night had been a moment of weakness, and she was eager to put the boundaries back in place.

Watching us wasn't on.

By the time we returned to the house, she was beyond agitated and so was I as her emotions fed into me. I focused on the positive; we could use the bikes and the car now, not brilliantly – but good enough.

Next on my list was learning to use the guns they had locked away in the back of the shed.

With all the training Cody and I had done, I realized it wasn't just a release from our stress or to prove to him we were equal – if not more dominant. Her whole reason behind it was preparing us for the fight she knew we would find ourselves in one day.

She had always wanted revenge.

It was why we could never live in the wild forever, for every inch of wolf – there was just as much human there and it wasn't just me who was affected by it. Learning to use the vehicles was another part of this training; the more familiar we became with not only our own strengths and abilities, but all that was available to us the better.

Everyone was tired, despite being used to farm work none of them put much more energy or time into their fitness. It was why Cody had been impressed I had been Connor to do some training in wolf form. They expected Cody to protect them, they never considered there could be another threat waiting around the next bend and as we were a small pack, they couldn't be so weak minded with their thinking.

If they had to live in the wild, they'd be dead.

There was no such thing as an easy meal, even on the days when you could relax you still had be alert for another predator lurking in the shadows or ready for when the weather changed and the herds disappeared.

They did what they had to and only because Cody made them.

"Bianca, come here!" Connor whisper shouted from the top of the stairs and seeing the trio collapsed on the sofa and Cody was still outside doing something with one of the bikes - I followed him into his room.

"It was too easy! Is this him, Ethan Forrest?" Turning the laptop to face me, I nodded.

"Yes! That's him!" it was his driving license photo and while he had lost that youthful edge to his looks, there was no doubt it was the same guy. "Where does he live?"

"A long way away, he has moved overseas. Six months ago his passport was used and he is on a student visa."

My hope dimmed, I wasn't sure what I had expected. Being on the farm over would be nice. I hoped to meet him and for the answers to all fall into place. Now we had the Atlantic between us.

"Does it have that face log thing? Can I contact him on there?"

"And say what? If you tell people you're alive when someone thinks you're dead, you're asking for trouble."

Connor had a point.

"The gypsy said once I found him, my journey begins. Do you think this would count?"

"I don't know. Give it a couple of days and see if any other signs pop up?"

"Thank you."

I left him trying to hack into Ethan's Facebook, the more I knew about him now the better. No one had moved off the sofa and since I could shift again, decided to go for run. No one was interested in coming with me so left my clothes on the veranda and let me wolf out.

We headed down the driveway that went to the rear of the property where Taylor had taught me to drive and I was glad no side effects seemed to exist from taking the plant.

The whining howl had me looking behind us and Cody came running up the track. We leapt forward, bowing playfully and as he got close enough we nipped his ear and sprinted down the track. He gave chase and unlike Jay didn't start to tire as we left the property behind. We finally slowed and panting heavily took a break, still wrestling in play when the scent of someone else came to me.

I paused, growling and sensing my change he stopped too. His head was lifted to the breeze and a few seconds later he growled too. We headed in the direction the smell came from and Cody took the lead which had me over taking him. The sounds of wolves up ahead had me dropping low, and he mimicked my actions and crawling through the bushes we saw the five wolves playing as we had been.

They were shifters too.

The breeze was blowing in the wrong direction for them to catch our scent, although from the shifters I'd met so far I doubt they would even notice their surroundings like their wild cousins did.

Cody nudged me and we moved away, to my surprise Cody shifted.

"Did you want to meet the neighbors?"

I shook my head and turned to go back where he had come from. His wolf reappeared at my side and we headed back home. The less people I met the better – so far there were only six people who knew who I was and I wanted to keep it that way for as long as I could.

-

The next week went by much the same.

Sleeping with Cody became part of my routine only I was always up before him and carried on with Connor. It was on Sunday morning he was actually waiting for me and while I could sense his excitement, his fear was thicker in the air around him.

"What is it Connor?"

"You know how I said wait for a sign? Well, Ethan flew into LAX last night."

"What? I saw Damon shoot him – they're right near there!" I started pacing, worried it might all be over before it could even begin.

"He's already gone though, from there he went to Canada and if his flight is on schedule, he'd be touching down any minute now."

Canada?

"Why would he go there?"

"I don't know, but if we give it a few hours I could probably check his credit cards and find out more."

"You can do all that?"

"I'm not just a pretty face." He joked. For all his weaknesses, he was stronger than most of us. He was smart and while he lacked the strength and ability to lead – he was good support. I likened him to the Beta of my wolf pack; he had the potential to take over only he didn't. While the Alpha's looked after all of the pack, he looked after them.

"You're really not."

"Oh and Bianca, don't even think you're going to Canada."

That's what he thought.

"Thanks Connor, let me know if you find anything else out."

We parted and I decided to try working the coffee machine one more time. Ten minutes later I was about to give up when Cody came down.

"Please step away from the coffee machine before you hurt it."

"I was just trying to get it ready for everyone." I didn't mean to pout, but I did.

"You've done the filter right, hit the green button until the light comes on and make sure there is enough water and you're done!"

Sure enough the water started to filter through the machine, coming out as the brown liquid that everyone seemed to love here.

Eventually everyone was up, the routine chores taking place and come mid-morning, Taylor surprised me with her suggestion.

"Cody, how about I take Bianca into town. She needs some clothes of her own and now she has some weight on her I'm sure she'll like having something that fits her rather than being too tight or loose or guy clothes!"

"You want to take her shopping?"

"Yeah, I think it'll be good to get away from you lot for a day!"

Cody looked at me, but I couldn't hide my shock at her suggestion and didn't answer.

"I don't think it's a good idea." Adam spoke up first and I knew it was because he didn't want me alone with his sibling.

"You're right. No." Cody decided.

"She can kick your ass Cody; we're not weak defenseless females you know!" Taylor challenged and his eyes narrowed in on her.

"She is right, I think we should go." I sided with her and that only annoyed him more and the tension in the room tripled as she didn't back down thanks to my support.

"I can go with them?" Connor piped up trying to clear the air, "I need some stuff too so we can do our own thing and still be close by?"

"Fine!" Cody growled and headed down stairs.

"That was intense." Jay looked at Taylor who only shrugged.

"We can't be kept here like animals in a cage. He needs to loosen up." She growled and turning to me she smiled. "Give me five and we'll go before the big bad wolf decides to blow the house down."

-

I walked behind Connor and Taylor who argued over something that happened on one of the TV shows they watched. The town was a hive of activity and just like when we got the festival, I was struggling to adjust to the crowds.

Taylor saw some of her friends and seeing how uncomfortable I was, Connor told her we'd be fine on our own and took me to one of the quieter stores.

"So what clothes do you like?"

"I dunno, jeans are good."

More surprising than Taylor wanting to take me shopping, which was really code word I want to see my friends – Connor knew a thing or two about fashion and I was in the change room checking sizes when another shifter came in.

"Connor, how are you? I haven't seen your brother in some time." The female voice had me curious and I peeked out from the curtain.

"Yeah good Anya, he's just been busy with the herds." He lied.

"Might come by soon to say hi. Did you hear about the shifter attack that happened a few towns over? It was during some festival and the Alpha down there is pretty pissed about it." Now she had my attention.

"No? Well with those packs it doesn't surprise me." Connor muttered yet the change in his tone made me nervous.

"True, so glad we're here and not closer! Is Taylor here?"

"Yeah, she asked me to check if something was in stock. I think she's up at the café though with her friends."

"Oh cool. I'll go see if I can find her then. Tell Jay I said hi!"

Relief came over me at the mention of Jay, not Cody like I had expected. Where did that even come from? Taking a deep breath, I squealed as the curtain opened and Connor was glaring at me.

"Know anything about that dead wolf?"

"No."

"You're lying, I can see a flicker of your wolf's eyes in yours when you lie – what did you do?"

Clever wolf.

'Go away. I can lie on my own.'

"I'm not lying Connor!" I stared at him hard, keeping a straight face and he watched me closely. He had made a mistake in telling me about that as from now on, my wolf knew to hide.

"Fine." He looked at the outfit I had on, becoming distracted. "Those jeans are definitely better than Taylors are on you."

"Thanks!"

We shopped for a little longer and Taylor found us as we passed a hair salon.

"You –in there!"

My hair was washed, treated, cut and styled. By the time we headed home I was in clothes that fit me and from having my hair done, I felt more like myself.

Jay and Adam played something on a PlayStation and Taylor went to put her shopping away. Connor helped me with my stuff and then disappeared into his room so I went back to the other two.

"Where is Cody?"

"Gone."

"Sulking"

They said at the same time, their eyes not leaving the TV where soldiers ran through a warzone. Adam glanced in my direction and had to look twice as I stood between the chairs.

"What?"

He looked away, but Jay was quick to take advantage of his distraction and his character was killed.

"Yes! Take that..... Woah!"

"What?" The longer they stared the more self-conscious I became and crossed my arms defensively.

"They're amazed you actually look like a girl, not a tomboy wearing her big brothers clothes for dress up. I think it's the hair, it doesn't look so feral anymore." Taylor flicked the back of my hair as she passed, jumping onto the sofa between the guys.

"You've seen me naked and now you stare?"

"Well, in our defense, your hair hid your boobs and that shirt doesn't!" Jay admitted and I couldn't stop myself from turning red.

"God you two are morons. I think there could be something in this working out thing though, you do look good Bianca!" Taylor smiled before snatching the remote from Adam and taking his place.

I didn't know what to say to any of that, the attention was more than I was used to and made me beyond uncomfortable.

"Bianca, can you tell me what you think of this shirt I bought today?" Connor called out, and looking back towards the stairs he waved his hands around frantically. He didn't want to talk about clothes.

"Sure."

"I've been keeping an eye on Damon and he is on the move. He just boarded a flight to Canada!"

"I need to warn Ethan." We both went quiet, before I had an idea. "Can you make me a fake face page? Can people easily do what you do? Can we make it secret?"

"More than half of people's profiles are probably fake ones and I could probably set something up so it will be impossible to trace here?"

"Can you do it? Then I can try to warn him without telling him who I am!"

He started to tap away on his laptop and with all the things going around on his screen I had to look away as I couldn't keep up.

"It'll take me a while, I'll let you know when I'm done just keep them away cause I need time to set it up and if they know what I'm doing, they're going to have some questions."

"Ok, I can do that."

I left him in his room and Cody was coming up the stairs, his reaction much the same as the others.

"Ah, you look nice?"

"Thank you."

"Have fun?"

I nodded and stood awkwardly between him and Connors door.

"I was going to ask if you felt like doing some training, but you got your hair done."

"If you're scared I can still beat you – even looking like a girl, I get it." I teased.

"Not at all, see you there in five?"

He went down to his room and I went into mine, slipping on leggings and a sports bra he was already down there putting on gloves when I walked in. The others were still playing their video game so at least now Connor could have the time alone he needed to set it up.

Cody didn't go easy on me, not that he ever did and I returned the gesture. The downside to constantly working with the same partner is you get familiar and as good as it was, I knew his moves before he knew what he was going to do and while he hadn't worked out my pattern yet – he was getting close.

I thought back to when I made my first human kill, fighting a wolf had been too easy like when Taylor had come for me in the hall. If I took the plant, I wouldn't be able to shift either and the more I thought about it, the more I wanted to do it.

"Can we try something different?"

"What did you have in mind?" He asked curiously, we were both breathing heavily and he undid his gloves, tossing them onto the table.

"Let me fight your wolf."

"Ok? How is that different?"

"I'm staying human."

He paused, trying to work out if I was serious.

"Why?"

"I want a challenge."

"You could get hurt. I'm not going to put you at risk!"

"I won't be at risk."

"You think you, as a human could beat my wolf?" He asked in disbelief.

"I don't think - I know."

His wolf was aching to come out, his eyes were changing to the amber of the animals and the more I mocked, the more likely this was going to happen.

"Outside, in that empty paddock. No holding back. If you're worried you might hurt me – don't forget I can shift just easily."

"I really don't like this idea."

Nothing in his voice made me believe him.

Submit; tell him we'll submit.

"If I have to shift because you're winning or about to win - we'll submit to you."

It was a tempting offer, even to the human and I saw the muscles in his arms tense as he tried to hold back from shifting then and there.

"Fine."

I headed upstairs, knowing full well he'd want to chase and quickly went to see Connor.

"Almost done, what do you want to say?"

"Just tell him Damon is coming and could possibly kill him. If he asked who we are, tell him someone from the pack and we'd tell him more later."

The howl the tore through the house was my sign to go.

"What are you doing?" Connor asked, getting up to follow me down the stairs and the trio joined us as I went outside. The black wolf of Cody stood waiting, and at seeing me his lips pulled back into a snarl before he ran over to the paddock, jumping the fence easily.

"I'm keeping everyone distracted."

Sure enough the trio followed me to the fence, not sure what was going on and Connor muttered something about not being able to watch me be stupid and went back to his room.

Climbing the fence, there were few bits of debris down the other end and otherwise not much I could use as a weapon. This was a test, so I'd have to make do and Cody gave me a wide berth as I walked towards the center of the field.

"Why aren't you shifting?" Adam called out, and glancing over they sat on the top panel.

"Because I'm fighting him human Adam!"

I didn't listen to their arguments that followed, something about me crazy, about Cody being an asshole for doing it and as I stopped to face him, I narrowed my eyes and growled.

He started to trot towards me, quickly closing in the distance and I turned to run to the other end. He was faster than I could be and suddenly veered left, he slowed and jumped towards me. I fell, turning as he came over already looking like he'd won and as he went to come in to attack, I bought my legs up and kicked him hard on his snout.

He yelped, not expecting it and I quickly got up and kept running. Taylor was screaming for us to stop and as the fight progressed, the screams turned to cheers as each of us got in hits and nips. Like the other night I found a decent enough branch and didn't swing as hard I could have.

I didn't stop moving the whole time and while I was starting to wear Cody down, I was getting tired too. With the sun started to set, we kept on and he got a good scratch down my leg which had me crying out. My scream gave him new energy and my own wolf was eager to get out and teach him a lesson now. If we shifted – it was over and that was the only thing that held her back.

His control was practically non-existent on his wolf and I expected and hoped for as much. Not being able to take me down was driving him crazy and I knew he wasn't holding back. That kill had been easy, and at least now I knew how hard it could have been.

I was lucky; I could have been the one to die that night instead of him.

As we ended up back down the other end where the three had turned to four, my attempts to end this were becoming more desperate and getting in a good hit with the branch, the next swing had Cody taking it in his jaws and I pushed it backwards, making him take it and as he stumbled and dropped it with me letting it go, I jumped onto his back, pushing my knees under his ribs and every inch of strength was put into holding him by the neck.

Just when I thought I had done it, he threw his head back and I was knocked off and he pounced quickly to pin me down.

"He's lost control; he's going to kill her!" Jay yelled, and pushing my hands up under his chin I kept his jaws away from my face. My arms were trembling with the effort as he tried to move away to try again, but thanks to my legs being around him, I was dragged along.

Let me take over.

It wasn't just Cody I was fighting, my wolf wanted out.

'No. I will not submit'

Her will became too strong and I couldn't hold both of them back any-more and as I shifted, I heard Adam cheer while the other three gasped.

'What have you done!'

I couldn't fight her anymore and I was pushed aside. Cody lunged forward to pin us down again, his tail curling even further as he knew he had won and going against the deal she met him half way, knowing him over.

Growling he got up, his movements slower than before and his hackles rose along his spine making him appear even larger.

She lowered her form, her tail wagging so low it swished against the grass and went near him, lowering her ears and she licked at his muzzle, rubbing against him like a cat.

My wolf was submitting to him, but on her own terms.

He stood there holding his head higher, growling lowly as he accepted it and he must have realized the same time as me and decided against it. He lunged for her to try and knock her over, and sensing the change she moved out of the way and instead knocked him down.

As he stood, she did the same thing again and after the third time he gave up – shifting.

My wolf stood beside him and he didn't look impressed at all.

I couldn't shift; she still had too much control.

"Shift."

I couldn't even make her shake her head.

"Bianca, shift."

Instead she dropped to the grass, rolling on her back and started wriggling around like a pup, whining as she did so and I was surprised to find Connor and Taylor shift and come running over.

"I give up!" Cody muttered, sitting down Jay and Adam came over to sit beside him and watched as the three of us ran around in wolf form.

Finally she gave me the ability to shift back and the other two tried coaxing Jay and Adam into shifting. It didn't take them long and the four ran out of the paddock, giving into a game of night time chase.

"You said you'd submit if I was winning."

"You weren't winning - I lost control. Do you have any idea how it was to keep you away while fighting with a voice in your head? She wanted to submit on her own terms, I think that was her plan all along."

"Your wolf is too smart for her own good and I was winning."

"Keep telling yourself that." I teased and the sound of the others playing came from somewhere near the bike shed. "Good fight though."

"Next time let's see how your wolf goes against fighting me."

The thought excited her and I knew we'd have him submitting for real within minutes.

"I don't think you could handle it."

I went to walk inside, limping slightly from the scratch on my leg and the bruise that started to come up on my hip, not expecting all the aches and pains to be forgotten as he grabbed my arm and pulled me around to face him.

"I think I can."

And then he kissed me.

Ethan >>>

Nine.

And then he kissed me.

--

What to do next was lost on me, so I simply froze. A part of me wanted to run, another was urging me to mimic his actions; give in to instincts I was still rediscovering.

Having him so close was nice.

Just like sleeping beside him each night was nice.

Comforting.

I took too long to react. I could sense his emotions as they passed and my wolf was more in tune to these than I was, so I felt each thing. Lust, anxiety, rejection; anger. My lips felt cold as he moved away; I don't think I even blinked as he struggled to look at me. Shaking his head, Cody stared to go up the stairs and finally my instincts kicked in making me chase after him. He clearly didn't know, stopping abruptly I practically walked into him as he turned.

Now all he felt was confusion and he wasn't the only one.

"Sorry, I don't know what I was thinking." He growled lowly, clearly frustrated.

"Cody, I..."

"It's ok, forget it."

I let him go and he went to shower, skipping dinner and going straight to bed. No one said anything, assuming it was because of the fight and I didn't bother correcting them.

"Why are you up? You've been normal lately." Connor came over to where I sat in the living room. The TV was off, but I couldn't bring myself to go to bed alone and I was scared to be alone with Cody. So now it was gone one in the morning, and I was still up.

"Thinking."

"About?"

"Everything."

I couldn't let Cody make me feel like this, just like he shouldn't feel any of these things for me.

"Well, while you're thinking I heard back from Ethan. He knew he was being followed, but is wanting to know who we are."

I only nodded.

"Bianca, we should tell my family. Maybe we can bring Ethan here?"

"No. I won't' put any of you at risk." It was a stupid suggestion, who knew what Ethan was like now and even Damon was following him I certainly wasn't going to lead him here.

"Talk to them first and see what they think. We could come up with a plan together?"

Connor was hopeful and I understood why. Together; our kind generally works well together, another trait inherited from our wild cousins and I could just imagine how sitting around the dining table and discussing it would go. They kept to themselves for a reason and I wasn't about to change that.

"A plan for what?" Jay startled us both as he appeared, yawning he stretched as he came to sit with us.

"Nothing." I snapped.

Connor looked between the pair of us and I knew what he was planning.

"Nothing Connor."

"You two are up to something, just tell me." Jay yawned again and Connor and I yawned with him.

"We found someone from Bianca's old pack." Connor blurted out and that woke Jay up.

"Really? So what does that mean, are you going to go back to them? I don't think that's a good idea considering everything else."

"Jay, relax. I'm not going back to my old pack."

The brothers looked at each other and Connor shrugged.

"We'll talk about this in the morning, I think it's time we all got some sleep." Jay concluded.

"Good idea." Connor agreed and they got up to go back to bed.

"I'm not ready for bed yet, good night."

At the sounds of their doors closing I got comfortable on the sofa, trying to work out just what I was going to do. I could leave them now, track down Ethan myself. I still wanted to learn how to use a gun, maybe Ethan could teach me. The fear he wouldn't want to have anything to do with me was lingering in the back of every plan I could come up with, but the gypsy told me it would all start once I found him. I wondered who else in my pack survived, he wouldn't have killed them all. Were any of my friends still around?

My wolf became alert and sitting up, Cody stood in the doorway.

"Are you alright out here?" While his voice was raspy with sleep, he didn't look like he had been asleep at all.

"Yes."

There it was, disappointment. My mouth wasn't my own as I spoke again.

"Did you want to sit with me?"

Cody hesitated, before moving to sit behind me. Instantly I leaned against him, curling up against his side like it was the most normal place to be. His chest vibrated with the smallest hint of a growl, only there was nothing alarming there. The contentment that passed between us was completely mutual and regretted not going to bed sooner.

"Can we sleep in bed, this is killing my back." He whispered a short time after. I didn't want to move, not willing to wake myself up as the exhaustion of the day had finally taken over. Instead I was lifted carefully and I struggled to keep awake as he headed up the stairs. He was right, being in bed was so much better and it didn't take long for me to find my place beside him once more. I was barely conscious as I felt his lips on my forehead, and with that final gesture we both fell into a deep sleep.

-

Everyone let us sleep. We were normally up by five and it was nine thirty when the bikes being fired up woke us. The extra sleep left me feeling amazing, and it was obvious Cody felt the same as I had never seen him so well rested.

"Morning." He smiled slightly, rubbing his eyes and as he stretched , I did the same.

"Morning."

We didn't mention the kiss or the fact neither of us seemed capable of sleeping without the other close by. It didn't matter either. We went our separate ways, the shower had never felt better and the new clothes were just as delightful as the water against my skin. Breakfast had been left in the oven and I had managed to eat nearly half of the bacon and pancakes before Cody came down. What was left didn't long after his arrival.

He head out into the paddocks where Jay and Adam could faintly be heard arguing and to my delight, Taylor was walking around with a gun.

"What's that for?" I asked curiously, silently praying she'd offer to teach me.

"Defence. I like to take it out every now and then to stay sharp. I know we're wolves, but a bullet works just as good!"

The clop of horses hooves sounded from around the corner of the shed and sure enough, Connor appeared on the buckskin while Taylors black mare followed it obediently.

"Did you want to come?" Taylor offered.

This day was getting better and better.

"Sounds great!" And looking at the horses, I decided I might shift and run with them.

"Jump on behind me then." Connor offered, and Taylor grinned, clearly seeing my shock at having to ride the horse. He extended his hand and I watched as Taylor mounted easily. Taking a deep breath I followed his instructions and he hoisted me up. The second the beast started to move I was gripping onto his waist like my life depended on it and I guess it really did. These things were unpredictable. If it got spooked it could throw us off and trample us with its hooves.

Who knows what else they were capable of.

"Bianca, you're hurting me." Connor whispered, trying to loosen my grip.

"Why do you ride these things?" I hissed back. The cousins only laughed at me, deciding it would be even more amusing to make the animals gallop. By the time I got down I was shaking and furious, my wolf assessing each of the animals as they were tied up nearby, for the quickest way to take them down.

Connor went and set up some tins a few yards away and Taylor began to tell me how the guns work, how to load in bullets and a bunch of other stuff she thought important. I was still trying to get over the ride up here to give her my full attention and that all changed as she fired the first shot, easily hitting the can.

It wasn't long until it was my turn. The other two made it look as easy as riding the horse, so experience told me it wasn't that simple and it wasn't. The first attempt had me stepping backwards from the ricochet of the shot, but at least I knew what to expect and with Taylor guiding me my next go was better. I still couldn't hit a can, my wolf eager to take over and I felt my abilities improving as she pushed through. With her senses at the front, my hearing was better and so was my balance and crouching low, I hungrily eyed up the can like it was a fresh piece of meat. Or a horse.

"Just lower the tip slightly," Connor instructed, coming up behind me and checking my position.

The wind picked up as I went to fire, and turning the tip slightly to the left as the bullet left the gun, the can went flying off the tree log. Taylor cheered and Connor grabbed me in a hug, while I was grinning like a mad man. We were still celebrating when Adam came running over in wolf form and shifting he looked at us all curiously.

"Bianca hit her first can!" Connor enthused.

"Yeah, only took her two hours." Taylor teased.

"So you teach the crazy one how to use a gun?"

Instantly I growled, he was teasing like his sister and my good mood began to slip.

"The crazy one still has the gun Adam." I warned, making a show of reloading.

"And that's enough for today." Connor snatched it from me and quickly shut it down. It didn't matter, I didn't need a gun to hurt Adam and as I continued to stare at him, he knew it too.

"You're such a shit Adam. What do you want?" Taylor snapped.

"Cody wants to speak to Connor and the neighbors are coming over to sort out the transport of the cattle to market next week." Adam shifted, looking at me once he started to leave. There was no way I was going back on a horse and quickly stripped, shifting.

"Oh he is in so much trouble." Taylor whispered to Connor as I took off after Adam. It didn't take him long to realize I was following and the harder he ran, the more fun I was having. I nipped at his heels, teasing him and before we hit the house he stopped and submitted. I took that as his apology and let him up, bouncing playfully forward, I didn't understand why he continued to dislike me. It took a little coaxing and I managed to make his wolf respond.

"Never thought I'd see this." Jay mused, coming near where we were playfully wrestling. Distracted I looked in his direction and Adam took a cheap shot, biting too hard on my leg. A short whine of surprise and pain escaped me and he decided to take his chances and leapt up to grab at my neck. He shook his head, his teeth breaking the skin beneath my fur and I was struggling to keep control of my wolf who had no patience left for him. Jay came running over as I managed to push him off me. If he thought because he was a bigger wolf he might stand a chance, he was wrong and this time when I pinned him we just held him like we would a dead rabbit. The internal struggle between human logic and wolf law was raging in my mind and finally I got her to let go.

Adam was quick to start trying to suck up. Like my wolf had submitted to Cody, he moved around me slowly. He seemed to shrink in size as he licked around my muzzle and reluctantly his apology was accepted.

Shifting he didn't say a word, and Jay only shook his head. Glaring at him I shoved him roughly in the chest, making him stumble backwards.

"Do that again and you're dead. Every time you push, I am losing control of my wolf." I warned.

Not the wolfs fault.

I understood what she meant, it wasn't his wolf at all driving him to constantly test us. It was why he was so quick to submit and why she hadn't killed him yet. It was all human.

"You should listen to your wolf, he is the one with the brain!"

Adam said nothing as he went inside and Jay began to apologize, but I stopped him. I didn't want to hear it. Taking refuge in my room, I went back over everything Connor had given me regarding my mate. I knew each word on all the pages now, but still I read it again. The death of that shifter left me wanting more, a successful kill made you hungry for the next. Life is unpredictable. In the wild the wolves understood the seasons, but they still treated each kill like it would be their last, even in the spring when food was in abundance.

I just started my own cycle, I knew my prey, I had made a kill – I wanted more.

I sensed Cody before he could make it to my door, quickly shoving everything under my pillows I looked at him expectantly when he entered.

"Sorry about Adam."

"Don't be. He is his own person."

"The neighbors are coming over, did you want to meet them?"

I shook my head, thinking about taking some more of the wolfs bane.

"I'll keep them out of the house then."

Leaving me alone, it was Connor who came in next and in his hand he had my clothes I had taken off to shift.

"Thanks."

"Ethan has left four more messages, what do you want to do?" Connor paused as the sound of the car came from down the drive and moving to the window we watched the neighbors arrive.

"Can I talk to him?"

We went into Connors room and sure enough another message was flashing on the screen.

"Do you think I should tell him who I am? No one can track where we are can they?"

"Not unless they're really really good and even then I've set it at a location in town. It's up to you what you tell him." Cody's voice came from outside, calling Connor. He grabbed the file next to the laptop and left me alone.

Ethan Forrest: Who are you?

Please tell me, if you know Damon is following me are you in his pack from the takeover?

Are there more of you?

Hello? Answer me!

Daisy Duke: There is only me and I am not in his pack. I run alone.

Ethan Forrest: Who are you?

Daisy Duke: I can't tell you on here. I want to meet, in person.

Ethan Forrest: How do I know this isn't trap?

Daisy Duke: You don't.

What could I tell him that would make him willing to do this? I had no idea, but he was the one person that might be able to help answer my other questions.

Daisy Duke: Did the Alphas have the funeral they deserved?

Ethan Forrest: They did. It was done before the takeover happened.

Daisy Duke: Did Leanna?

Ethan Forrest: I made sure she had more pink roses than she could have dreamed of.

My tears were burning as they ran down my cheeks, just thinking of the funeral I hadn't been able attend broke my heart. Thankfully the pack had looked after them and closing my eyes I could just imagine a beautiful white coffin with bouquets of pink roses which were her favorite flower, all over it. The image Connor had found of her at the crime scene flashing into my mind, and I fell to my side sobbing.

I missed my parents; the sound of Mums voice waking me up, the comforting scent of my Fathers hug. I missed birthday pancakes, made in love heart shapes and covered in chocolate and sprinkles. I missed the feeling of their love, their presence. I missed Leanna, and sleep overs and gossip. I missed school. I missed all day shopping trips to the mall and talking about what our future would bring. I missed her companionship, she had been like my other half and I wouldn't even care if she was late if I could just see her one more time.

The ding of another message had me snapping out of my pity party, wiping my eyes I was positive my heart stopped as I saw his next message. How stupid had I been to ask those questions?

Ethan Forrest: Bianca, is that you?

Daisy Duke: No.

How did he know Leanna's favourite flowers? We all knew each other, but we weren't really friends.

Daisy Duke: How did you know Leanna's favorite flowers?

Ethan Forrest: She was my mate, the night she died my wolf felt it and I had a dream about her.

My heart was breaking all over again, not just for Leanna, but for Ethan too. She was the one destined for her perfect fairytale ever after with the future Alpha and it took me a few minutes to work out what to say.

Daisy Duke: I am so sorry.

It wasn't enough. I could never tell him how sorry I really was. It was my fault he lost his mate.

Ethan Forrest: I want revenge 'Daisy' and I know you do too. I am willing to meet you in person, where do you want me to go?

Daisy Duke: I'll be in contact soon.

I tried to work out how to delete the conversation, and satisfied I had managed to do it closed off the laptop. My wolf was willing to take over, feeling my pain and distress, but she couldn't ease this pain. I thought I was getting better, but all of this just shattered my world all over again. Sitting by the window, everyone had disappeared and going down stairs, their voices were out on the verandah.

Since I couldn't leave without being seen, I went downstairs and sat in the corner of the gym hiding. It wasn't long until I started to cry some more and eventually I fell asleep. Ethan knew too much now, I either disappeared into the wilderness or go find him. I knew he would be looking for me since he knew I was alive and I couldn't risk Damon following him here.

My wolf wasn't responsive, retreating into the back corners of my mind and I was left on my own.

"If she's gone, we'll just have to hope she comes back." Cody woke me up, the pain clear in his voice. Opening my eyes everything was hurting. I had a pain in my neck and shoulders from where I had slumped over, my eyes were burning from the crying and my legs were cramped from how I had curled up.

"There is no fresh scent anywhere Cody, it's like she just... hid." Blinking a few times the pair of them stood by the door and Connor pointed in my direction. "Why are you hiding down here? Was it the neighbors?"

"No," I coughed, trying to make my voice work properly from the squeak that came out "No I wasn't hiding from them."

"Are you hurt?" Cody asked, sniffing in my direction.

Yes. I was hurting in ways I couldn't even begin to tell him and fresh tears were brimming at the edges of my eyes.

"No."

"I got this Cody." Connor came over and helped me stand, his eyes searching mine it wouldn't take a rocket scientists to know what had upset me. I barely got to move my arms to hug him back when Cody was pulling him away.

"Leave us."

I couldn't even argue, yet Connor didn't move.

"No, you don't understand."

"Why don't I understand? You two have your secrets and I've had enough. I demand to know what's going on. This is MY house and I am Alpha here!"

I was close to blurting it all out and wouldn't blame Connor if he did. Cody was beyond angry, his command would have a lesser wolf in tears or shifting out of fear.

"It's not my place to tell you."

My mouth dropped as Connor managed to fight the command and that was all Cody needed to tip him over the edge. His fist came up to punch Connor, or maybe shift - i wasn't sure and I quickly pushed him down out of the way to take the hit for him, falling beside him my jaw exploded in pain and I spat out the blood filling my mouth. My wolf was quick to take over, ready to defend her vessel and her friend and growling Cody hesitated.

His regret was obvious, he would never hit his brothers, his anger had got the better of him. His dominance was understood never enforced and while we fought in training and would rough each other up, that hit had been different; not intended for me.

Connor's fear was like a fog, seeping in the room and while it helped to calm Cody, it only made me angry.

Anger felt better than broken.

"Leave us." Cody commanded again, the edge to his tone more deadly than the rage that had been there seconds before.

Connor didn't fight this time, inching himself slowly away from me, the second he passed Cody he ran up the stairs and I heard him close the door.

I was expecting another fight, maybe some yelling, but instead he sat on the mat in front of me and just stared. Slowly I got the power back to shift, my jaw barely a bruise as my wolf had been quick to heal it.

"I'm sorry."

"It's OK. We've all felt like that before, your wolf got the better of you."

He only nodded, and while he was calm I could sense his wolfs unrest. We sat in front of each other for a few more minutes, neither one of us saying a word.

"What's going on between you two?" Cody finally asked.

"What do you mean?"

"You get up early together, stay up late. He always offers to go everywhere with you and I hear the whispering in his room and you defend him all the time."

He is jealous.

"He's been helping me." I started.

"It's been a couple of months now Bianca, how much does he really need to help you?"

"More than you'd be happy knowing."

He growled, and I realized how that would sound.

"He found someone from my old pack. He's been looking up things about my past; the people in it."

It felt good to tell him the truth, well the start of it and I don't think he really understood what I told him as he seemed more relieved than anything.

"That's all?"

"Yes Cody, that's all."

"Then why are you down here, what happened?" His anger had completely gone, and I stood up set on running away once I told him what I had decided.

"I've decided it's time for me to leave."

"Oh. Wait, what?" He stood as I began to leave the room, quickly stopping me. "Why?"

"I don't want all of you to be involved, Connor has done enough and I need to find someone."

"We're already involved, the second you stepped foot in this house we got involved. We will help you."

Packs work together.

'It's too dangerous'

Better than being alone.

"You don't even know what you're agreeing to Cody." He had warned me against going down the path of revenge. It hadn't helped him and maybe one day I will agree with him, but not now. Not until it was over.

"You want to go all lone wolf and act a hero? That's stupid Bianca, we can help you!"

He was getting angry again and my wolf warned me to tread carefully.

I could just lie to him again.

"I'll think about it."

I had every intention of doing just that, until it all went out the window thanks to how close he was standing in front of me. I had to look up at his face otherwise I'd be pressing noses with his chest and now the look in his eyes had my body feeling numb for completely different reasons.

"Good."

My lips parted in preparation for what was coming next, his warm breath mixing with mine as there was practically no space between us.

This time I kissed him.

Cody had me feelings thing I didn't want to even know about, not helped by the rush of acceptance my wolf hit me with. Cody was strong, dominant and she saw him as her equal, worthy of us. Would it have been like this with my mate? The love we would have developed should have been greater than anything else possible, but what Cody and I had was completely natural. The human part of me couldn't deny he was attractive, despite his rough exterior his heart was in the right place. Even if he was as damaged as I was.

If I had met him before his own families attack, would he really be different to the man he was now?

I couldn't imagine him any other way.

I didn't want him any other way.

We gave in to our own primal urges, the contact of skin on skin offering a way to connect completely. Pain soon gave way to pleasure as we wrestled on the mats, not training this time although we ended up just as sweaty. For all of my own virgin inexperience, he was there to guide me; teaching me something completely new and this time when he pinned me down, I wasn't struggling to get free. Instead I wanted it, begging him to keep me beneath him as the pleasure only intensified.

By the time we finished, still clinging to each other, I knew more than ever that it was time to leave.

--

I woke up first, barely an hour later and carefully getting up I headed upstairs. Finding the laptop in the living room, I gave Ethan the details on where we would meet and deleted the message as soon as I got his reply. Once that was sorted, I went to my room to pack a few things. Using one of the backpacks from by the front door for storage, I shifted and grabbed the bag, disappearing into the night.

The letter I left on the kitchen table explained everything and I promised I'd return one day.

I just hoped that when I did, they'd still accept me.

<h1 style="text-align:right">Ten.</h1>

We didn't stop till mid-morning. If we planned this right and Ethan was able to do as we planned, I'd be seeing him by nightfall. What I didn't expect was the familiar form of the Alpha's daughter trailing me and our reunion was soothing to my soul. Following her, the pack was nearby and I didn't like how low they'd come so early. The reaction I got at returning to them was of pure joy and the pups were now mini wolves, actively joining the pack. I was glad to see they had all survived so far, it would appear this year was being kind to us all.

I stayed with them for two days, heading in the direction I needed to go and as night fell the single howl had them all responding. I kept quiet, listening to make sure it was the one I was waiting for and shifted. My own song sounding out after the pack and the response was quick to answer. The pack followed me as I took off towards Ethan and it took it me longer than usual as I convinced them to stay back. My power with them was weak and while they didn't stay at my side, they did linger nearby.

Old habits die hard.

I dropped my backpack nearby, easily finding Ethan who was looking around cautiously. I watched for a few minutes, assessing the wolf in front of me. He was a little taller, thinner and while I knew he felt he was being watched, he made no attempt at finding the source. I circled him, purposefully making noise when I wanted him to hear it and all I seemed to be doing was making him even more scared.

Weak.

'Give him a chance.'

Everything was riding on what this meeting could provide us and putting him out of his misery, I emerged from the bushes. He spun around instantly, growling with warning and I didn't flinch, shifting instead. He instantly stopped, shifting and running over to me.

"Oh god Bianca!" While I had become familiar with the others touch, and despite the fact he was of my original pack, I shied away from his hug. He didn't seem to notice. "I can't believe it's you! We all thought you were dead!"

"I should have been. Are you alone?" I glanced around curiously, I knew he was, but he could always have some waiting a howl away.

"Yes, it's easier to move around undetected when you're on your own."

"Come, I know somewhere we can stay the night and talk."

Shifting, he followed without complaint and finding the pack he went on attack mode. The wolves all responded the same and shifting I tried to encourage him to do the same.

"Your place to stay is with wolves?" He asked in disbelief. I tried to calm the pack and the longer I was with them, the more they listened and finally moved away from us.

"They saved me Ethan, do not think less of them because they are only animals." The edge my tone had him silencing and I wondered if he really could have taken the place of my father at the head of our pack.

Weak.

My wolf didn't think so.

"Can you tell me what happened and where you've been the last five years?" He asked, glancing towards the wolves who watched him like an easy target. We found a nice patch of grass to sit down on and I told him parts of what had happened. Despite everything, I didn't trust him.

"How did you know Damon was coming after me if you've been playing wolf all this time?"

I decided against telling him about the gypsy. For some reason I felt like that was my one advantage over all of them, so I lied.

"A dream, it was almost like a vision. Damon shot you, and since I've been tracking him – after that I looked for you. The fact you'd both went into Canada was to convenient."

"I knew he'd be after me the second I decided to come back home. I'm not going to make it easy for him to kill me." He growled. He had my story, now I needed his.

"Why would he want to kill you?"

"It was a week after we buried your parents he appeared. He declared he was going to take over and merge the two packs. The survivors were thankful, but I recognized his scent of Leanna and put two and two together so to try and defend our pack from his take over, I challenged him."

"You were to young!" I gasped, he had only been a shifter for a month and that challenge would have been asking for death.

"I know. So did he and the pack, my challenge was revoked with his permission. Only because I had done it, clearly I'd try again when I was older so he made my life hell. I just want revenge for my mate and to take back my pack."

It's not his pack.

'It's not ours either'

She snorted in response and I focused back on Ethan.

"Four years later I was visiting Leanna's grave and he was there, him and his thugs. If you challenge him it's not a fair fight, he uses safety in numbers and is never without them around him. A couple of weeks ago a wolf was killed that was part of his group. I sent a bottle of champagne and I think he thinks I did it."

I regretted not doing something the same, and made a mental note to do that next time.

"So I'm at the grave and he asks me if I still wanted to fight him and I said no. I'm not stupid. He admits to me he was there when Leanna died, that she had begged like a whore for them to let her live and that our Alpha's had fought like weak mutts. I knew what he was doing and before I could respond they jumped me, he kept saying something about a gypsy telling him that I was a threat."

Again my wolf snorted.

"Then what happened?" I asked softly, his rage thinking about the comments about Leanna obvious.

"I got one of them, managed to shift and ran. I went home, got a few things and headed south to a human friends place. Six months ago, I got the hell out of here and headed to Europe."

"So why did you come back?" He had an out, he would have been safe over there.

"I got a letter telling me my parents had died, foolishly I came straight home and getting to the airport I knew it had been a set up. I got the next flight out of there as the place was crawling with his pack and as soon as I could, I phoned my parents to tell them. They're currently in New York and are heading over to my place in Germany."

"Why haven't you left?"

"Because when I was arranging my flights I got a message warning me about Damon coming and decided to find out what that was all about. So here we are!" He waved his hands around the clearing and I only nodded. "Whats your plan?"

"I'm going to kill them all."

"Bianca, you're a girl. You've been running around the forest with wolves. What chance do you have of taking him down?" His disbelief annoyed me and I growled, not caring enough to stop my wolf coming out.

"Because I'm the one who killed that shifter and that's how I'll get him. Take away the pack, he is nothing."

I didn't think Ethan was going to be much help. My wolf was right, he was weak and while I was glad I knew his story; it provided me with nothing.

"Then you're going to need my help."

"Why?" I couldn't hide how skeptical I was over that declaration.

"Because I have another one of those guys tailing me. He lost me back over the border, but he is a keen tracker. I can lure him out and you can kill him. They will think I did it, playing in your favor and so when they come after me, you can get them."

All I heard was me kill them, and while he clearly wanted the glory, he wanted his hands to stay clean. Had he always been like this? Either way the result would be the same.

"Deal."

A few hours later Ethan was back to asking me questions and while I answered them simply or not at all, he finally asked something he should have done in the beginning, despite my vague description of what happened that night we were attacked.

"Do you even know why he chose us?"

Don't tell him.

My wolf didn't trust him, neither did I. Even if he was meant to be Leanna's mate, he wasn't so I had no reason to believe him.

"No idea, but he made a big mistake leaving me alive."

And that was the truth.

-

Crossing the border was easy enough and stealing a car, I left that side of things to Ethan. He did let me drive for a while and the open country roads gave me time to adjust to driving on actual roads and also to be alert for road signs. The first town we came across we booked into a hotel, figuring they were probably tracking his accounts like Connor had.

Just thinking about him made me think of Cody and a week later, I was missing all of them; even Adam. Ethan was nice enough, our travelling in human form left us with time to talk and he filled me in on what he knew of our pack that was left. Many had died in the fights that followed the takeover but Damon had the numbers we didn't and with no Alpha to lead, the pack submitted.

It was the smart thing for them to do.

"Do you ever sleep?" Ethan asked as we found our room.

"Yes?"

"I mean for more than an hour at a time."

I struggled to sleep without Cody. I don't know how that happened, and I hated it. Exhaustion eventually made me stop, but it never lasted. I needed to be stronger if we were going to have to fight and despite requesting separate beds, we were given a small double. Turns out it wasn't Cody I needed, just someone beside me. Well that was what I told myself. In reality my wolf took over, imagining Cody beside her and it worked. We slept for nine hours straight and I felt more human the following day.

"Daisy Duke keeps messaging me, I just got reception back on my cell." Ethan handed me his phone and all of Connors messages came through in a rush. A week without checking had let them pile up and by the end there was over sixty. He could obviously tell we had seen them as the phone vibrated in my hand and he sent through another two.

Daisy Duke: Please just tell me you're ok

I know you have seen this message!!

Ethan Forrest: I'm ok. I'm sorry but it was better this way.

Daisy Duke: It's really not. My brother is a mess

We never used names, even in all of the messages he referred to them as only his cousins or brothers and so I made sure I didn't either.

Ethan Forrest: I'm sorry.

Daisy Duke: Just come home.

Ethan Forrest: I cant

Daisy Duke: I thought you were a better person than this.

His status changed to offline and I hated disappointing him. Before I could give Ethan the phone back, Connor was messaging me again.

Daisy Duke: I told him everything and I mean everything. He hasn't spoken to me for a week. I don't know what happened between you two but you need to come back. We all need you.

"Ah Bianca. We have company." Ethan called from the window and I turned off the phone. Standing beside him we peeked out of the curtains, the two men were easy to spot amongst the humans in the street.

"There are two of them." I hissed, he had told me there was only one.

"Max and Kyle. Kyle is the one you need to watch, Max must have joined him for support since I got away."

"This changes nothing."

I found the wig we picked up the day before, hiding my dark hair the blonde didn't really suit me, not that it really mattered. As Ethan put on his cap and sunglasses, I had to roll my eyes at how obvious he looked. Discreetly I tore a tiny piece of the wolfs bane leaf off, and followed Ethan out of the hotel. We split up and thankfully he didn't notice anything different about me as we parted.

I walked past Max and Kyle, my wolf anxious to catch their scent and we were not disappointed. Kyle was one of the ones there that night, Max was just unlucky. Did Damon always send his most trusted men to do his dirty work?

Coward.

I wondered what he had on them to make the oblige or were shifters really that stupid. If Ethan was considered strong enough to be an Alpha, what did that make Cody and I? Just thinking about Cody distracted me and I tripped over a crack in the pavement. Surprisingly Max was there, helping me up.

"Careful Miss." He smiled, and there didn't seem to be a single thing vicious about him.

He dies too.

He knew my face, he would think I am only human, but we couldn't leave loose ends. We wouldn't make the mistakes they did.

"Thank you." I mumbled, praying my hair hadn't moved.

"Sorry, but do I know you?" He asked and Kyle looked me over for a second. I had no idea where Ethan had gone, so looked confused.

"I don't think so?"

"Oh, do you have a sister who is stripper? I swear I saw you dancing just last night down the road there!" Kyle piped up.

A stripper?

"Sorry, wasn't me!"

They didn't try and stop me, carrying on down the road towards a bar. Obviously the strippers weren't open yet, but it gave me an idea.

Ethan was easy to find, the guy had no clue on keeping out of sight and I had no idea how he wasn't already found. Clearly they had something more important to do before finding him.

"You ok?" He asked, having seen it all.

"Great! Come on, we need to do a few things first."

-

This was it.

If I did this, there was no going back.

My wolf was in the front of my mind, a constant pressure on my temples as the scent of Kyle had her fighting for freedom.

Ethan had managed to do as we planned and had slipped something into Max's drink at the bar. Kyle had ruined that for us, as he had already left. He would never know his pack mate had found himself being thrown into the hotel pool for one last swim. The spare seat beside him told me Max was definitely expected so I had to move quick before his presence was missed.

Max was probably the luckiest out of all of the Damon's shifters, it was bad luck for Kyle he didn't get the same fate. We also knew the chlorine would make sure Ethan's scent had been removed from the body. Thinking back, Kyle had been more of a watcher than a participant and had started to leave when the others decided to throw me over the edge.

I guess he wasn't as bad as the others, but he still hadn't stopped them.

And the pair of them had been here to find Ethan.

"You going to wait those tables Daisy or you here to watch the show?" The bartender poked my arm and I didn't hide my wolf tonight. There were no other shifters here, so as I got closer to Kyle he easily scented me.

"Well she-wolf, you wanna find out who's top dog around here?" He slurred, the putrid stench of alcohol on his breath had my stomach churning.

"I don't come for free." I purred back, winking and as another patron slapped my ass I prayed Kyle couldn't see my annoyance.

"Of course not." He signaled the man with the DJ. I only met him once earlier this afternoon and to get hired all I had to was tell him I'd be willing to wear the ridiculous piece of string they called underwear and smile nicely at the guests.

"How much?"

"Daisy here is a ripe little flower, ready for the taking!" He mused, looking in my direction I kept my face still. "What are you wanting my good Sir?"

"What can a thousand get me?"

"Daisy, take the man to room three and show him what a thousand gets him."

The room smelt like sex and decay, the disinfect was only there if you searched for it through the rest of the smells and I wished we had been able to drug Kyle too, just so I didn't have to breath this air.

Thankfully human diseased didn't affect us and I kept telling myself that as I touched the pole. I had no idea what to actually do with it so I walked around it, waiting for him to sit down. I didn't have to wait long.

"First day?"

"Yes."

"I can tell you're nervous. It sounds cliché, but what are you doing in a place like this?" Kyle wasn't as old as Max or even the first shifter I came across. He could have been around thirty, maybe just under. While he wasn't handsome like Cody or good looking like Ethan, he had something about him that was interesting to look at.

He waved his hand, and I realized he wanted me to stop walking around the pole.

"I could ask you the same thing, I came here because there were no other shifters." I growled and he nodded, the drinks he had already consumed had opened him up and he was rather chatty.

"I'm here with a friend on pack business. We're looking for someone. My Alpha is a bit of a hard ass and the pup pissed him off. Haven't seen him have you? Blonde, I guess he looks like he belongs on a beach in California."

"No, you're the first shifter I've met. What you going to do with him?"

"Honestly, kill him. If we do it now it will be kinder than what the Alpha has in store. We'll just bullshit we didn't have a choice."

I wasn't expecting to hear that.

"Don't look so surprised princess. He killed one of our own." Kyle sighed, "He was a dickhead, but he was still pack and despite that I don't want to have to see anyone go through the torture the pup has waiting for him back home."

He was showing mercy to Ethan?

Where was your mercy?

I had been so lost in thought, I didn't see him move from the chair and growled while trying to push him off as he picked me up and took me to the bed.

"So what does a thousand get me?" His lips on my neck made my skin crawl and pulling my legs up slightly, I got ready to get him off me.

"A quick death." I whispered in his ear.

"Wha..."

I kicked hard in his stomach and with a groan he fell to the side. Disorientated and slightly drunk, his movements were slow and I had him pinned easily.

"Want to know the real reason why I'm here?"

He fearfully nodded, my wolf was growling in preparation to be let out.

"My mate killed had his pack kill my family and then rather than killing me, someone said. Now what was it? Oh let the wild animals out there have at her, maybe an eagle or something?"

"You're her! The alpha's mate!" He started squirming underneath me and I punched him hard in this side of the head.

"Well done."

"I'm sorry, I am so sorry." He started to apologize, begging for forgiveness. "Please, just let me live."

"I'm pretty sure I begged like that and you know the answer I got!"

If I had thought it would be easy, I had underestimated the idiot. Getting a hand free, he gripped my throat and I as I let him go his threw his own punch. He got me hard in the ribs and I fell backwards.

"Think you're tough little she-wolf?"

"Prove me wrong shifter." I challenged and leaving the room, he was quick to follow. No one said anything as we ran out and hitting the tree line I shifted.

Kyle did the same, the brown and white wolf was surprisingly smaller than I was expecting, barely bigger than me. In seconds were nothing but a snarling mess of fur. He was quick, but I had the strength he lacked. He managed to knock me over, pouncing on my I rolled up to face him and leapt for his muzzle. His whined, panicking as I gripped onto his lower law, the sensation of bone cracking under the pressure of my own making my wolf feel even more dominant. He wasn't whining now, he was yelping and his paw came up to try and scratch at my face.

It worked, I let him and he ran eager to escape me.

That wasn't part of my wolfs plan and licking the blood from around her muzzle she ran faster, leaping at him her weight made him stumble and we rolled for a couple of meters before stopping. Getting up I shook my coat, the few odd wounds already starting to heal, as were his. This time as I came forward, he couldn't move at all, the fall had weakened one of his legs and the sensation of ripping his throat out had my wolf going in frenzy.

Blood covered the white fur as the limp figure of my opponent was torn apart. Finally getting control back, she stepped back panting and the sight we left behind sickened me to my core.

He deserved it.

'Not like that'

Throwing her head back, her howl screamed of her success and leaving the corpse behind, I didn't like how much joy she had taken from the kill. There was only one death she needed to enjoy and it wasn't Kyle's.

Ethan was waiting with a car as I emerged from the forest and seeing me he got out, offering me a dress to put on.

"Come on, we need to go." He urged, and getting in the car Max's scent was everywhere.

"Who's car is this?"

"Theirs, I figured they wouldn't need it anymore. We just need to get away from this town, then we can shift and head back towards home."

Not bothering to argue, I sat back in the chair. Did Esmeralda know this what was I'd end up doing when I found Ethan?

With him driving, it didn't take me long to fall asleep. Only now I had new nightmares waiting for meand I couldn't blame Damon for these ones; they were completely of my own creation.

Eleven.

A week later we were back in the US and finding a new hotel, we paid cash. Ethan was getting on my nerves, and I wished I had stayed on my own and ditched him at our first stop after the death of Kyle and Max. I wondered if that was why we had never been friends at school, though I hardly remembered him from back then.

Imagining him as Leanna's mate was even harder, he was an ass.

"Why are you going to the gym?" He followed me down the corridor to the elevator like a lost puppy and I was close to knocking him out for five minutes alone.

"To keep fit?"

"We're shifters, all that running we did the last few days will keep us in shape." Having been a swimmer, I was surprised at how narrow-minded he was in regards to fitness.

"You're an idiot."

"You keep saying that." He teased, and continued to follow me anyway.

By the time I had enough of punching a bag while imagining his face, my wolf was itching to go for a run too. Now we were in more of a city, there wasn't anywhere for a wolf to go that wouldn't look strange. Getting back to room I did it there, sitting out the balcony we just observed the town below us. It wasn't long until she turned her nose into the breeze, inhaling deeply as it felt like she was looking for something. Her disappointment surprised me before my own sadness kicked in at realizing what she was doing.

Cody.

'You wanted to go too.' I reminded her. In fact the night we left she had been the one more in control.

"What are you doing? Someone might see you!" Ethan came to stand beside me and instantly I growled before turning back inside.

"I don't understand shifters." Slipping on an oversized t-shirt I went to get my hairbrush and paused by the dresser where his wallet was open.

"What don't you understand? I guess not having one to help you must've been tough." He locked up the balcony door and I pulled out the picture in his wallet, my lip instantly shaking as I tried to hold back my tears.

Leanna was frozen in time, smiling her perfect fake smile, it never quite made her eyes and I could just imagine the way she'd burst out laughing or pull some stupid face the second the photo was taken. This was the taken the year before she was murdered, the hot pink streak she put down the left side had been to annoy her Mum. Her head was tilted slightly to make the most of it and the fight she had with Aunt Alice when the pictures were sent home had been one of their most epic battles.

"It's the only picture I had of her, your house was boxed up before I could find any others and her Mum kind of burnt their house down."

"Aunt Alice survived?" I just presumed they had all died that night too, the prospect of being able to see her let the tears win.

"Not quite, she died a couple of days after that. I'm sorry."

Of course she did. Why would I think I still had family out there, someone who would care that I was still alive?

Cody.

'Not now.'

"It's fine." I lied, wiping my eyes. I dropped the photo by his wallet, unable to make my hands work enough to put it back in the holder and curled up with a pillow in the corner of the bed against the wall.

"You don't have to talk about her Bianca, but I just." Ethan sighed, rubbing his eyes and groaning went to leave.

"She loved sunsets and could paint really well. I don't know if you ever saw the picture outside my Dads office, but she painted that. She must have been the only person in the world to hate chocolate and on the night of my birthday she told me she was scared of dying during her first shift."

He stopped by the door, turning back to where I sat and ended up lying beside me.

"She hated chocolate?"

"Yeah, the only dessert or sweet thing she'd eat was ice-cream and she could eat a tub to herself in less than five minutes on a bad day, six on a good."

Ethan and I had something in common; we both lost our mates before we could even know them. The only difference was, I knew what he was missing out on. It felt strange talking about her, like I was betraying her by gossiping behind her back. The cruel reality was this was her only way of existing now and sharing her memory with Ethan gave her new life.

It was bittersweet. She made us both so happy yet for every smile and laugh, there were just as many tears.

"Thank you for sharing her with me." Ethan finally got up and went to his bed, laying so we were still facing each other. My pillow was damp from all the crying and even with the lamp off I could still see him well enough.

We went quiet for a few minutes, and for the first time since joining up with him, I felt safe enough to actually sleep.

"We will kill him Bianca; make him pay for what he has done."

It wasn't exactly the good night, sweet dreams that normal people would tell each other before bed, but it made me smile.

"I know."

-

While I finally slept during the night, I was awake by three and taking Ethan's phone I slipped into the bathroom. I dialled in the number I had learnt to heart and waited.

"Hello?" The anger was clear, despite the sleepy slurred nature of his voice. "Hello?"

I didn't know what to say, I just needed to hear his voice.

"Bianca?"

Hanging up, I put the phone on the counter and slid down the cabinet to the floors, somehow falling asleep and come morning Ethan gently woke me up.

"We do have beds to sleep in you know?"

I didn't offer him any explanation, kicking him out of the bathroom so I could shower. After breakfast Ethan wanted to check in with one of his contacts within the pack and I stayed out of it, listening in from a safe distance.

"There have been more shifter deaths, the Alpha is furious. You should really get out before he blames you." The woman was nervous and I wondered if she knew anything about Ethan's plans.

"I want him to blame me, my parents are safe and there is no one left for him to hurt to get to me. I will be challenging him again; I just need to get my timing right."

My wolf tried to growl, but I managed to hold her back. Ethan wouldn't be the one to kill Damon and he certainly wouldn't be doing it by challenging him. I wasn't even sure he was up to leading a pack, despite our bonding session last night; my wolf and I didn't think he had it in him. He still thought because I was a girl, I wasn't even capable of taking down a male shifter.

In his mind there was nothing wrong my luck.

"With Kyle and Steven out, Aden and Simon are being extra cautious, but nothing like Damon. He has put out a reward for any information on the murders." The woman had our interest, if he was scared it could make him slip up.

Even though the pack will work to separate one deer from the herd, sometimes opportunity comes with another as they panic and break out from the safety of the mob. Maybe if we could spook Damon enough, he would split and make a run for it on his own.

Later that night Ethan wasn't sold on my theory and the only pissed my wolf and I off further. Despite being the one to take down two of Damon' guard dogs, he still didn't think I had it in me and he kept telling me to buy a lotto ticket.

Now we knew where we were at with the pack, we headed away from the city and the second we hit the national park, I had shifted and made a run for freedom. My wolf had missed the wilderness, even if she was constantly telling me we belonged in the city and with other people.

She easily found something to hunt, and was about to give chase to the rabbit when instead Ethan tried to tackle her. The response he got told him it wasn't playtime and the tension I had been trying to avoid with his comments and assumptions exploded instead.

It wasn't a pretty fight and surprisingly he held his ground so any chance of taking it easy on him went out the window. The fight only excited my wolf, and Ethan began to tire before she had even peaked and this was what I didn't understand about shifters. It was like they forgot they were part wolf, neglecting their skills and condition, presuming because they were better than humans; that was enough.

My wolf kept at him until he ended up collapsing, no longer showing any signs of even thinking of getting back at her. My wolf while tired, was not going to let him know it and ended up finishing her hunt and by the time we got back, he had only just managed to shift.

"What was that?" He growled.

"I told you not to underestimate me Ethan."

"You're the alpha's spoilt little girl who goes shopping and throws parties and walks around school like she owns it. You're not a fighter, I was always meant to be the one with the potential to lead the pack!"

"Don't you get it? I'm not that Bianca anymore and the only pack you're fit to lead is the hypothetical one in your mind. If my father was still here, I would never let a wolf like you take his place!"

Somehow, this managed to surprise him.

"You're a bitch, a crazy fucking bitch!"

"That's it? That's all you can say?" I yelled back.

He shifted, clearly sulking and started to walk away. Grabbing my backpack, I followed him and we headed on to lower ground. Setting new tracks, we didn't mention our fight again. We used his credit cards at each town and finding a suitable one to stay at, got comfortable in the hotel at the edge of town and waited.

As expected it only took two days for shifters to start arriving and it wasn't just one or two, but they came in lots of three. Some Ethan was able to easily identify from the pack, others were locals and they were keen to assist at the mention of the reward.

While Ethan stayed in the human run hotel I knew just the thing to get around unnoticed.

"There may come a time when you need to be human, walk amongst the wolves without them knowing who or what you are."

Now was that time.

I walked confidently through the streets, my mind set on going to get some groceries to take back to our room. Anytime I passed a shifter I tried not to flinch, but even the humans seemed to give them space and I didn't have anything to worry about as none of them even looked at me.

Stopping by a café, I went inside to order a coffee. Not because I wanted it, but the smell reminded me of being back at the ranch.

"Do I know you?" Turning the woman behind me was looking at me curiously and I wanted nothing more than to put some distance between us.

"No sorry, I don't think you do." I answered with a smile, glancing towards the barista who seemed to be taking his time with my coffee. I didn't need it; I could just leave now only that would only raise her suspicions.

"I'm pretty sure I've seen a picture of you somewhere, did you go to UCLA?" The edge to her tone told me wasn't going to drop it until she worked it out and she didn't have the patience to play guessing games.

"No, I've just come down from Alaska to visit family. Have you been there?" I asked, trying to stop myself from sounding annoyed. I soon noticed the large diamond on her finger and her Gucci bag, which seemed a little out of place in a town like this. She clearly had money and that wasn't anything new amongst shifters, especially if they were connected with an Alpha position. My wolf recognised her as a threat, not just for snooping, but also for the wolf within her.

"Oh no, never mind." Her smile was fake, and as she left the café I kept the red head in my sights she went over to a couple of other local shifters. I was human now; she shouldn't have been able to sense anything about me. At least no one else had been able to and thankfully none of them looked in my direction before they walked away.

"You don't want to get caught staring at her." The barrister startled me and he glanced back out the window where they had been standing.

"Why?"

"Let's just say, her partner runs this town and they're not the nicest of people." An Alpha's mate; it made sense.

"Thanks for the coffee." I mumbled distracted, and dropped a few coins in the jar beside him as a tip.

Leaving the café the cup felt warm in my hands and walked down the street, it wasn't hard to miss the leader now I knew who I was looking for. They seemed to join up with a few of the other shifters from Damon's pack and went into a bar. Ditching the coffee I waited a few minutes and went in, finding a spare seat at the bar and ordered a drink.

"Thank you for your assistance; we appreciate you letting us in to your territory." Listening was easy enough, as humans were limited in their numbers, they spoke freely in the corner and glancing over the bartender had already put a few glasses of beer down on the table.

"Any shifter murderer deserves what they get. Caprice is our best weapon; maybe she will be able to lure him out." The red head nothing from where she sat beside her mate and the more I observed, the more I realised she was the dominant one out of the pair. Shifter men, like Ethan too, presumed women to be weak and that their testosterone made them better than us. Maybe in human form we were smaller and maybe even a little more defenceless, but as a wolf – it didn't matter.

I could see her assessing each of the men around her, judging them silently. Only a couple held my own interest as a possible threat, the others were nothing.

"If you think she was up for it?" The man wasn't showing her enough respect and she leapt forward, ramming his head against her knee before pushing him down against the table.

"What Alpha sends such a worthless shifter out to do his work?" She hissed and I found myself liking her, if only for the fact she wasn't putting up with their shit.

"Do not speak of our Alpha that way!" Another retorted. Their voices began to rise and as the first glass got smashed on the floor the few humans left, clearly not strangers to bar fights happening around here.

"You do not speak to ours with such disrespect!" One of the locals piped up and all the wolves in the bar started to move closer.

I didn't leave, instead moved towards a table by the door curious to see how this would work out. The locals clearly were in this for the money, not the glory and as the fight began I watched in awe. The locals were good fighters, dominating over Damon's pack.

No one seemed to rush in to break it up and I guess it was part of a territorial dispute. These things had a way of working themselves out as soon as the intruders know they were outnumbered and a minute later that was exactly what happened and before anyone even had a chance to shift.

I'd have to watch the Alpha's while I was here, they were not a force I wanted to stand against on my own. If we were to kill anyone while we were here, I had a feeling their punishment would be quick and just as deadly. This was the wrong place and getting back to the hotel, I had to convince Ethan to leave.

"It works in our favour; they'll probably end up fighting with each other even more the longer they're here. The distraction will benefit us!" The threat outweighed the slim chance we had to succeed and I decided if he wouldn't leave, I'd go without him.

"You're stupid to think that, these are smart shifters."

"But we're smarter. I know this is the right place to be!"

'Leave.'

My wolfs wants were obvious and I agreed. There was a part of me that didn't want to see Ethan hurt, and I felt like I owed it to Leanna to watch out for him.

"It's not Ethan, and I think we should go. I'm not going to leave you though, but if anything happens no arguments!" I demanded.

"Good. Now I've been watching closely and I swear I saw Aden. He never leaves the hotel across the road without a hat on and at least three others with him." We went up to the roof and looking down the three stories, it was easy to watch them all. Sure enough come nightfall, the group of shifters emerged.

What was even more interesting was how we'd missed Caprice joining them. The red head lead the pack, almost as if she was escorting them out. With Aden was there, I wondered if that was exactly what she was doing. I had taken half a leaf and still had three hours or so of human time left, so dressing to go out for dinner ended up finding them at one of the nicer restaurants in town.

Sitting alone in the corner, I studied the menu like I was about to tested on it and with my back to the group, relied on the mirror behind the bar to let me see them. Despite the hum of chatter, it was easy to focus on the voices I wanted.

By the time my mains arrived, nothing interesting had been mentioned. Generally it was more polite chit chat than a get to know you and I decided to order dessert, just in case. It was a good gamble and paid off, the lowering of their voices instantly had me interested.

"So tomorrow night at the end of the wine festival, Aden will present the trophy to the best vineyard. If we're right, and its Damon's guard that are being targeted, I doubt that shifter will not notice him being here." One of the locals started going into their plan how they were going set up the bait.

Even if I hadn't heard, I wouldn't have been stupid enough to fall for it. Ethan on the other hand would have, I knew it. He didn't think ahead, focusing on the moment not the outcome. It was why he was a terrible fighter and preferred to throw his weight around rather plan his next move.

"So we'll keep everyone on guard as he goes back to the hotel, if not at the festival it'll be when he leaves. If he goes alone, it'll be hard for him not to attack."

"How did the others die?" Caprice wondered, and the group fell silent. The voice I knew as Aden was the one to do the talking now.

"Kyle was left ripped to pieces in the forest and Rowan had his neck snapped." There was no missing the sadness in his voice at his dead pack mates.

"Wolf or human?" She asked, not showing any signs of sympathy.

"Wolf."

"Then don't shift. Clearly he will try and lure you into the fight. We're shifters and sometimes the human is the better option."

This had them all talking, her pack agreed with her while the others didn't know what to think. It made sense, but at the same time when we were in trouble our wolf was our first choice of fighting form. It had been too easy really, so maybe Caprice was onto something.

"Damon is trusting your pack will end this, he can be very generous to his allies." Aden reminded her.

"That's what I'm counting on."

With Caprice's answer I got up and went to clear my bill, trying think about the best way to go about getting Aden off our list. Ethan was no help; I had to tell him a hundred times we were not going to risk taking the bait. The second I could shift I did and my wolf spread over the single bed, letting me sleep while we tried to come up with something.

Rowan, the first shifter had been easy. Kyle had put up a fight, but in the end we were better. Getting to them had been simple, unmated wolves could be easily distracted by a piece of ass or if they had a high prey drive and a lack of morals like Rowan, it wouldn't matter what his prey was.

Caprice warned Aden to stay human, thinking he had a better chance of survival if he didn't shift like his pack mates. I didn't think it mattered, but if they wanted to play human – so would I. Thankfully my wolf found the solution and the vision of the silver gun in Damon's hand that he used to shoot Ethan came to me in a dream.

Shifting, I quickly tried to wake Ethan, knowing exactly how we were going to kill Aden.

-

We checked out early that morning and while Ethan found us a new car, I went to the grocery store to get a few supplies. In reality, the lemon, lime and paprika filled tomato juice was just a disgusting mix of ingredients. To Ethan, I convinced him it was a magical concoction that would allow us to be human and walk in the streets without anyone looking at us.

I used a full leaf of the wolfs bane for each of us this time, and with him keeping his own hat and sunglasses on, we enjoyed the day tasting some wine and local produce. This side of Ethan was fun, he could be a nice guy and I knew Leanna would have made sure he wasn't a jerk as often as he was now. It was when Aden went up onto the stage we left the party, nothing more than a happy couple walking down the street after having too much wine. All day we had watched the local pack set up, wolves patrolled the forest that surrounded the way out of town. Shifters wandered in groups of four and what had my attention were the ones with guns that had been spaced along the path Aden would take to go home.

"Go to the car and make sure you're ready to go when I get there." I commanded and Ethan obliged. I had my suspicions he had a hard time killing, he was happy to help just not actually commit the crime and I didn't care. My wolfs bloodlust outweighed my own reservations and as he carried on down the street, I climbed up onto the roof where one of the guards was waiting.

"Sorry, you cant be up here." He growled, sniffing the air cautiously he relaxed.

"I didn't realise anyone was up here. I was hoping to watch the fireworks from up here. This is the only building that had a ladder for access." I paused, spying the rifle that had been leant against the side of the wall. "Is that a gun?"

I wondered if I could be an actress after this, the hysteria in my voice even fooling me.

"I said you can't be up here." He warned.

"I'm calling the police Mr! You're all in black, what are you some kind of sniper? Oh my god you are!" I turned to run back to the ladder and apart from a grunt, he didn't seem to report this to anyone so he was probably not wired. He tackled me to the ground, the rumble in his chest unmistakable.

If I had been a human, I would have screamed and demanded the attention from everyone in town. That should have been his first clue of what was about to happen. With a kick between his legs which more force a human should have, I punched him under the chin and he fell backwards awkwardly.

"Sorry about this." I muttered, finding some rope and tying his wrists. My wolf was urging me to kill him; he was a witness and would be able to tell them it wasn't Ethan doing the killings. It wasn't his fault he was here and I knocked him out instead. By the time he woke up, we'd be gone anyway.

I had no idea how to use this kind of gun. The barrel was already loaded and it took me a few minutes to turn off the safety. Watching the street, it was empty now and I couldn't believe my luck when the fireworks started and the lone wolf appeared opposite me on the street.

"Please let me hit the can!" I whispered, firing my first shot I hit the pole behind him and panicking he foolishly ran into the middle of the road. Another shot missed and I tried to pre-empt his next movement and again. From behind him, a wolf appeared and a couple of humans, all looking around for the shooter.

I missed Connor, and titling the tip slightly I managed to hit him in the chest. I had hoped for a headshot, but I'd take what I could get. My plan had been getting him in one shot and running, instead four shots later I was on the roof with everyone emerging from their hiding places.

Keeping the gun with me, I jumped down and ran behind the building, through the alley way and listening around took a risk and ran to where Aden had just shifted. The scent of his blood hit me first and crouching behind the bin, I couldn't miss with this range. By killing him, I gave away my position and ditching the gun, heading towards the hotel. The footsteps all stopped as they reached his body and going into the building I tried to walk calmly towards the elevator, smiling politely at the receptionist who had been on last night. More bangs were faintly heard from outside, the fireworks masking the noise well and stopping at the first floor, went out the back way to the pool area.

It was then I realised something about the conversation in the restaurant. They had never mentioned Max's death, only the other two. We were miles away from that hotel, but surely if a body had turned up in a pool it would have made the news no matter how the shifters tried to hide it.

My wolf growled in warning and from the dark, the pool light caught the reflection of yellow eyes in the night. As calm as I could manage, I stripped off and jumped into the icy water. Any scent of the gun would be lost in the water, and after a few laps another hotel guest appeared to join me, her eyes confused as she realised I wasn't in a bikini but actual underwear.

Getting out I gathered my things and grabbed a complimentary towel, drying off quickly before wrapping my clothes in it and dumping it in the bin by the gazebo. My wolf was still alert, well aware of the wolves prowling outside. Shifters tend to stay in hotels where their own kind is. If shifting accidents happen, it made explaining it easier and things were in place to accommodate those mishaps.

I didn't smell like a shifter, I was in a human hotel and as more humans appeared, they left. Stealing the woman's kaftan I slipped it on with her flip-flops and disappeared back inside before she could notice. This had been close, to close for my liking and after a few minutes went back outside, avoiding the path to the pool and jumped the fence to the alley.

I had to go up two blocks to where Ethan was waiting and I could see the car when my wolf became alert. Daring a look behind me, Caprice stood with her mate who was yelling at some of his pack while she was simply staring in my direction. Getting to the car, Ethan started it and the second my door closed he had us speeding down the road out of town.

"What the hell happened?" He screamed as I put on my seatbelt.

"I need some more shooting lessons."

It only took us about a minute to work out we were being followed and as we approached a service station, I got him to pull over. We were human; they had no business with us. Before we stopped, I grabbed a pair of pants from my bag, pulling them on awkwardly before we got out.

I didn't expect one of the wolves to be Caprice and as we entered the diner at the side of it, she was slipping on a small dress and walking inside.

"Whatever happens, follow my lead." I muttered to Ethan, taking his hand in mine I started laughing as she entered with her mate behind her. "So did you want to share a burger?"

"Sure babe." Ethan answered, glancing over the menu.

"Oh coffee shop girl. What are you doing here?" She greeted, her eyes meeting mine I felt the challenge and prayed the leaf hid all signs of my wolf that was willing to accept it.

"Just grabbing a late dinner before carrying on our way." I smiled, and her eyes turned to Ethan.

"Why the hurry to get out of town?"

"No hurry, we stayed for the festival and if we want to get home for my boyfriend's Grandmother's funeral, we couldn't afford to stay one more night." I lied, "You know what, I'm Daisy. This is Alan and the more I see you, the more I think I do know you from where!"

She smirked, not buying it.

"Did you used to work at Hooters?" I asked innocently.

"Oh, from the calendar. Miss March!" Ethan piped up. Her mate glared at Ethan, who didn't fold under the pressure of his gaze and Caprice didn't let her eyes leave me. She looked at Ethan one last time; the way her nostrils flared told me she was buying the human cover. Unable to find anything, she leant closer down to my ear, and I gripped Ethan's hand to the point I may have dislocated a finger, trying not to bite back.

"No." She answered unimpressed and pointed a perfectly manicured fingernail in Ethans direction. "Your lucky I'm not taking you to see a friend of mine, because I know you're hiding something from me. I just don't know what it is. Come back to my town again, you'll find us less welcoming." Her threat was obvious and rather than keep on poking at her, I did what any human would when someone spoke to them in such a deadly manner.

I cried.

"Wow lady, I have no idea who you are but I think it's time to go before I call the police for harassment!" Ethan warned, getting up he moved to my side and I threw myself against him as he comforted me in the chair.

Caprice said nothing, shaking her head in disgust at my weakness and a few minutes after they left, the sounds of their howling echoed outside.

"Don't mind them love, there are some weird things in this town and those two seem to the king and queen of it!" The slim waitress tried to comfort us as she came to our order and the voice didn't match the body, which was much older than she would have you believe. Ethan quickly ordered something we actually had no interest in and she left us alone.

"That was way to close!" Ethan breathed out heavily and skulled a glass of water as if that would fix our problems.

"She is smart, any other time I think I may have liked her."

"Sorry to interrupt your social life." He growled. I only rolled my eyes, and seeing the food arrive I realised I was actually starving. Just to annoy him, I made sure I hate everything and excusing myself to go to the bathroom, I stopped by the payphone. It had been close tonight, things were only going to get worse and there was something I needed to do.

"Hello?"

"Hi."

Silence.

"Pretty sure you were meant to hang up, not answer me." Cody muttered bitterly. It was the most I had heard him say since the night I left, and it was hard to miss the resentment in his tone. Either way, I just wanted to hear his voice, even if he hated me.

I deserved it.

"I'm sorry Cody and..."

"So am I."

Cutting me off, he then hung up. I hesitated before finally putting down the receiver and went back to Ethan.

"You ok?" He instantly asked as I got to the table. I only stared at him, completely lost as to how he could be such a jerk one minute, but then this really observant sweet guy the next. He got up and gave me a hug, leading me out of the diner. He didn't speak until we were half hour down the highway and I wished he hadn't.

"Why the sudden change, you were all I want to be that woman's friend and now you look like your best friend died." He cringed as he realised what he said.

"It's nothing." I slumped further down the chair; pushing the seat back slighttly I stared out into the darkness.

"Wanna drive? That usually makes you happy?"

"I'd rather not."

He gave up trying to talk to me and once again I fell asleep in the car, dreaming of the day Cody would want me again.

"f you want something done, do it yourself" Damon muttered under his breath, snatching the bouquet of white roses from his housekeeper. The growling snarl that then erupted from him had her running down the corridor and even the guards that had followed him into the foyer all cringed away as the vase was thrown across he room. It smashed instantly upon impact, the roses falling apart as they hit the tiles to lie in ruin amongst broken glass and a puddle of water.

"HOW IS THIS HAPPENING?" He roared, his face turning red as his anger had complete control. His eyes were wide with fury and blood dripped from his clenched hands where his nails cut into his palms.

"Alpha, Caprice doesn't think it's the shifter pup. Two humans..."

"I don't give a FUCK what that bitch thinks. " Saliva sprayed from his mouth as he continued to scream at Simon. He was the last of his most trusted advisors, the last part of what had been a well thought out plan of dominance when Damon gained control of his Uncles pack. So far the others had failed in bringing down some egotistical pup and the only solution was for Damon to take care of it himself.

"Sir, she thinks he has humans helping him. She never caught his scent anywhere, yet there were two..."

Simon didn't get a chance to defend the towns Alpha's as Damons fist connected with his jaw and he fell to the ground with a growl of his own.

"A town run by shifters, with MY own pack there to assist and they think, HUMANS were involved?"

"Aden was shot down, Kyle mauled and Rowan could have found his end with humans hands. The pup could be using them help him, I think you need to talk to Caprice and learn what you can from her." Jordan spoke up, choosing his words carefully and staying out his Alpha's reaching distance.

The flash of red amongst the white roses caught Damon's attention and ignoring the broken shards of glass on his bare feet, he went to retrieve it. Even though the water had started to turn the card to mush, he managed to get the envelope off it and the blurred writing was still easy to read.

Three down, two to go.

xx

"Bring her to me, if she refuses kill her." No one moved at his command, and growling he screamed again. "NOW!"

As chaos ensured around him with everyone disappearing to fetch the Alpha, he held up the card again deciding it was time to pay a certain gypsy another visit.

Twelve.

The fall had been warmer than most and leaving the cabin; the winter had finally managed to tighten its hold over the lands; just like Damon. Ethan had managed to get a hot tip from one of his pack contacts, and I was almost sad to hear that things hadn't gone well for Caprice after our departure. At least while they had been focused on all of that, we managed to disappear again.

Ethan hated it, yet with the pressure on he didn't want to risk missing his flight back to Europe should it be picked up he was on the move again. Our plan was to wait out the winter, let things settle before coming back out.

Well it was my plan; Ethan wanted to get it over and done with.

The cabin we were in had been long forgotten within the boundaries of the national park. With a bit of a cleanup it offered us some protection from the cold winds and weather. Even better than that, my pack had already started their move to lower grounds for the winter months. Seeing them was like returning home, the pups were still in good condition and only one wolf was missing. In some ways I wished we could communicate, I wanted them to tell me what happened and all the things I had missed out on being away. While they couldn't understand me, I shared with them everything that had happened in my own life.

I would always have a home here, the forest was my sanctuary as much as it was theirs and leaving Ethan, I travelled with the Alphas daughter. Despite heading towards her second year, she was already showing promise of dismissing her mother from the lead which impressed me. She had always been my shadow, and even after being away for so many months that hadn't changed.

For two nights we made the travel back towards their summer lands, avoiding the other wildlife and a few lingering humans until we hit the true wilderness.

My wolf knew exactly where she was going, rarely stopping we were both exhausted by the time we got to the river. Finding a place out of the rain and wind, we slept the day away and come night we were nearly there.

The wooden fence was the first sign that we had made it, her whines stopping me as she got nervous heading towards the humans territory. I was feeling it too, and unable to hide it left her even more skittish. We followed the fence along the edge of the property and my wolf was absorbing the scents of our human pack as if she only just smelled them for the first time.

Leaving the property behind, we headed to higher ground and with nightfall a few rodents dared to come out to try and feed. It was enough to fill our bellies, and finding somewhere to sleep I decided I just needed to see them one last time before we went back to Ethan.

Once more ended up taking two days of stalking.

Jay and Adam came up the back to fix a break in the fence on the first day, Taylor and Adam rode the horses down to the river in the afternoon and that night all of them went for a run.

Cody wasn't with them; if he had been maybe I would have gone sooner as he was the one I wanted to see.

It was on the night of the second day, when I started to regret staying.

"Do you guys feel that?" Connor asked as he shifted, looking around his eyes lingered on the bush we were hiding in. The others all shifted, following his lead.

"Probably nothing." Taylor stretched, shivering as the cold hit her skin.

"No, he's right." Jay had been the one to sense me when we first met; his instincts were strong even if he rarely used them. "I think there is another shifter out here."

Busted.

My wolf decided now would be a good time to tease me and nudging the wolf, we took off at a sprint. We lost them easily and with the control back in our hands, we followed them to the fence line. Connor kept looking behind to where we hid, the others too distracted with their play and it wasn't long after they disappeared a howl interrupted the quiet of the night.

From where we laid, I stood up quickly and the wolf with me only yawned, her ears twitching slightly. The call meant nothing to her, while my own wolf was standing there like a fan girl meeting her idol. Her whole body was trembling, and then she started whining. I was fighting to stop her from answering, and with the energy she was creating my companion final stood too. She didn't know what was going on, but found herself getting caught up in my hype and this time as another howl sounded out it was her who answered.

It wasn't Cody who returned her call.

The pack answered their wolf, much closer than they should have been and she took off in their direction. Reluctantly I followed and I soon realized they must have been tracking us. It was stupid of me to think they'd let her randomly run off, even with me and the connection the wolves had to one another made me miss being a part of them so much more.

To my relief Ethan wasn't with them, yet as they all wrestled and ran back the way they came it was hard to miss his scent. Leaving them again, I tracked him easily enough and getting near the fence I froze at the savage sounds of a fight that waited me. My wolf leapt into a run, our heart stopping as Ethan was surrounded by the others fighting Cody.

Connor noticed me first and his growl turned into more of a yap which woke me back up from my shock.

I had no doubt Cody could beat, even kill Ethan, but that didn't mean Ethan would go down easily. As Ethan saw me running over I could feel his relief. He thought his cavalry had arrived and he took advantage of Cody's own shock to lunge at him.

It wasn't Cody I went for, getting Ethan to let him go instead. I couldn't let Ethan hurt him or meet him. I didn't want him even knowing who these guys were. Ethan only knew the basics of my story; he didn't even know Damon was my mate. He presumed my own revenge was based solely on my parents and family.

He did as I wanted, yelping as I knocked him over and as he stood I nudged him back towards the forest, urging him to run. Slightly dazed, he didn't move as quickly as I wanted and with that distraction, Adam went to take a shot at me.

Connor held him back, his own growls more savage than I ever thought he could manage and finally able to process a thought, Cody shifted.

"Bianca?"

The anger and disappointment from the last time we spoke was gone, he was in complete disbelief and with him shifting so did the others. Ethan looked at me and back to Cody stopping his growling, but not his defensive stance.

"What are you doing here?" Connor asked; ignoring the look Cody served him with as he took a step closer to me.

I had two options, shift and talk or turn and run. Really I only had one choice and before I could run, Ethan shifted.

"Who are you?"

"This is our territory, we ask the questions." Jay warned, the four moving to stand either side of the still dumbstruck Cody.

"Well you can…"

I growled, mouthing his hand in a bid to drag him away.

"Shift." The command in Cody's tone was obvious and I fought it with all I could as my wolf was happy to oblige. "I said, SHIFT!"

Taylor's mouth dropped open as I actually did what he asked, and while Jay and Adam looked at each other doubtfully, Connor smiled.

"Holy shit, you are still alive!" In seconds he was hugging me and I hated how good it felt to be amongst them, almost as good as the pack.

"Connor, back."

Cody seemed incapable of more than one or two words in a sentence. That said I don't think I could manage much else either. This time was wolf was willing to submit, completely, and I prayed he wouldn't ask or demand it of me.

"Sorry." He mumbled, going to stand beside Jay. The air suddenly got thick; you could practically see the tension buzzing around us like electricity as we stood in a stalemate.

"Wanna tell me what the fuck this is about?" Ethan growled beside me. I had almost forgotten about him and snapping back into reality, my wolf allowed me some control since she was certain I wouldn't run.

"It's nothing. Just a small pack I came across. Sorry for trespassing, we will go." I quickly mumbled, shoving Ethan hard towards the forest and he obliged.

"Nothing?" Cody snapped, following after us. His anger broke the tension in the air, causing it to explode as his temper came out.

"What the hell? She said we're sorry, back the fuck off. We're going." Ethan challenged, and right now even my wolf was willing to run to avoid Cody's wrath. The fact she was equally excited at experiencing it didn't help.

"You're not going anywhere. Not until I say so."

"Please." I turned and instantly stepped backwards into Ethan as Cody was now right in front of me. I wasn't expecting him so close and thanks to the cold, the heat from his body was like a magnet.

He was the perfect specimen of an alpha male, the power was intoxicating and I had been in wolf form, she'd be begging him for a second chance. I couldn't take that risk, not now and not with Ethan hovering around behind me looking to start another fight. My guilt made me feel weak, just like my desire which was breaking down my resolve to stay away with each second I was stuck there.

"Bianca, let's go. There are only five of them; none are a threat to us." Ethan concluded.

Cody only glared in his direction, his eyes turning to the more golden hue of his wolfs and before another fight was break out, I found the will to move away.

"Shift!" I yelled, pushing Ethan as I did so and we took off into the trees. Sure enough the pack followed and calling out, the wolves answered. In seconds we were surrounded. We had power in numbers and my wolf was keenly keeping her mind locked on Cody as they chased after us.

My wolves were not ones to be chased from the territory and it didn't take long for them to turn on the intruders. Thankful of the distraction, I didn't stop to help the, and made sure Ethan kept going too. We stopped once I was certain enough distance had been put back between us, calling my wolves to retreat their replies told me they hadn't be injured and as we shifted back to our human forms the next howl told me it wasn't over yet.

"Who were those people? They all knew you!" Ethan growled. "Are they the ones who helped you find me?"

"Just the one who hugged me, his family is harmless. He is harmless. I don't want them to be involved."

"Do they know about the pack, about everything?" He asked finally.

"No, they never asked. He only did what I asked him to do." It wasn't a complete lie.

"People have a habit of doing that with you don't they?" Ethan snapped sarcastically, yet it wasn't intended to be vicious. The first sounds of the pack had us hiding, and satisfied they were alone we started the journey back to the cabin. The trip would still take a good day or two and with the night on the way out, it wasn't long before we all found a place to rest.

Sleep never found me, and getting up I headed for higher ground. A few wolves raised their heads, but none followed me and shifting I welcomed the cold to try and cool me down. I had wanted to see Cody again, now I had it only messed my mind even more. On the horizon the darkness began to fade to a purple before violet streaked with the orange promise of the dawn. Being here felt right, it felt like home.

"Bianca."

I instantly cursed my wolf for not keeping her guard up, and it didn't take me long to work out it had been her intention the whole time.

"Cody, I..."

"You don't have to apologize."

He sat beside me on the hill, and I was well aware of the millimeters that kept our skin separated. While the forest felt like home, he smelt liked it and as I moved to lean against him his arm was already pulling me closer.

"Where have you been?"

I didn't want to tell him. I didn't want him to judge me.

"Around."

"That was that Ethan guy from your old pack?"

"Yeah."

We stayed quiet, the first sounds of a bird breaking through the silence of the moment.

"I've missed you." His admission was barely a whisper, and I heard every word that went with it that he didn't say.

"I've missed you too."

Looking up his head was already lowered, and the second his lips touched mine the horrors of the last few months slipped away. Moving over he let me straddle him, and the sensations of being the one in control was intoxicating. I kissed him hungrily as his hands went all over my body, almost like he was checking it was all still there and my guilt for leaving was replaced with regret.

It was that regret that made me stop our reunion from going any further and Cody said nothing as I pulled away. Instead, we just sat together trying to ignore everything that was wrong with the whole situation and everything that needed to be said. Cody made sure to hold me that much tighter and with the sun finally rising to the sky, we fell asleep.

—

The wet sensation on my cheek had me stirring and blinking a few times it was the alpha's daughter that greeted me. She licked my cheek again, her tail wagging as she noticed me beginning to stir and yawning Cody jumped at the sight of her.

Seconds later my name was being called out from below and glancing at the sun it had to be a couple of hours since dawn.

"Come home, you don't need to do this anymore." Cody sat up, rolling his shoulders and pushing the wolf away gently as she tried to clean his face too.

Stay.

My wolf was on his side, and honestly so was I.

"It's not that simple."

"Yeah it is. Even blondie can come with us." Cody offered.

"I don't want him too, I don't trust him."

"So you've been gone for months with someone you don't trust? Makes sense."

I only rolled my eyes, and the sound of Ethan's voice was getting closer.

"I'll come back; I just need to work out what we're going to do." I decided.

"No, don't give me that bullshit Bianca." Cody growled, clearly not trusting me either. I didn't blame him.

The sound of his growl had the wolf returning it, moving to put herself between us as she watched him like a hawk.

"You still run with the wolves," He shook his head in disbelief and I instantly took offence. "How long have you even been around here?"

"A few of weeks, but further north."

Some of the pack came running over and it wouldn't be long before Ethan found us.

"Cody, I've done some stuff and I'm not proud of it. I can't come back yet, I'm not putting any of you in danger. I promise I will come back once it's done."

"You don't get it do you? You think you're the only one who wants to, and can, kill? I've done my own fair share sweet heart; running around with that idiot is the one way to make sure you get yourself killed. Come home, I will help you."

Do it.

'What if they get hurt?'

They won't.

There was enough confidence in her voice that made me think she was right, and if that was the case, I had no idea why she made us leave in the first place.

"Fine, let me deal with Ethan and I'll be there by nightfall."

His surprise at having me agreeing with him obvious and not saying anything else, he shifted and ran. I was certain he didn't actually leave, and it wouldn't surprise me if he followed us all the way back to his place. It didn't take long for Ethan to appear with the rest of the pack.

"Can you ever just stay in one place when you sleep? Even in the hotel you'd wake up in the bathroom or on the balcony."

"I'm a restless sleeper. Look, what if we went back to my friends? We could wait out the winter safely."

I knew the prospect of living in a house and not roughing it the way I had originally planned would appeal to him. I just had to make sure it went as simply as I hoped. Adam wouldn't like it; I couldn't imagine any of them would be thrilled at their new guest. Or the return of their old one.

"Friends?"

"I lied; they took me in from the wild. They helped me be human again."

It was the biggest part of my past I had really shared with him so far and he seemed to recognize that too.

"I don't like it, can we really trust them? Damon has scouts all over the country trying to find me." While he was trying to delay it, I already knew we'd be leaving the wolves and heading home.

"I trust them with my life." And more than I trust you, I thought to myself. We still had to go back to the cabin and get what things we kept on us. With the decision made, we started off and just as I suspected Cody followed.

By the time we arrived back at the cabin, Ethan knew we were being followed and I was almost disappointed in how long it took him to realize that. Cody was right, sticking with him would end up getting me killed and I could see why Damon visited the gypsy each year. Wanting to know the future was addictive. Knowing all I did now made me want to see her again so once we got settled, I decided to ask Connor to come with me to see her again.

I still didn't trust Ethan enough to know about her or to leave him with everyone without a more dominant shifter around.

By the time we returned to the ranch, Cody was waiting for us. Ethan instantly went into defense mode and I spied the others were all waiting by the fence. I growled at Ethan, reminding him off his place. To my surprise he calmed down, almost to the point of submission.

Cody was quick to take advantage and set upon him, forcing him to completely give in. Despite how proud his wolf was, it knew the basic law of the wild and did what he was required to do. So did I.

Satisfied he left us and went back towards the house. Jay leapt towards us first, and while I was busy greeting them all again I kept an eye on Ethan. If he growled for a second to long at any of them, I was on him. Typically Adam was there testing the limits, again only not with me. Ethan easily overpowered him, yet I continued to interrupt. Peace keeper seemed to be my new job description and Ethan soon clicked on. Despite being confused about it, he followed my lead and Jay ended up taking us to our rooms.

I almost expected to be taken to the cell downstairs near the gym, but Ethan got the room I had been given before. Taylor seemed almost happy to be sharing hers with me. Just like with the wolves, it was like no time had passed since I left. We were accepted with less tension than what I was prepared for too. The guys all seemed to fall into line within minutes and Ethan clearly appreciated being amongst others; in an actual house.

It helped me relax slightly and after showering, I stayed in Taylor's room trying to avoid Cody. Staying here for the winter made sense, our survival was guaranteed if we didn't have to live in the wild. I had done winter in the forest, it wasn't easy and I honestly didn't think Ethan could do it.

"Bianca?" Connor appeared cautiously looking around the room until his found me sitting on the floor in the corner by the window. "Can I come in?"

I nodded and he closed the door behind him before coming to sit beside me.

"I'm glad your back."

"It's only for the winter." I reminded him.

"Do you know what it was like for us?" He sighed heavily, running his hands through his hair roughly and I kept quiet. I didn't want to hear it, my guilt was bad enough. "Cody flipped, ran out of the house and was gone for two days. When he came back, he wouldn't talk to us and stayed in his room all day. When he came out, he demanded I tell him what I knew so I did. All of it."

I could just imagine how that would have gone.

"Did he hurt you?"

"No. Well not really, Jay stopped him. He was beyond furious; I've never seen him like that before." Fear still lingered in his voice and I only nodded.

"Then he acted like nothing had happened which was worse until Adam mentioned you and he bailed me up again, trying to find out if we could track you. I had kept an eye on Ethan and then you finally messaged me back. Just not knowing where you had gone or if you were even still alive was the worst. At least with your prank calls we knew you were still around and then even they stopped."

"I'm sorry." It was a weak apology and stood for nothing even if I meant it.

"But you came back." He pointed out.

"I shouldn't have. I'm just going to leave again and this time I might not come back."

"Where did you go? Can you at least tell me that?" He was almost begging and my wolf was pushing me to tell him. "I won't tell anyone, not even Cody if it means you'll trust me again."

"I do trust you Connor, why would you think that?"

"Because you left without saying goodbye, and I told Cody everything last time."

"I'm glad you did, I should never have asked so much of you. I didn't say goodbye because I didn't trust you, I just had to go."

"Fine, then tell me what's been going on so I can trust you again."

He had me there and I wanted us to go back where we used to be. I was sorry and I did miss him.

"Promise you won't hate me afterwards?"

Connor put out his pinky finger, and I linked mine in his so we shook on it.

"I promise."

Before I could even start to tell him, Taylor came in and seeing us she squealed in surprise.

"Connor! Get out of my room!"

Rolling his eyes he reluctantly got up, extending his hand to help me stand it was clear he wasn't going to let me get out of telling him anything.

"Not you Bianca, you can stay."

"It's ok, I need to check on Ethan anyway." I lied, and followed Connor out. He kept behind me as I went into the living room, and my wolf was eagerly searching for Cody with no luck.

"Why couldn't we have come here sooner?" Ethan greeted, tapping away at the gaming controller beside Adam. I was impressed at how quickly he was able to fit in whereas I was still trying to shake off the weirdness from being back. I wanted more resilience; I wanted Connor to be angry at me and for Taylor to refuse sharing her room. Adam hadn't even tried to test my patience yet and Cody was avoiding me as much as I was him.

"You know why." I snapped. Part of what I told Ethan on the way here was that I didn't want them put in any danger and to say that in front of them only annoyed me. Or maybe I was just looking for a fight since no one else seemed keen to do so.

I felt guilty and hated how easy they were making this for us; for me.

Leaving them to it, I followed Connor out the front and the cold wind greeted us brutally compared to the warmth inside. Connor didn't flinch and neither did I as we headed over to the barn where the horses had been put away in. The stench of the creatures had me wishing we'd stayed inside and said nothing as Connor led me upstairs to the loft. Amongst the bales of hay the horses weren't so bad and instead it was almost comforting being up there. It would be easy to nest and get comfy to sleep which made me wonder why I'd never thought about it before.

The whiney from below reminded me why it hadn't happened.

I hate horses.

"OK, spill." Connor leant back against one of the bales and sitting on the dusty wooden floors I got comfortable. I started with finding Ethan, and then about our first kills. He kept silent through all of it right up until the part where the wolf and I stalked them, concluding with our arrival here. Connor's gaze rarely left mine, occasionally his mouth would open and close, but he never interrupted or gave me a clue as to what he was thinking.

"And that's all of it." I finished, now trying to avoid looking at him. I didn't want to see his disappointment or his fear so when he moved and grabbed me in a hug, I nearly cried with his acceptance.

"I don't approve of what you're doing, but nothing I can say will stop you."

I didn't understand.

"You don't approve? How is that all you can say?" I stopped when I realized I was yelling at him.

"Because it's all that I can! I'm not going to say well-done, good job. You killed those shifters. I understand why, but I don't like it. You've always been different, to us anyway. Cody? Not so much. He has done this too Bianca, he is still my brother and I know it haunts him, but if he didn't do what he did," He paused, sighing sadly. "We probably wouldn't have him with us now."

Now I understood.

The urge to kill from my wolf had infected me, removed the guilt that already lingered in the back of mind threatening to take over. She would make sure that didn't happen, like Cody's. They couldn't stop it completely, but enough to let us live with it.

"Thank you for trusting me enough to tell me." He finally broke the silence that settled between us. This time he was the one surprised when I hugged him.

"You know I still need you to do your computer stuff on Damon right?"

"Good thing I never stopped."

Thirteen.

With my new hiding place decided upon, I spent my nights sleeping in the barn. The urge to go to Cody was hard to ignore, so at least with the distance between us it was easier to stay strong. I even decided horses weren't that bad, as long as I didn't have to ride them. When Ethan and I weren't helping out around the farm, we were training. Occasionally one of the others would join us, but never Cody.

He was virtually invisible since our return and it was killing me. It shouldn't even be possible not just for me, but for my wolf to have this attachment to him. I didn't really understand the mate thing, other than they were meant to be the perfect partner for you. Once the bond was established between the two, it was unbreakable. They were your true love, your life and shifters were meant to spend their lives searching for their other half; not searching to kill them.

It was something Damon and I had in common when it came to each other. Since being told I would be the death of him, he had searched for me. Now I wanted to make sure I did just that, I searched for him. I didn't have to do too much, he rarely left his state though his transactions never revealed any kind of pattern.

Using what contacts he had, Ethan found out minimal information. I found out some of what Connor knew about things happening within packs was actually from some calls Cody had made. The search for Ethan hadn't eased up and the reward Damon was offering only kept climbing. There was also the alert about being aware of humans as he had two, if not more helping him.

All I could think about was Caprice. Did she know who Ethan actually was? The fact she had only seen him as a human probably didn't help her when Damon had taken her in or maybe it did. The descriptions put out for those humans were nothing like us, which only made me even more curious about her.

"Can you find out anything about the Alpha Caprice?" I didn't know her last name, but if she was an Alpha of such a large area, it might be easier than I expected it to be to find her.

"Why?" Connor asked, looking up from his computer.

"I need to know if Damon killed her."

All eyes turned to us and I regretted not waiting until later to ask.

"What does it matter?" Ethan growled, getting up to come over to us. Sure enough Taylor, Adam and Jay all followed.

"She is a smart wolf, and don't you think its strange the two humans that apparently 'helped' you were described as a dark skinned male and a blonde female?"

"I hadn't really thought about it." Ethan admitted and clearly none of the others had either.

"That is why she will live and you will die." Cody muttered as he passed, heading outside. It was the most he'd said to either of us in the last couple of weeks since our arrival and it silenced me completely.

Ethan only growled, not impressed.

Before I knew what I was doing I was running out after him. Cody headed to one of the paddocks, and I followed. Behind me the others were trying to keep their distance, but they failed at not being obvious. There was something about Cody right now that had me on edge and not in a good way.

"Feel like some training?" He asked flatly and I hesitantly nodded. "This time, I fight your wolf."

"What?"

"It's only fair." He taunted, climbing over the fence.

Do it. He's right.

'I have a bad feeling about this.'

Do it.

Her eagerness was almost desperate and so I shifted, leaping over the fence to join him. Just like I had done, Cody stalked towards the center of the field and my wolf keenly studied his movements. Already she was in attack mode and faintly I could hear Ethan yelling something.

"Come on she-wolf." Cody growled, squaring out his shoulders there was no hesitation as I started to circle him.

"This is fucking insane! Stop them!" Ethan screamed.

"They've done this before, let it go." Jay answered calmly, but I didn't think this was going to be like last time at all.

Tuning them out, I struggled to keep control of her. I didn't think my wolf could be this focused on killing something. Not even with the arrival of the first deer at the end of winter had her this riled up and I constantly tried to remind her it was Cody. Not one of Damon's pack; not a threat.

She taunted him a few times, jumping in and then back as if playing. In doing this she caught him off guard when she did move closer. Grabbing his arm I cringed at the sensation of bone in her mouth, yet his fist connected with the side of her head just as quick and instantly she let go. The taste of his blood was spat out of her mouth as she snarled, coughing saliva out more in display and started to circle him again.

Breaking the pattern, Cody ran towards an old panel of fence and I quickly cut him off. Stalking towards him he hesitantly stepped backwards before I lunged again.

He managed to dodge the next few attacks and instead she started going for his legs, reasoning if she got him down she could keep him down. It took three attempts before he realized what her plan was, and when he did fall; he shifted.

Things only got worse from there.

The last few months seemed to explode via his wolfs attack. As if that wasn't bad enough Cody had the same control over his wolf as I did mine. None.

The next few minutes went by in a blur of fur, teeth and claws. I didn't know if the yelps were my own or Cody's as we battled it out. Adrenaline made us stronger, numb to the pain. The wolves didn't quite know how to release their frustrations. Humans could talk it out, and so the animals forgot their true nature, reacting more like humans than anything. He wanted me to hurt like he had, where as my wolf was more focused on staying alive.

By the time we stopped, steam was rising from our bodies as the color began to fade from the sky.

We were both panting to the point of collapsing and finally I took a second to look around. Somehow we had left the front paddock. My legs were trembling beneath me and my chest was on fire. Numerous wounds were tingling as my body began to heal and I felt dizzy from the frantic pace of the panting.

There was no chance of being able to shift, despite having control back and we stood barely a meter apart, trying to work out what the other was going to do. My legs were aching in protest at having to remain standing, and I moved first.

Standing at his side, I whined as I fell and he followed. I rolled onto my side, the damp cold ground beneath me felt nice and slowly we began to calm down. Slowly Cody shuffled closer, reaching out to lick my muzzle and I returned the gesture before dropping my head down to lie on my paws.

The pressure of his head resting against my neck sent a new rush of emotions through me and with a deep content sigh, human and wolf were finally on the same page with that magic word lingering in the air.

Sorry.

--

No one said anything when Cody and I finally managed to get back to the house the following morning. Dried blood covered our skin along with the dirt and as I walked past Ethan he opened his mouth to say something. I quickly shut him up by holding up my hand.

"Not now."

Cody only growled and when he went into his room, I claimed the shower. The miracle of having the warm water wash over my skin was a sensation I had not yet grown tired of. Especially when every inch of me was aching and it took a few minutes of scrubbing before the water began to run clear again.

I had just finished washing the shampoo from my hair when the door opened, and knowing who it was I held my breath before the curtain was pulled back. Cody said nothing as he stepped in beside me, and I prayed he wouldn't hear how hard my heart was beating. Guilt filled his eyes and I knew he hated losing control to his wolf as much as I did.

"I…"

"I know." I answered, already knowing exactly what he was going to do. He didn't need to apologize, his wolf was as strong as my own and if she could understand it – so could I. "How do you feel now though?"

"Better." Wolf and man were once again at peace with each other. It explained why he had worked so hard at avoiding me too. "I really thought he was going to kill you, and I couldn't stop him."

"I thought the same thing before you shifted. It's done." I didn't have control the second I followed him out of the house, maybe on another level our wolves could communicate and that had been their plan all along.

With the wolves satisfied, it was time to take care of the humans.

Soaping up the wash cloth, I moved so he was the one under the shower-head and began to wash away the dirt. Despite how tense he was to start with, by the time I finished he was completely relaxed. Washing him down like this left us both feeling vulnerable. He was letting me take care of him, yet my wolf was trying to make me understand it was me who was submitting to him.

He stepped forward, the warm water still running over his shoulders and down his chest. The sensation of the warmth against my own skin felt nice until I found myself being held against the cold tiles behind me. I soon forgot about the burn of hot on cold as his lips claimed mine possessively and I wilted against him. The smell of the soap was still fresh on over his body and my hands ran up his muscular arms before snaking through his hair, pulling him to me.

"Stop, we can't." I managed to mumble as his lips moved down my neck steadily. Tilting my head back, I closed my eyes, trying to find the will to stop him before we went too far or worse – someone heard. My thoughts must have been obvious as Cody sought to put me at ease.

"No one is here, they all went for a run." His voice was raspy with need, and that was all the convincing I needed until the hot water ran out and the icy change had us both jumping away. Cody turned off the taps, and as we left the shower recess he instead scooped me up. Ignoring my protest, we moved quickly to the end of the corridor and into his room. He put my down gently, yet thanks to the height of his shoulder I still bounced as I hit the mattress. He was on top in seconds, the cold of the room forgotten thanks to the heat of our bodies and even if they all came home now there was no way I was going to let him stop.

-

The others didn't come back for a couple of hours and hearing them outside I left my place beside Cody on the lounge. He didn't even stir, his soft snores giving away how deep of a sleep he was actually in.

"Everything ok?" Jay asked first, as the others all shifted behind him.

"Fine, have a good run?"

"Yeah, cold though." Adam piped up which surprised me, since my return he had changed and I had no idea what to make of that.

"Can you be quiet when you come in? Cody is crashed out on the lounge." It was hard to ignore the look that passed between them and the growl was sent out in warning.

"OK." Taylor growled back, shivering she only wanted to get inside and the group all went in quietly - disappearing into their rooms. I checked on Cody, glad he was still asleep and went into the kitchen for a drink. Connor was the first to reappear and the look on his face told me had news.

"Is this her?" He opened his laptop and on Damon's Facebook page a picture had been posted of him with the other alpha pair. It was only dated a few hours earlier.

"Yeah it is." Her smile was clearly fake and her mates eyes gave away his rage.

"Apparently he loves having house guests and they will be there for Christmas." Connor scrolled through the page a little more and I wondered what the point of this all was. "He must be doing it for show. The fact he is keeping them with him would also make him look harder to get to. If he has a powerful alpha couple as well as his pack nearby, who would even try to attempt anything towards him?"

"What if the alpha couple were to leave?"

Connor looked at me nervously, already my mind was forming a plan.

"Unless he lets it happen, they're not going anywhere."

"That's what he thinks." Despite our run in earlier, something about Caprice made me want to trust her. I knew she would be a strong ally and my wolf agreed. So far all the information that had been passed around the packs was completely fake and I knew it was her doing.

"Do not do anything yet. We will work this out together, understand?" Connor warned in a tone I didn't know he was capable of producing. If it had been Adam to talk to me like that I would have put him in his place quickly, but Connor had the ability to get away with it. "And I'm telling Cody when he wakes up. No secrets."

"Fine." I mumbled, leaving him to go outside.

It wasn't long until my time with the horses was cut short as Cody came storming in.

"So Connor told you?"

"He did. We're doing things differently this time Bianca." He warned.

"I know."

It felt nice to have his arms wrap around me and to feel his body back against mine. Things were definitely going to be different this time.

-

"I don't like it, if you can get them out – why not just kill him then and there?" Ethan demanded. Jay started to clear the dinner plates and to say Ethan didn't like my latest suggestion was an understatement.

"Because we don't know what it's even like in his compound. They do and if he is keeping them in the guest house at the back of the property, we won't even have to go near the main area and risk exposure." Connor pointed at the satellite image of Damon's mansion, circling the smaller house in the corner.

"This is stupid and we're going to end up getting killed." I didn't like the way he was talking to Connor and only glared at him. "If only he had a mate, we could have got hold of her and put her to ransom."

Jay dropped the pile of plates he had in his hands and the clatter had us all jumping out of our skins. The awkwardness that followed made me sink lower into my chair and everyone besides Ethan turned to look at me. Their question was clear, what the fuck?

"What? It's the oldest trick in the book!" Ethan hadn't noticed and Adam and Taylor got up to help Jay sweep up the broken crockery.

"Yeah, if only he did." I mumbled, not wanting to linger on the topic. "We're getting nowhere. Let's just sleep on it."

I didn't move from the table and neither did Connor or Cody. The TV was soon turned on and with the others distracted, Cody pounced. "He doesn't know?"

"No."

They both shook their heads, the family resemblance uncanny.

"Let's keep it that way." Cody finally decided.

"Don't you think..." Connor started.

"No. You heard his idea. He is scared and desperate to put an end to this so he can fly off into the sunset. If he finds out, I think he really would do something stupid like put Bianca up for ransom." That was the one thing I hadn't thought of yet and Cody had a point.

"You're right. I'll tell the others." Getting up, Connor squeezed my shoulder as he passed and Ethan walked in as he walked out.

"Fancy a work out?" He offered, ignoring Cody. The growl was obvious as it sounded from his direction and with clenched fists Cody left us alone.

"Yeah why not." We headed downstairs and I didn't miss the way he always looked at the cell curiously as we passed it.

"Do you ever stop?" Ethan was breathing heavily after half an hour.

"If you stop in the wild, you die." I snarled, taking another swing. He was getting tired and he didn't block me as well as he should have. With another hit, Ethan was knocked over. "Let's call it a night."

"You're something else Bianca." He stayed down for a few minutes, taking off his gloves and tossing them to the side. I extended my hand to help him up and instantly stepped back from how close he was to me. "You should be careful with Cody. He has a temper and I don't trust him. The way he looks at you, you need to be careful."

"The way he looks at me?"

"You're smart, but really stupid if you don't see it. I think once this is over, you should leave with me. There is nothing here for us once we have revenge for Leanna, for the pack." He was to close again and I stepped back, my wolf coming to the front. She didn't want me to retreat, she wanted to fight.

"You want me to leave, with you?"

"I think you had the vision for a reason, it bought us together. Maybe I was meant to help you and take you away. What if your mate is waiting across the ocean? This could be part of a bigger plan."

"My mate isn't waiting for me across the ocean Ethan, this is my home now." I answered coldly, narrowing my eyes at him.

Leave.

She was right, I needed to get away before he kept poking and I slipped up.

"Good night Ethan."

"I'm just trying to look out for you, pack sticks together!" He yelled out after me. Packs do stick together, and that's exactly what was happening now. I had my pack, and I wasn't leaving them again.

Fourteen.

T he next few weeks went by quickly. Thanks to the distraction of
the holidays a fake calm settled over the house. Thanksgiving was
simple, uneventful and Ethan didn't mention me leaving with him again.
That's what I most thankful for.

Waking up, the first snow had finally fallen over night and looking out
over the fields of white was beautiful. I never really appreciated the beauty
winter offered, it wasn't a time to enjoy rather one to focus on surviving
and going downstairs my change in circumstances boosted my mood.

It didn't take me long to work out the coffee machine, and for the first
time completely unassisted managed to make, and not burn breakfast for
everyone. Cody was down first, heading straight the coffee machine it
was obvious he was impressed yet he said nothing as he made his coffee.
It didn't take long for everyone else to start emerging from their rooms
and the whispers that erupted among them at the smell of breakfast was
amusing.

"Who cooked?" Adam asked curiously, taking a seat there was no stopping
him from digging in.

"I did." I couldn't help smiling as they all looked at each other. Taylor lifted a couple of pieces of toast checking for any hidden burnt bits and at finding none they all laughed.

"Thanks Bianca!" Taylor got up to give me a hug and as everyone started eating, I realized Connor was missing. It didn't take long for me to find him. The sound of the printer the first clue and going into the main study, he was just taking something off the printer.

"I cooked edible food and you're missing it." I whined, walking over to him. I nudged his arm playfully and he only smiled.

"Jay will save me some, and I have this for you." He handed me the printing and I read over it quickly, before going over it again not understanding.

"Congratulations on being a successful applicant... what am I a successful applicant for?"

"Well I saw a job ad being advertised for wait staff and since Daisy is a whiz with a drinks tray, they couldn't really say no." He patted my shoulder and headed to the kitchen.

"Daisy is a whiz doing what?"

"What's going on?" Taylor asked, openly chewing on her breakfast.

"Bianca's got a job." Connor took his seat and ignored the silence that followed as everyone looked at me. I didn't quite understand what he was talking about so joined in the staring. "Show them."

Cody took the print out and read over it before Ethan snatched it from him.

"This is his party." Ethan pointed at the address.

"Yup." Connor sipped his juice, looking more than pleased with himself.

"You're not serious?" The growl that came from Cody had Connor dropping his relaxed attitude and now everyone was silent for a different reason.

"It gets me in." I shrugged.

"And then what?" Cody's question didn't seem directly related to the job, meeting my gaze my wolf was getting anxious and I wasn't going to be the first to look away. She seemed to understand something I wasn't and was waiting for me to work it out instead.

"Then we kill him. Fuck Caprice, you're in. Finish it." Ethan demanded. Cody broke our staring contest and I quickly moved to stand in front of Ethan, blocking him from Cody. My good mood was quickly disappearing and so was everyone else's.

"We have two weeks to work out what to do; Connor got me the job so we will make the best use of it. How we all decide." My word was final, but clearly Ethan missed that message.

"There is nothing to decide. This is just prolonging the inevitable and putting us in more danger. He needs to go, this is our chance!" The more he argued, the harder it was to contain my wolf. She wanted out to put him in his place that he had clearly forgotten. The others all backed off and I was left playing peacemaker between Cody and Ethan.

"If you are so keen, do it yourself then Ethan. Your hands are clean so far maybe it's time you got them dirty!" I snapped at him.

"Maybe I will. This has been our goal, why are so hesitant on getting this done?" He yelled back.

Taylor was moving towards the way out while Adam stood up beside Connor, keeping himself in between our fight and Taylor. My wolf was on high alert, quickly assessing each movement and emotion with those around us and even doing that, none of us expected what Jay added to the argument.

"Because he is her mate and we have to be careful so he doesn't find out!"

Taylor gasped and Adam quickly got both of them out of the kitchen as the colour left Jay's face. Connor slapped his hand over his mouth and shook his head, while Ethan's dropped open like a goldfish.

"Mate? You're his mate?" Ethan asked in disbelief, reaching out to grab me by the shoulders Cody had him stumbling across the room before I could blink. The fight that broke out between the pair of them was expected and instead I grabbed Jay and Connor, getting them out of harm's way since they were frozen in place.

"I am so sorry; I don't know why I just did that!" Jay apologized.

"It's ok; he was going to find out eventually." While I was trying to comfort him, my tone only reflected how annoyed I was. The stumbling behind us disappeared and the sound of snapping jaws and growls took over.

We looked out the front window as the black wolf gave chase the white and brown, and Adam and Taylor came to join us.

"You might want to break it up Bianca." Adam muttered as Cody took Ethan down. He was going to give up so easily and managed to take hold of Cody's front leg.

"What makes you think I could?"

"Because one of us can?" He answered sarcastically, rolling his eyes and I saw Taylor take his hand.

They were scared, for themselves, Cody or maybe Ethan – I wasn't sure, but he was right. They needed to stop before it got really out of control.

"Stay inside." I ordered. My wolf was eager to take over. I couldn't let her do that, she was too hard to read at the moment and losing my own control wouldn't help. Slipping on a pair of boots and a jacket, I ran outside towards the fighting wolves.

It was hard to determine who was winning, for every hit Ethan took he managed to give one back. If I had shifted, I would have easily broken them up. In human form, it wouldn't be so easy and I needed to break their focus on killing each other.

"STOP!" The command was obvious and I was surprised how much I felt my own wolfs presence in my voice.

Ethan did, slipping out from underneath Cody he was quick to move behind me. His coat was damp with a mixture of saliva, blood and melted snow. In seconds Cody spun around to pin him down again and spying me, he clearly hadn't heard or noticed my arrival until this point. Now I knew who was winning, the way Ethan hid behind me made it obvious. I was his Alpha now; he needed me to protect him. I would have loved to know what Ethan was thinking about this, his actions clearly his wolfs.

Cody stood defensively in front of me, his amber eyes glowing as he tried to assess the situation. I met his gaze, not backing down and his puffed up tail arched towards his back in his grand display of dominance that was completely for show.

"Shift."

Ethan whined behind me, not thrilled on the idea of turning to his weaker human form with Cody still in attack mode. I refused to break Cody's gaze, challenging him further and the sounds of Ethan shifting behind me told me enough.

"Go inside Ethan."

"But..."

I only growled and he slowly headed towards the house. Cody made an attempt to lunge after him and I threw myself in his path, getting knocked over in the process.

"Asshole," I muttered, yet he stopped pursuing Ethan. Standing over me, I only glared up at him. "Can I get up?"

Obediently the wolf stepped back a few steps and standing I brushed the dirt and slush from my hands before rolling my shoulder to try and work out the ache from hitting the ground. To my surprise Cody moved forward, leaning against my legs like an overly affectionate pet dog and instinctively I ran my hands through his fur.

Rubbing behind his ear his head rolled back to look up at me, the goofy expression on his face made me laugh breaking my mood. His tongue rolled out the side of his mouth and just like that his fight was forgotten.

"Come on Rover, get inside." I teased, with a final pat I headed inside and the wolf trotted alongside me until we hit the veranda. Shaking his coat I left the door open and was met with five sets of eyes and pointing at Ethan, ignored the others.

"You. Upstairs."

I could feel his anger, and knew his pride was wounded. Closing his bedroom door Ethan sat on his bed, pulling the blanket around himself he didn't say a word.

"I'm sorry for not telling you." I admitted.

"Guess I look like a jerk for suggesting using well you as bait then?" He growled. "I kind of knew something had to be up because of their reaction. Why couldn't you have told me?"

"I don't know. I guess I didn't trust you enough, I didn't really know you at the time and never really had a reason to bring it up." I took a seat beside him and he only sighed.

"Do you trust me now?"

The fact I hesitated wasn't missed, yet surely now and after everything we had been through I could give him the answer he wanted. "Yes."

"Then trust me when I say we shouldn't be here." He took my hand cautiously and I only frowned.

"You don't understand, this is my home now. You do need to be careful around Cody though, I won't always be there to protect you." My warning was clear.

"Fine, as soon as this is over I'm out of here anyway."

"That's your choice Ethan." He let go of my hand and got up to get changed so I left him alone.

"Maybe it will be yours too."

--

A couple of days went by and Cody and Ethan gave each other plenty of space. There were no further upsets which helped settle everyone else down. For the day after it was as if everyone was walking on eggshells and it only thanks to Adams suggestion of getting a Christmas tree sorted out that ended it.

And that's where I chose to sit at night, beside the Christmas tree. I couldn't stop staring at the lights. The tinsel Taylor had obsessed over making sit just right glistened in the soft glow. Sitting on my own and with the house asleep, I didn't hold back my tears.

My last Christmas had been when I was fifteen.

The decorations were beautiful, yet with each laugh and smile that was shared; a dark cloud shadowed all of us in the house. While the cousins still had each other, they all lost parents, aunts and uncles. A mate.

I wasn't prepared for the sight of the tree. Seeing the guys drag it inside triggered memories of my Dad and Uncle taking Leanna and I out tree hunting. We'd always pick the same one, argue until we ran out of breath and then give in to each other. Because the main Christmas lunch happened at our house with the majority of the pack in attendance, I would always be the one ending up with the prized tree.

Now I'd give Leanna every tree in the forest if it meant she could be sitting beside me now.

"Couldn't sleep?" Ethan startled me, and I quickly wiped my eyes.

"No, just thinking of the lunch we used to put on." I smiled weakly, knowing he would share the same memory.

"Oh right. God that feels like a lifetime ago."

"You're telling me."

Ethan sat down; turning away from the tree he noticed I had been crying.

"I know it's not much, but did you want hear some ah, not so bad things about him? You know, like you did for me with Leanna?" He didn't need to say Damon's name, and I quickly shook my head.

"There is nothing I need to hear. Unlike you, I don't want him. At all."

"I miss my Mums hot chocolates and gingerbread cookies." He finally broke the silence and clearly some part of my stomach remembered the cookies too as it growled hungrily. I appreciated the change in topic and a tiny smile appeared.

"Those were the best. I don't know how she had the patience to decorate them all."

"She acted calm once we arrived, but at our house she was a maniac. She doesn't bake like that anymore." The sadness was obvious, only I couldn't find a way to feel sorry for him. He still had his Mum; mine was dead.

"I miss trying to sneak a peek into the presents put under the tree with Leanna. Mum always managed to hide a few so we were still surprised Christmas morning."

"I miss your Dad dressing up as Santa for the pups on Christmas Eve. I was devastated when I found out it wasn't actually Santa."

"He loved doing it too." The thought of my Dad stuffing the over sized red suit made me smile; yet a new stream of tears ran down my cheeks at the same time.

If only killing Damon would bring him back, just so I could hear him walk through the front door wishing everyone a Merry Christmas one more time. If I knew that was going to be my last Christmas with them I wouldn't have begged to leave the lunch earlier so Leanna and I could go into town to meet up with some of our school friends. I would have sat by his side being Santa's helper all god dam day and in the ridiculous elf outfit that came with the suit. I wouldn't have rolled my eyes at Mum when she asked me to help her with ham and I wouldn't have teased Aunt Alice about drinking too much champagne.

There were so many things I regretted taking advantage off so I focused on Ethan's memories. Sure we were from the same pack, but his memories were different with people I wasn't so close or connected too. Even so it was hard for me not to talk about them too. Like in the hotel room when I told him about Leanna, it was a way for them all to live again.

It hurt, a lot.

We shared missed memories for a good hour, and I had never felt so homesick. This was the Ethan I liked, and I just wished he could be like it all the time. Things would be so much easier if he was, but nothing in my life had been easy these days.

I had been so distracted that when the pressure of my wolf in my mind finally hit me, I realized she had been trying to get my attention for a while and turning around; Cody was leaning against the door frame.

"Hey." I whispered, my voice still broken from the crying.

"Hey."

"Try and get some sleep, I'll see you in the morning." Ethan was quick to get the message and got up, leaning down he gave me a quick hug. "Did you need someone to walk out to the barn with you?"

"No, I'm fine. Goodnight Ethan." I felt a little guilty, from where I had found a new place to sleep everyone presumed I was still out there. I was always awake and in the kitchen or living room by the time everyone got up so they wouldn't know any better anyway. Now the air had been cleared with Cody, his bed had become mine again.

Just because I had a bed, didn't mean I was ready to sleep.

I never really established a normal sleep cycle; I'd still be the last to bed and the first to rise. I would take naps during the day, but to actually sleep for more than four or so hours was unheard of. Now it was nearly one o'clock and I knew he'd be here to tell me it was time to go to bed. Only instead of calling me over or giving me some other sign it was time to go, he moved to stand before me. It was hard not to be distracted at the sight of his bare chest. The house was kept warm, not warm enough to walk around in nothing other than sweatpants though.

We hadn't done anything since our truce was passed, more content with the company than anything else and a part of me wanted to change that.

"I heard you two talking, are you ok?"

All thoughts disappeared with that. He was too coming off to calm and gentle. I'd seen a softer side of him before, just not like this. The pain the holidays bought all of us was clear in his eyes and while I knew we were all hurting, I never expected him to actually show it.

"Yeah, it's just hard."

"I wish I could tell you it will get easier, but it won't. You just lean to deal with it." He took Ethan's place beside me and as his arm lifted to the top of the sofa I crawled to fit beside him.

"My Mum sounds like yours, she would spend days preparing the food and shifters from all over this region would come around. We used to use the barn on my Uncles property. He and some his friends had an old high school band and they'd perform all night. I miss hearing my Mum sing with them, she had a beautiful voice."

I wasn't sure what to say, he never spoke of his family. What I did know was from Jay and a little from Connor.

"And I miss sitting back on the fence having a beer with my Dad. During that beer we'd solve all the world problems, plan the cattle for the next year and yeah. It was like our own little tradition, you know?"

"Yeah, I know. I'm sorry you don't have them here anymore." I rested my hand over his heart, feeling it pounding underneath his skin. Bad things happened to good people. It just wasn't fair.

"Don't be sorry, they had a good life and went down fighting. It sucks that they didn't get to see Connor shift, he is smartest person our family has ever produced." He chuckled softly, and I loved seeing the affection he had for his brothers. "Jay is just like Mum. Everything he does reminds me of her. Patient, kind, a good cook."

I laughed with him. Everyone always teased Jay when it was his night to cook. He would put on the apron and even something as simple as steak and veg was treated like it was being prepared for the most gourmet restaurant in the country.

"Adam and Taylor took it hardest, but they're tough. My Uncle took shit from no one. Had we actually been part of an active pack, rather than a family unit – he would have been alpha. We were lucky to have what time we did with them."

"That's a great way to think of it." I had been lucky to know my parents, to have them raise me and give the memories I now ache to relive. Not having those would leave me with nothing.

"Like I said, you learn to deal with it."

We stayed cuddling on the sofa in silence and I realized he never mentioned his mate. I wanted to know about her, who had the fates chosen for him? Was she strong, an equal or was she more like a calming presence keeping him in line?

"Bianca, why don't you talk to us like you do Ethan?"

"What do you mean?" I sat up slightly to look at him better.

"You never cry in front of us. You don't really trust him, yet he sees you at your weakest?"

"I guess cause he knew them all too and he was Leanna's mate. I feel like I owe it to her to protect him. I know he wouldn't be such an ass if she were here with him. We were always getting in trouble, but she was this beautiful creative person too. She was strong and wouldn't take shit from anyone, yet she was a bit like Jay, always looking for the best in everyone. She would have had him wrapped around her finger and he wouldn't even know it." I could imagine her throwing a tantrum at him when he started letting his own ego take over. She hated people like that and would have beaten it out of him if she had to.

"Makes sense, you see him as a link to her. I just hope he thinks the same. I don't trust him." The growl that rumbled through his chest was hard to miss. The feelings between the pair were mutual and I doubt that would ever change.

"What was your mate like?" I blurted it out before I could shut my mouth and held my breath, as his eyes seemed to glaze over. He shifted away from me slightly and I knew I had over stepped a boundary. "Sorry, you don't have to answer."

"No, it's OK."

Silence followed and I moved away, only to be pulled back into place at his side.

"I'd only known her for six months. She moved to town with her grand-parents and the world literally stopped when I saw her. She was the most beautiful girl I had ever seen and I felt compelled to go talk to her. I helped her take her groceries to the car and the next day we went out for coffee. By the end of the week, it was obvious who we were to each other. Jill was amazing. Nothing ever made her angry, always ready to laugh and have some fun. I hated being away from her. She had this, innocence about her that drew me in. I don't know how to explain it. In some ways she was, weak I guess. I knew I could protect her and I knew that was why she was mine." The affection in his voice was obvious, yet there was something else that my wolf picked up on and I was missing. Just like in the kitchen a couple of days ago, there had been a double meaning in his question that I still hadn't worked out.

"She moved in with us a month later, it's weird how one person could just take over your world like that."

"Weird?" I was expecting wonderful or amazing. My parents always told me they were in love within days of meeting, that a lifetime would not be enough time for them to be together. They weren't the only ones. Mates were valued within our society for a reason.

"This is between us, if Tay found out she'd kill me." I nodded and sighing he carried on, "It was weird. I didn't like how out of control it left me. I didn't even know her last name when I realized I could love her. When she moved in and she was suddenly apart of our life here, it happened too easily. She fitted in, Tay was like her sister and my parents loved her as much as I did."

"What is wrong with that?" Confused didn't even start to explain how I was feeling. It made no sense.

"I don't know. It's why I felt so guilty when she was murdered. Not only was I not there to protect her like I promised her I would, but I mourned for my family more than I did her. She was my soul mate. What kind of shifter am I if I can get over the death of losing that?"

No words left my mouth as I opened it; I had no idea what to say. I didn't know many shifters that lost their mates. The ones I did were never the same person afterwards and Cody had a darkness about him that would keep smart people away. It only came from suffering, and it was how we first bonded. I was just as broken as him.

"You want to know the real shitty part?" I knew it was rhetorical and sat up, finally putting some space between us. "Since you've come into my life, you've challenged me, beaten me and showed me up in front of my family. And I like it, welcome it – hell I want it. When you left, I felt more fucked up inside than when Jill died."

He didn't look at me, despite the fact I was staring. I couldn't move. I couldn't process a single thought.

"Better than that, I know you will see your mate again and I know you say you want to kill him, but you won't. I know he will see you now and be unable to resist the bond that will draw you together. He is a strong wolf; you're made to be an Alpha female Bianca." He turned to look at me slowly, the pain in his eyes broke my heart and I knew I could never feel anything for Damon like what I felt for Cody.

He was wrong.

Before I could tell him that, he got up and went to bed. The sound of his door closing snapped me out my trance.

My mind went crazy with a rush of thoughts and questions, while my wolf was lost in the mess. This was the part where I wanted to run, truly forget the world away from the forest. I don't know if it was my wolf or just the logical part of my human brain that stopped me, I couldn't keep running. I was acting like a spoilt child who didn't get their own way and I needed to start facing the things I found hard. Fighting, I could handle. This emotional and mental aspect of life had me stumped.

Wolves weren't complicated like this. You know what they're thinking; their body language is easy to understand. Humans hide too much and show the wrong things, but right now only one thing made sense and that was Cody.

Slipping into his room, he sat up slightly. Crawling in beside him, the tension in his body was obvious. Not all body language could be easily hidden and as he laid back down I was glad he didn't refuse me joining him. My wolf told me I was stupid to ever think he would.

Lying alongside him, my arm hugged his chest, as I got comfortable. His arm came around my back and finally he sighed, relaxing.

"You're wrong Cody." I whispered, feeling his lips on my forehead.

"We'll see."

And I finally knew what had happened in the kitchen. 'And then what?' was not about the party or getting into Damon's place, it was asking me what would happen when I finally saw him again. The truth was I had no idea. The pain that had controlled my life was too strong to simply disappear, I was happy here. I was happy with Cody. That didn't stop the slow slither of doubt as it began to work its way into my mind.

Maybe things would change once I met my mate again.

Maybe there would be the ever after I had been raised to believe in with him.

Then what about Cody?

He could never love me like he had Jill. I never got to establish the bond with Damon to know him, love him so I would never get to experience having that connection to someone. If Cody was right, maybe I would, but I didn't particularly want it.

Cody.

My wolf seemed to think that wasn't the case. Her mind had been made up; it was Cody who had bought us back here. It was Cody who had been on my mind, even when we'd been hunting down Damon's pack.

"Go to sleep." He mumbled, turning slightly onto his side so my head turned to lie against his chest. I smiled as the sound of his heart beat filled my ears. We both struggled to sleep without the other.

Surely this connection stood for something too?

What do you think? Is Cody right and will the mate bond be strong enough to get Damon and Bianca together?

Finally get to meet him in the next chapter... da da da duuum.......

Fifteen.

Walking down the stone steps to where the winter wonderland marquee had been set up my hand was trembling. Normally this would be fine, I could hide them in my pockets or fiddle with something. Instead I had fifteen champagne flutes gently clinking together, sending streams of the three hundred dollar a bottle bubbly liquid down to pool at the base of the tray.

"Daisy right? I'm Becky." The over enthusiastic brunette balanced her own tray in one hand, extending the other to shake hands. I stopped walking, struggling to keep the glasses upright as I took her hand. "First time at one of these parties?"

"Yeah, it's a bit much." It wasn't a lie. There were too many shifters and the crowd took some getting used to.

"I've done heaps, the celebrities are the worst though. This crowd seem pretty tame. I did this one party for this awesome band, Taking Over Monday, that was out of control. Have you heard of them?"

"Can't say I have." I mumbled, focusing on the steps while I tried to keep hold of the tray with one hand like my coworker. This was a mistake, no one would believe I had waiting experience and my wolf wasn't helping my balancing skills.

"How is that possible? Beau the lead singer is hot, but I like the drummer better..." Becky's chatter about her favorite band carried on until we hit the marquee where pale blue fairy lights dripped around the edges like icicles. Under the tent was warm thanks to the fire pit in the center of the room and from the stage the band played Christmas songs.

"OK, so the best thing to do is keep moving. People will take glasses as you pass, and give you empties. To save going back to the main house, in the right corner there is another bar. Dump your tray and grab a new one. If Peter catches you standing still or talking to guests, he will put you on rubbish duty." Some of this had already been mentioned earlier in the afternoon when we had a run through. None of it sunk in and since I hid my wolf, she was too busy sulking at not getting her chance to rip Damon apart should we see him.

Clearly Ethan's own ideas had won her over.

Following Becky's instructions I kept walking, making sure to smile politely at the guests and gave up on being one handed. Holding the tray with two hands wasn't encouraged and after my first lap, Damon and Caprice were nowhere in sight.

An hour passed.

I knew Cody was outside the fence of the property with Jay and Ethan. They kept close enough to hear any commotion, but far enough away that they wouldn't alert any of the guards. Cody even got in Brett and Kane to help out, the pair who used to help guard the property spent most of their time over in the house that Taylor and Adam were raised it. The extra muscle could prove useful if things went south.

Connor had also bought some new equipment and he was able to hack into the security systems. It was amazing to see how intense Damon's security set up was, comforting too. Adam and Connor had a clear view to the tent, of the yards and in the house. Every now and then I made sure to head to the edge of the marquee so he could see I was still OK but otherwise, I was earning my wages.

Two hours in Damon hadn't made an appearance, yet I did spy a familiar face. Instantly my wolf stopped sulking, all my senses coming back to life and I even found the ability to balance the drinks tray with one hand. Getting closer one of the other waiters was distracting the trio with bits of pastry and meat and I could openly stare at them.

He is supposed to be dead.

'I know.'

Max stood laughing with a couple of others, and my wolfs fury easily transitioned through me. The angrier I got, the more I could feel my face flush and my breathing altered. I had to tell Cody, any sign of trust for Ethan disappeared and now I felt like I had been thrown to the wolves all over again.

"Hey Becky, can we take toilet breaks?" I whispered as I found her by the bar.

"Sure, he isn't that much of a tyrant. I need to go too, I'll show you where we can go."

We headed back to the house and I nearly died as I my wolf fought against whatever barrier was in place to hide her. Damon walked down the stairs with Caprice between him and her mate. There were no smiles or talking as they made their way to the party, and as we passed Caprice's mouth dropped slightly yet I was too busy fighting the urge to look at him. Glancing behind us, he was doing the same thing and thankfully something Becky said made her laugh snapping me back to look at her.

The sensation of his eyes burning into the back of my skull didn't stop though and I was scared to look back again.

I knew she had been talking the whole time, yet I didn't hear a word of it. "Don't you think?"

"Sorry, what?"

"Never mind. You ok? You were kind of red down there and you look like you saw a ghost!" She was right. I had seen a ghost, one called Max.

I needed to try and tell Connor I needed something, but he wasn't the only one who could be watching the camera's. The house was like a palace. My own home had been impressive, yet compared to this is looked like a cottage. Art lined the walls and everything was finished in white and gold. Becky led us to busy kitchen, it was huge and I expected this is the kind of commercial kitchen you'd find in restaurants not in a home.

While following her, I couldn't help but wonder if things hadn't gone this way with Damon and I - would this be our house and our party for our pack?

Coward.

My wolf was back, not impressed with his standard of living even though I had felt her watch him with the same level of shock when we passed.

Behind the kitchen was a laundry, the other door that led into the area was closed and a few other waiters all stood around having something to eat. Becky disappeared into the toilet and looking around I noticed the camera in the corner of the kitchen. I hovered by the door to the laundry, smiling awkwardly at my co-workers as they passed and spying some paper near a workbench, was able to write a quick message.

"It's free now." Becky smiled, making her the most friendly human I had ever met. I dropped the pen and tucked the paper in my hand.

"False alarm, but I know for next time. What's with the security?" I pointed out the camera, flicking my middle finger up at it which only made her laugh. Connor would know I needed something though and leaving the house we just made it outside when I heard Taylor. I had also given her a tiny piece of the leaf incase of this very reason and told Becky to go on without me.

Taking a deep breath I turned towards the front of the building and there she was, dressed exactly how I was.

"Ask her, she knows me! Daisy!" She waved and the guard at the door only rolled his eyes. "Please tell him I'm meant to be working right now. Peter is going to fire me for being so late!"

I had to give it to her, she was a good actress.

"Sorry sir," I smiled innocently at him and even tried to flutter my fake eyelashes at him. "Megan, you're too late. He's already fired you. Just leave, call tomorrow and beg for your job back."

Maybe I was too.

"You heard the lady, no work for you. Move on sweet heart!" The guard growled, literally, which was weird considering we were human. So we acted like a human would. We looked scared and she nodded fearfully, tossing her own blonde wig over her shoulder she looked close to crying.

"Call me later OK?" I mimicked how Becky talked, and hugged Taylor while slipping her the note about Max being alive and that I've seen the other Alphas.

"OK." She nodded sadly and turned to leave. The guard looked like he wanted to say something, but we both moved away quickly and I headed back to the party.

Heading back into the marquee, one of the guys shoved a tray of tiny pieces of toast with tomato on at me and started up the stairs so I started doing the rounds again. Some of the gowns were beautiful and spying Max again, I realized he was near Simon. He was also on my hit list and as he moved away from the ghost, he went to Caprice. She paid him no attention, looking over the crowd as if she was searching for someone and shivering she turned in my direction. Her eyes widened slightly, the fake smile disappearing as she stared at me. Her mate followed her gaze and I quickly turned to disappear among the crowd.

If I knew her, she'd be on me in seconds.

She didn't disappoint.

"What are these?" She asked, not looking at the tray as she searched my eyes for something and the way her nostrils flared made it obvious she was trying to catch my scent.

"A way out if you're interested." I met her gaze, not backing down and her partner looked around cautiously.

"Interested." She smiled, if anything she looked relieved. "I've seen your work before, clearly you won't disappoint."

Carefully she lifted one of the hors d'oeuvres off the tray, passing it to her partner as she looked at them all over again.

"I have some others I can shift to over by the bar if this isn't to your liking." I offered, smiling as someone else walked past to take some of the food.

Her gaze dropped down and pointing at one of the tomatoes, she stepped side ward and glancing down she lifted her gown to reveal some kind of handcuff on her ankle.

"No need.' She growled and I understood. "I may retire for the evening, in our guest house by other side of the property. I may ask my host if some of these delicious treats could be bought over to my room. Parties bore me."

The pair left me and I carried on walking around, avoiding Damon at all costs. Twice I caught him staring at me, and the urge to throw up only began to grow the longer I waited. I was nervous, this wasn't good and my wolf was to distracted watching him to help ease my emotions.

It wasn't long until Caprice went past him and after stopping for a few minutes, half an hour later the couple were leaving. Going to get a fresh tray of food, I saw one being made up with a variety of samples being put on.

"What's that for?" I asked curiously and Peter looked up, his stress obvious.

"Some princess what to eat privately. Apparently these things aren't for her, so this and this are to be taken to the guest house. Don't go through the house, follow the lawn until you get to the pool and it's just behind there." An ice bucket with a bottle of Bollinger and two flutes were shoved under my arm and he passed me over the silver platter.

"Sure thing boss."

This was it.

Glancing around Damon was by the stage talking to some people with Max and sticking to the outside, prepared to sneak out to the guest house. What

I didn't expect was Simon to appear. His eyes ran over the tray and the ice bucket before he smiled.

"Would you like a hand with that Miss?" He offered, reminding me of Kyle a little bit.

"Thank you, but it's fine. I just need to take these to the guest house." I went to keep walking and he followed.

"They're not nice people, I can come with you to make sure you make it back in one piece." He purred, taking the tray of food from me.

"Not nice how?"

"Well, they're kind of part of a gang. Politics and all that. Sometimes they just need a reminder they're not top dog around here." His double meaning wasn't lost on me and he picked at some of the food as we walked.

"A gang?"

"Nothing illegal." He assured me, "My boss just has a lot of business deals around the place. This party is just him treating those within his employment how much he appreciates them."

"That's nice of him."

"He's a nice guy."

We walked in silence and spying the pool, Caprice stood on the other side of the gate out of her gown and in a light sweater and a pair of leggings. It was too cold to wear something like that outside, so clearly she had no plans to stay around for long.

"What are you doing here Simon?" She growled, instantly standing taller as her mate appeared in only his cotton shirt and suit pants.

"Just escorting the lady here." He taunted, the way he narrowed his eyes at her wasn't missed by any of us.

Looking at Caprice she nodded and swinging the ice bucket, I whacked him in the side of his head. The tray of food fell against the pool decking with a thud and the bottle of champagne smashed amongst the ice and glass with a fizzy bang.

"I told you I would be fine." I growled, straddling him I grabbed the broken bottle and held it to his throat, letting it cut in slightly. "How do I get the cuffs of them?"

"Keys." He gasped, his eyes unable to focus I realized I hit him harder than I should of before getting my answers.

"Where?" I demanded.

Touching his pocket the jingle was undeniable and getting them out, I threw them to Caprice.

"You, you won't get away with this." He stuttered, with each word the glass cut deeper into his skin. I leant down lower to his ear as he closed his eyes, barely conscious.

"Just like how you didn't get away from the one who has been killing your pack?"

The struggle to open his eyes was as clear as the fear that started to radiate from his body and despite hearing Caprice and her mate telling me it was time to go, my wolf was too focused on the kill.

"No. Please don't." He mumbled, his begging the weakest I'd ever heard.

"I asked for the same kind of mercy and instead I was thrown off a cliff."

Now his eyes opened, meeting mine - they were the last thing he saw before the bottle was rammed the rest of the way in. Looking up the alpha couple didn't hide their own horror at what I just did, the warm droplets of blood making my skin tingle as it splattered across my face.

"Can you shift now?" I asked them, ignoring the look.

"Yes, the bracelet is connected to the fence, it's all electric. If we had shifted or gone near it, we would have been electrocuted" Caprice explained.

"They're going to think this is our pack freeing us. Is it worth escaping?" Her mate argued as we ran past the pool. It was risky, but with the cars and limousines filling the driveway, we could use them as cover to get to the main gate.

"I will not be held hostage." Caprice growled. "If we get home we will be ready for them this time. She just killed Simon, he is going to be out for blood and act reckless. Now is when we take him down."

From speaking with Connor, I knew the section of the decking Simon was didn't show up on the camera's. This was going against the plan, but even with blood on my hands, I wasn't ready to leave yet. If I avoided the humans, the shifters wouldn't call the police and my wolf was eager to see the spoils of my kill.

"There are some others waiting for you, do not let them come for me. I will meet them at the destination."

They both hesitated and it was her mate who spoke up. "Shouldn't you stick to the plan?"

"I can't."

They shifted by the cars, and wasted no time in running to the one fence that wouldn't shock them. I watched them jump the black bars before turning back to the house, working on my tears I headed to the rear of the house and screamed, running to the backdoor. By the time I got there, one of the guards appeared to open it and looking at me I saw the flash of his wolf in his eyes.

"They they killed him. Call the police, call an ambulance!"

My hysterics drew on the others, they all came over curious as the first guard left me sobbing in the doorway and two others ran out after him.

"Calm down, what happened?" The tallest of the men asked. Despite his size, he was actually one of the less threatening of the guards and I didn't stop sobbing.

"That red head woman, she just attacked him! I was pushed away and they they, they killed him!"

I was led inside and into the nearest room. It was a library of some kind and the frantic shouts and rush of activity thrilled me. My wolf was proud, finally able to enjoy the mayhem the deaths caused and there was only voice she was listening for. Ten minutes later, it came.

"Where are they? I don't care who sees, get the trackers out there after them!"

"I can't believe they would do this." Another voice yelled and then the words human, inside, saw everything came to my ears. Clinging to the guard, I screamed as the door was thrown open.

"Is this her?" Looking up my eyes were aching from the contacts being in with all the crying. The pain and rage amongst the shifters was intoxicating and my wolf was inhaling it with each breath I took.

He mouthed the words human to the guard comforting me and I felt him nod.

"Miss, are you OK? I am an off duty police officer. The minutes after witnessing an attack are the most important, could you please tell me what you saw?"

So I told him about taking the wine and food to the guest house, Simon offered to walk me and when we go there they were standing by the pool. I was pushed out the way when they snatched the champagne I was holding and how they killed him, took something and ran off.

"Did you see anything else, unusual?"

In other words, did you see them shift into a wolf.

"No, I couldn't stop staring at the bottle. It was just, rammed in there like it was nothing." I started crying again and they all left the room with an older woman soon appearing with some tissues and a glass of water. She said nothing, yet the fear in the old shifters eyes was undeniable. Getting up I stood by the curtain and from that angle, could barely make out Damon who was waving his arms and screaming at the group. Even from here it was an impressive sight and looking to the desk, I saw the writing set.

After leaving a quick message, I left the room. My wolfsbane would be wearing off as I had taken it early today when we arrived in the city and to be caught as a shifter wouldn't be a good idea right now. Sneaking through the hall I heard the sounds of the kitchen and breaking the lock on the door went into the now empty laundry. Looking around I found a cloth and going into the bathroom, cleaned up a little bit to walk out.

No one was around out the front now, and walking down the drive I was able to get out with ease. It didn't take me long to get to our destination and Cody and Ethan were arguing out the front with Caprice.

Cody saw me first, running over I was nearly crushed in his hug before the others all followed.

"We had a plan, what the fuck was that?" Ethan growled.

The look I served him had him backing down instantly and I was quick to push him against the wall of the motel room. He tried to push me off, but with my anger came strength and with the others behind me, he wasn't stupid enough to resist.

"Why was Max walking around and having a grand old time at the party? You were meant to have killed him!"

He was lucky I couldn't shift, as right now my wolf would be ripping him apart.

"I-I couldn't do it." He choked out.

"Obviously!" I growled, pressing harder under his chin, he tried to push my arm back. The biggest surprise came from Cody who was the one who ended up pulling me away from. "Back off, this isn't your business."

"Like hell it is, why didn't you leave with them?" He pointed at Caprice and her mate as they stood by the hire car with Taylor.

"Because I had something else I needed to do! Now move, this is between Ethan and me!"

"I'm sorry!" Ethan croaked, rubbing his neck he had the nerve to step completely behind Cody.

"Dam straight you are! You wanted my trust Ethan, guess what - you just lost it. Fuck you!"

"That's a little unfair, you kept things from me too!"

Cody couldn't stop me as I darted around him, throwing the punch Ethan fell to the floor.

"How about we use you as bait?" I yelled and grabbing me around the waist, Cody dragged me over to the car. I already had a kill tonight, I wanted more starting with Ethan. I was furious, shaking with the need to shift only due to the drug in my system I couldn't.

The others went to help him up and my gaze was intense as I focused on Ethan. My prey drive was out of control and I just a look in my direction had him cringing back behind the group. Cody blocked my view, his eyes meeting mine I didn't even realize he was holding my head in his hands for a few seconds after. Blinking a few times his gaze was almost hypnotic, and going to pull away - he kept me in place.

"Calm. Down." The more he said it, the more my anger only peaked before it began to disappear all the together and I focused on my breathing. Finally he let me go, pulling me into a hug instead.

"As sweet as this all is, got a plan to get us out of here human?" Caprice broke into the moment and pulling away, I did feel calmer. Looking me over, she raised her eyebrow curiously. "She-wolf?"

I nodded before pointing at Ethan. "This isn't over."

I went over to Taylor and got out the bottles of the concoction I made with the wolfsbane for everyone to take. If trackers were hunting down shifters, they weren't going to find any. Reluctantly everyone drank it and surprisingly the our new companions didn't even ask or complain.

Cody got into the driver's seat of the closest car and I slipped into the passenger side. Caprice and her mate got in the back of the car with Connor while Adam, Taylor and Jay took Ethan and Kane. The other guard was going to stay and keep an eye on things for us.

Leaving the city behind us we didn't have long until we made it to our stop for the night. It wasn't far from the town where the gypsy lived and I was interested to see her again. A lot had happened between my last visit and avoiding Ethan, I was glad Cody got us a room to ourselves.

"So, how was it?" He asked as I got undressed.

"What?"

"Seeing him again?"

"I didn't really see him at all. I was distracted by Max, Simon and getting Caprice out of there." Going into the bathroom, I was eager to shower and clean myself properly to get rid of any other traces of Simons blood I had missed. Of course Cody was there to join me and we just stood under the water together.

"Was Simon one of them too?"

"Yeah, that's all four of them now." I sighed, content with the thought I had taken down Damon's closest and the ones responsible for the death of my parents. "Do you think I could still be like this if the attack never happened? I would have gone to college, worked - had a normal life. Despite my Dad being Alpha, I never considered taking his place. Knowing Ethan, I couldn't imagine him leading the pack like my Dad. Leanna's mate or not, I couldn't let someone like that take the title. But then again, what would he be like if the attack never happened?"

"The fact you said you'd stop him and because of who your mate is, I think you would have found an alpha position eventually. What was your first thought when you saw your wolf?" The soft caress of the washcloth on my skin had me opening my eyes, and I realized he had washed me completely while we had been standing there.

"I thought she was beautiful and I was proud that she was mine. I didn't think I was worthy to have such a proud wolf."

"That's because you didn't have a reason to believe you'd be worthy of her yet. What do you think now?" He was doing it again, being too gentle, calm. Yet it was exactly what I needed and I wondered if he was more in tune to me than I thought possible.

"She's mine as much as I'm hers." For years I had been running blind, letting her be in control. She handed it back to me, like she knew she would have to do and there was no resentment there either.

We were one and that was how it was supposed to be.

The limp body was lifted from the decking and placed on the stretcher. The guests had gone hours before and extra guards were stationed around the property. Watching Simon be taken away was hurting Damon, nowhere near the level of pain the ones who did this were going to feel once he got hold of them.

"Sir, maybe it's time you came inside." Jordan kept out of reaching distance, not liking the silence that had fallen over his Alpha. For twenty minutes he had stood staring at the blood that had stained the decking and the loss of another pack mate vibrated through the whole unit.

"Fine." Turning to go inside, Damon stopped. "Kill the human, she will have to many questions."

"We ah, we lost her." Jordan muttered, yet Damon said nothing as he went inside. He went straight to the control room, and sure enough the trackers were already going through the footage of the girl.

"Who is she?" He demanded, freezing one of the screens her face was only fully seen in one blurry shot in the kitchen where she and another waitress were giving the finger to the camera.

"Daisy Duane. Only hired two weeks ago, this was her first job for Delight Catering Sir. So far all details on her file are fake. No one knows who she is." One of the guards told him, bracing himself for an attack that hadn't happened yet.

"And you let her just walk out of here?" Damon asked, the calmness in his voice worse than any anger could ever be.

"She avoided all the cameras leaving the library. She is human, she must be one of the ones working with Ethan or Caprice was lying and the humans work for her."

"Just find the bitch, both of them. Kill the human, save the shifters for me."

Going into the library there was a faint smell in the air that had his wolf fighting for control. He had only done that once tonight and it had nothing to do with the escape or the death of Simon. The waitress girl on the camera had been the one he had passed earlier in the evening.

Blue eyes haunted him, the more he thought about them the more he realized they were too blue, almost fake. Her brown hair held no scent as he passed, all of her seemed void of a true scent. The perfume hid anything else and it was that perfume he found in the room now.

Taking a glass of whiskey, he sat at the desk. Leaning back in the chair he started to think over detail of her, his wolf eager to do so there was something odd about how much he had remembered. The white cotton shirt and waistcoat didn't do much for her figure, yet she carried herself proudly and he had been watching her as she moved around the marquee. There was a sure footed, almost graceful way she moved you didn't see in humans very often. She had lifted the boxes of wine at the bar with more ease than the other girls, so clearly she was strong.

Putting down his glass Damon saw the writing on the paper and leaning forward, the scent hidden under the perfume met him and as he read the words, the world seemed to stop.

One to go...

"It couldn't be..." He muttered to himself. Closing his eyes he leaned down against the paper and breathed in deep. His wolf was eagerly absorbing the smell and the memory of clinging to something that could never be filled his mind as he had held his mate, his stupid weak little mate before he sentenced her to death.

She was human, but there was no denying it.

She was alive.

Alrighty..... What do you think about that? Should I have given Damon and Bianca more contact or happy with how that turned out?

Sixteen.

After dropping the cars back to the hire company, we found the cars and bikes and headed home. The roads were empty and the trip home wouldn't have taken long if not for a detour.

Faking it as a stop for breakfast, I was surprised there was actually a café open as we hit town. Not only that, but the main street was closed off with a Christmas market. A man was playing a saxophone near one of the food stalls and our group dispersed through the street.

Connor went with his family while Ethan stuck by Caprice and Brian. Cody and I drifted down to the closed up shop of Esmeralda, but not before grabbing some freshly made cinnamon donuts from a food stall.

"It's closed." Cody pointed out as we got to the door.

"She's a psychic, she would I'm coming."

"If she's not a fake." He muttered.

We walked down the side of the building and glancing over the park area where I had killed Rowan a shiver ran down my spine. The back door was unlocked and instantly I became alert.

Walking in the assault of incense had my nose burning and Cody pulled his shirt over his nose to try and save himself. Walking out into the store everything was dark and quiet.

"I don't think she's here." Cody's voice was muffled through the fabric and I was about to agree with him when the familiar jingle sounded from the backroom.

"Of course I am here." The blonde gypsy appeared dressed casually in jeans and a knitted sweater. Seeing her so normal was kind of unusual and Cody took my hand, pulling my back behind him slightly. "Settle down shifter. I mean her no harm."

Getting closer she looked a little older than last time, her smooth skin was becoming worn with wrinkles and I stepped back as she reached out to me. The hug was awkward and Cody's growl split us up.

"It is good to see you she-wolf, I have been keeping watch over you. Your fate has changed many times." Taking my hand she led me to the room where her crystal ball waited. "Shall we see if your vision has changed?"

Cody stood behind me, watching every move she made.

"Out." She pointed to the door and Cody shook his head. "Fine, but don't blame me if you see something you don't want to."

Just like last time she held out her hand, waiting for mine.

"Hand."

I did as she directed, déjà vu washing over me like the tingling that ran up my arm. She closed her eyes and same black mist began to rise from the ball. That wasn't where the similarities ended either as the vision of Damon shooting Ethan appeared.

I couldn't help feel disappointed that there wasn't anything new until the image seemed to expand.

"I know that place." Cody interrupted and Esmeralda's eyes snapped open.

"What?" I turned to look up at him and wish I hadn't.

"It's near the ranch, just outside the neighbors place. Will this happen?" he turned to Esmeralda and I was more worried about him jumping across the table to get her than what was in the vision.

"The future is unpredictable. Every minute that ticks by has the potential to change it all." It was the same cryptic message as before.

"That's what you said last time." I reminded her.

"It's true. I've seen you die, I've seen you survive. Your journey has begun, but how it ends has yet be decided."

Cody moved quickly, but I was already anticipating it and stopped him half way. Didn't help Esmeralda who fell backwards on the chair, cursing him as she landed.

"No more games!"

"Cody calm down." I managed to pull him away, pushing him out of the room and went to help her up.

"That one is trouble, you can't afford the distraction he brings." She paused, looking down at the ball. "He has been here you know, a couple of times since we last met and he'll back soon now he knows who you are."

"Now he knows who I am?" I instantly thought of Ethan, surely he couldn't have done something.

"His wolf knows who you are, they are the part of you that finds your mate. It's why it only happens after you shift and connect to your wolf. No amount of wolfs bane could hide you from him for ever."

"Did Ethan have a part in this?" I demanded. I was already furious with him, and this would change his fate. I would kill him.

"Not yet."

"Not yet? Not yet? This is my life, you can't do this!"

So far I had based months of my life around what she told me and now when there was even more death to come, she couldn't even give me a clear answer.

"You knew coming here wouldn't hold all the answers." She ran her hands through her hair before adjusting her belt.

"Then where do I get my answers?"

"No where, when."

"And when will that be?"

"When you know what you're going to do. Last night was more than ticking another name off a list and freeing the Alpha from the north. Tell me you didn't wonder what your life would have been like had you met your mate under better circumstances? Your house. Your party. Your pack. You and your wolf can deny it all you want, but you both wonder. You both want to belong; you just need to decide where that will be. Once you do, the rest will fall into place."

I wanted to slap the smug look off her face, but she was right. That hint of doubt only seemed to have managed to firmly lodge itself in my brain.

"Everything I said last time still stands Bianca. I'm hoping for one out-come, but nothing is set in stone." She rested her palm on my forehead and looking into her dark brown eyes, I suddenly felt dizzy.

Leave.

My wolf felt far away, just like the room seemed to disappear.

"He'll be here soon, you might was to leave unless you feel like changing the future already." Her voice was barely a whisper, taking the place of my wolf in my mind and I was loosing control. I didn't like it yet I didn't have the will to fight it either, because somehow I knew this wasn't bad.

"Bianca?" Cody's voice called to me now, more urgently. The sensation of freefalling hit me as Esmeralda's eyes were replaced with Cody's and the only kind of falling I was doing was into his arms. I hadn't even seen him come back in.

"Hey, can you hear me? Bianca?"

Slowly I lifted my head to find he was holding me up and the gypsy had gone.

"Lets get you out this place." He growled, and as we left the empty shop I had a feeling I wouldn't be coming back here again or that I would see Esmeralda again. Her final words came back to me as my wolf seemed to reappear too and I tried to tell Cody.

"We need to go, he is on his way here." I mumbled, not complaining as Cody carried me out.

"How do you know that?" He asked, the cold of outside woke me up and I wriggled out of his arms.

"She told me." The door slammed shut behind us and trying the handle, it was locked. "Didn't you hear?"

"No, you kicked me out and then it was like the room was sealed off. I broke down the door as you fainted. Come on, lets get out of here." I didn't protest, and we quickly found the others and carried on home.

"You ok?" Connor stopped me before we got in the car and I still felt spacy, not entirely sure what had happened.

"Ah yeah. I'll be fine. Tired." I shrugged.

"You know you suck at lying right?"

Connor had always been able to tell when I was lying, before he told me it was because my wolf showing in my eyes. I had no idea how he did it because I know she let me lie on my own now. So I tried to do what I was so far failing at, lie some more.

"Just thinking, it's nothing." Lie.

Spying Ethan in the crowd I hadn't calmed down enough to be around him yet.

"Down girl." Caprice whispered in my ear as she passed, finding it more amusing than alarming.

"She has a point, you look like you're about to rip him apart." Connor agreed, only he wasn't teasing.

"Could be a good idea." I growled and got in the car.

It was time to go home.

--

Night had taken over the world by the time we arrived back at the ranch. Ever since we had started travelling with Caprice, my fascination only grew. There was no need to establish who was more dominant. I respected her.

The feeling was mutual and once we were all settled, I found her out on the veranda sipping a hot chocolate.

Brian had spent the majority of his time on the phone organizing their pack for the expected attack. It surprised me she wasn't the one doing it considering he was more like her shadow. Thinking back to the bar she had let him do most of the talking, only taking over when she needed to remind them all of her place.

"Hey." She greeted, smiling as she looked up at me. To my surprise she extended her arm and welcomed me to share the blanket she had. I sat beside her on the bench, tucking my knees underneath my body and she threw the blanket over me. The warmth between us was nice and she leant against me, so we just sat in silence staring into the dark.

"When I first saw you in my town I knew trouble was following you. There was something in the air and the arrival of Damon's goons confirmed the newbie was behind it. Brian thinks he is the one in control, I let him think it. Every thought he ever had came from me, I love him, but thank the gods one of us has a brain."

I found myself laughing with her, not fake or forced, but the kind of laugh two girlfriends would share over brunch.

"I saw everything you did, right down to shooting that idiot. I had a feeling we would meet again which is why I let you leave that night."

"I'm sorry for the trouble we, well I caused your pack."

"Don't be. Things were getting boring anyway. Besides you fixed it, coming in like that took courage. I respect that." For some reason having her accept me had me glowing inside. "You have an ally with us. I will tell you everything I know about what goes on in that shifters pack, but I need to go back to mine."

"I understand. Anything you can tell us is appreciated." I smiled at her, a genuine kind of smile I hadn't done for a while. She put down her cup and wrapped her arm around my shoulders as Taylor walked out and she stopped cautiously.

"Join us." I offered, shuffling over. So the three of us sat outside, talking like we had known each other for a lifetime. When I first saw Esmeralda she told me my wolf would never do me any wrong and to trust my instincts. Caprice was the perfect example of that. Being older, there was a lot I could learn from her and I think that was exactly why I was destined to meet her in the first place. I learnt about her life, her pack.

She spoke of it all like a proud mother showing of her children. Caprice was firm, but fair and was very specific how her unit worked. I thought back to the barista's warning and never would have thought we'd up like this.

Brian appeared first. The alpha couple had to leave early to get home so he took her to bed. Taylor left me soon after and it was hard to think we hadn't gotten along when I first arrived.

Just like Brian, Cody came to put me to bed. We didn't say anything as we waited to fall asleep together and when he did speak, it was barely a whisper.

"Merry Christmas Bianca."

"Merry Christmas Cody."

--

When I got up, I was surprised to find drawings and pages of notes left by Caprice. It was not even five in the morning and they had left. There were details on the security roster, those Damon kept around him and basic drawings of the house layout.

They also left all their contact details and it was the folded piece of paper with my name on that I focused on first.

Bianca,

Apologies for our departure, I know you understand why we had to go. Do not be a stranger; I have a feeling we have many years of friendship ahead of us.

Drawing up the house plans I remembered why I thought I knew you when we first met. I do not know the reason for this, perhaps you will tell me one day. In the upstairs office on the desk there, Damon has your picture in a frame. Now after seeing you without a disguise, I know it is you.

Be careful, listen to your wolf.

I promise we will remain loyal, no matter the outcome of the days to come and we wish you good luck until we meet again.

Caprice.

I ripped the note up and threw into the fireplace in the living room making sure to the light the fire, I sat in front of it to watch the paper burn.

"Bianca, I'm sorry." Ethan appeared behind me and after sleeping on it; I no longer had the urge to kill him.

"So am I."

"What for?" Cautiously he walked around the sofa and we sat beside each other.

"One day something will happen and I might not be able to stop it. You're my last link to Leanna and despite everything, I don't want to loose you." I admitted.

"I don't understand."

"You will one day."

And then I hugged him, tightly. Twice I had the same vision, so maybe not all things can be changed or avoided in the future. I couldn't let him die with our argument still hanging between us, and while he was almost forgiven – it hadn't been forgotten.

If he did die, could I live with the regret of not trying?

The day was spent absorbing all of Caprices' notes. I wondered how long they actually slept for because she had left details for everything. My wolf poured through them like it was discovering the meaning of life and by the time the afternoon came around; a work out with Cody was what we needed to clear our mind.

It wasn't long before we gave in to our refreshed wolves needs and went for a run, all of us. We frolicked in the snow and raced along the flat lands. It was what we needed.

Fun.

Our wolves were bonding, celebrating the success in the release of the Alpha's. We all survived. No one was hurt. Now it was time to relax and enjoy the moment. I wrestled with Adam and even Ethan and Cody managed to be near each other without turning nasty. As the moon appeared in the sky we all sang out to it, a ghostly chorus that had what birds remained in the forest shifting further into their nests, the deer scattering and our neighboring pack of shifters, joined in.

There was only one to go now and his time was running out.

Seventeen.

W e turned New Year into Christmas to make up for the lack of it on the twenty fifth. The feast Jay and Taylor put out would rival anything my Mum could have come up with and there were even presents. It gave me hope for the coming year, a good start could only lead on to better things.

At least that's what I kept telling myself.

After washing every dish and piece of cutlery the kitchen possessed, I sat up on the bench and watched Cody finish putting the last few things away. Everyone else was playing a game or watching TV, I wasn't entirely sure. The laughter that came from them was nice to hear and I wanted the day to last forever.

Could this be how my life would carry out once Damon was gone?

Cody seemed to think so, coming to stand in front of me I wrapped my legs around him and welcomed his kiss. Though as his hands ran through my hair and he pulled me tighter against him, I made him stop.

"Anyone could walk in." I reminded him, looking towards the entry. I knew Connor had worked out where I slept again, but I wasn't sure about the others. Even at the hotel they had assumed we had a room each.

"I don't care anymore, why not let them know?"

"What will they think?" I didn't want this to change their opinion of me, I had worked hard to make them accept and respect me.

"Does it matter?"

He moved in again and the awkward cough from the doorway had him leaping backwards while my face went bright red.

Guess he did care after all.

"Oh please, don't mind me." Connor teased, going to the fridge.

"It wasn't..." The excuses were about to come pouring out of Cody and I couldn't hide my amusement.

"Yeah right. Keep telling yourself that brother."

"You knew?" I asked and Connor only nodded, taking a swig of the orange juice straight from the carton.

"It's obvious, always has been. The only one who hasn't clicked on is your friend, though he did work out the other day you don't sleep in the barn anymore."

He left us with that and Cody couldn't hide his embarrassment. Here we were, thinking we had everything worked out and hidden only they knew all along. I was almost proud of them, I didn't think they had it in them to be so observant. Neither did Cody.

Cody lifted me down and we headed into the living room, taking the beanbag Cody got comfortable and to his surprise I made sure to sit with him. Not next to him or near him, finding a place between his legs and leant back against his chest. His arms fell over my shoulders and I got comfortable too ignoring the looks from everyone.

Especially Ethan's.

After a minute, things went back to normal and slowly my eyes began to close. I was warm, comfortable and felt completely safe. Better than that, I felt loved. It was a strange realization to finally understand feelings I had forgotten. I loved my pack in the wild. We travelled, hunted and lived together for years. Yet the affection was different. It wasn't like the humans, like what I allowed myself to feel for this group. It was the same kind that hurt when I thought of my parents and family, of Leanna. If I lost any of this family, it would hurt me just the same. Actually it might hurt worse as I had only just rediscovered what it felt like and I couldn't lose it again.

Waking up I was surprised to find I was in bed, and glancing towards the clock on the bed side table it was eleven thirty. It was only eight when I sat down with Cody, and I couldn't believe I had gone to sleep so early.

"Go back to sleep." He mumbled, rolling over slightly the cold section of the bed had me following him to keep warm.

"I cant."

"Yeah you can. Close your eyes." He groaned. It amused me how much he liked to sleep for an early riser. His own sleeping pattern had changed slightly to fit in with me, but I still slept for only half the time he did. Although in the last couple of weeks though he woke at the slightest movement, and I knew it was because our bond was only strengthening. Sensing each other moods didn't even require thinking, I just knew. I could feel it and my wolf was even more focused than I was and it was obvious he was the same.

Downstairs I could hear the others laughing and had no idea how I had even managed to fall and stay asleep down there, let alone be taken to bed.

Safe.

I agreed with my wolf, I felt safe here. I trusted them.

"It's nearly New Year, want to join in the countdown?" Cody yawned, sitting up slightly. I realized that would involve getting up and biting my lip, there was one other way I could imagine bringing in the New Year. He said nothing as I moved to straddle him, giving me complete control our clothes were quickly discarded.

It wasn't long before down stairs were calling out the final seconds the year and as the chorus of Happy New Year met our ears, we were to lost in each other to even care. The party that we had going on between us deserved more of a celebration than the start of a new day and keeping in spirit of the night, we had a countdown of our own making entering its final stages. Hitting our peak, we fell together slightly damp, but completely satisfied to the bed and looking into Cody's blue eyes, my future was clear.

It would always be here, and any doubt I had about that was gone.

"Happy New Year." He mumbled, his breathing as erratic as my own and all I could do in response was kiss him. In doing that, it lead to one of the best mornings of my life and the perfect start to a New Year.

--

January went by in a blur. We trained, we spied more on Damon's movements only as the weeks went by, more attention started to go towards the things on the ranch that needed to be taken care of. With the worst of the winter over, it was time to check fences, ready the cattle and start to plan for the year. Jay and Cody took care of all of that and Connor had work to do on the accounts. His genius wasn't just with computer, but with numbers and I also learnt he did college by correspondence.

Everyone seemed renewed with the start of the year. Ethan and Cody were actually getting along, in fact we all were. Nothing felt fake or like it was about it to break. It was nice to be normal and we all benefitting from it. It was like the pack when Spring arrived, you knew the hard times were over and put aside the losses suffered in the winter and focused on the future. You knew food was coming, you knew the weather would be warmer. You found hope and the strength you'd been missing to keep going.

Even in the peace you knew not to let your guard down, and sitting on the veranda as everyone went about their business – I saw they all had. Now would be the time when another pack would come to move in on your territory, ready to go after the herds in your land or the rogues would slip in to lure others away for their own pack. Maybe the yearlings would leave, set on finding their own territory or be chased out from an attempt at taking the lead that went bad.

I knew all these things would be affecting my pack in the wild. The weather was still cold and the rain still came, though we had nowhere near the same snowfall as in previous years. I couldn't wait for them to move closer, desperate to check on them. They had all been in good health when I saw them last and to leave now to find them was something I couldn't make myself do.

We had our own pack to watch over now, our time with the wolves was over and as February arrived, the snow came back. Work stopped and for the others they spent more time in town with friends, simply living as they had before I came. Ethan and I trained with Cody, and I even made sure he went out with this family every now and then.

Alone time with Ethan varied as much as the weather and while a truce had settled between him and Cody, I knew they needed time apart. Sometimes

I'd go with Cody though he was rarely left completely alone. I couldn't turn off like the others. Any sounds at night had me up, any cars from the other properties that came within hearing distance had me cautious. In town I looked at everyone suspiciously and my trust in Ethan hadn't improved. While we were also in a truce, he had done nothing to help reestablish any trust. We still had our talks about the past, plans for the future and he didn't let up about moving to Europe with him either. Now he knew about Cody and I, it only annoyed me he would think that I would leave them all behind.

"We don't have to do Valentine's Day." I was lying. The prospect of celebrating the holiday with, well my boyfriend, had my stomach in knots. I understood what giddy with excitement was now and Connor only rolled his eyes as Cody and I discussed it in the kitchen.

"Yeah we do. I'm the guy, it's a day for romance." Cody argued.

"Just do it Bianca, Taylor even has something upstairs for you to wear out tonight." Connor joined in the argument and finally giving in, my grin made my cheeks ache. "God this is sickening."

"Shut up Connor." The brothers started arguing amongst themselves and I sat back to watch. While we were all content, the change in Cody was the most noticeable. Adam told me he hadn't seen his cousin like this in so long he forgot what it was like to see him happy. Taylor agreed and with frequent calls through the computer than Connor assured me where untraceable, the friendship I had formed with Caprice gave me hope this was it for us.

The attack on Caprices' pack never came, and while we both knew it would stupid of her to let their guard down – like us, it was hard not to do.

Forgetting about Damon would be easy, the others had already started lowering his threat level from his lack of action since Christmas Eve, but I couldn't let it go. I knew he was only waiting for the right time to strike and with the talk of our valentine's day dinner in town, I let that worry be put on hold.

Just for one night.

Taylor dragged me into her room around four thirty, an hour later she had put me through a variety of torture from eyebrow plucking to hair straightening. She even put make up on me and got me into a dress. Thankfully we negotiated on the calf length boots rather than the heels and after adding a jacket and scarf, I emerged looking more like my old self than I had since I was sixteen.

"Now that's the Bianca I remember." Ethan whistled as we went downstairs, "Good to see you looking like a girl. In a dress."

"Shut up." I snapped, but it wasn't serious. He had a point though, I used to live in dresses, high heels and my girly wardrobe put Taylors to shame. These days I was different, for tonight – I was the old Bianca.

Cody came in from outside, and sensing him before he entered I already moved to greet him.

"Wow, must be serious. He cleaned out his car." Adam mocked.

"Now make sure she's back by ten, a minute over and you're both grounded." Connor joined his cousin in the teasing, yet a look from Cody had them giggling to themselves as they retreated to the living room.

"You look, different." Cody stuttered, and rather than leave we stood there awkwardly. "I mean, good. But different. You don't look like you usually do."

He was nervous.

We both were.

This was all different and new. It was a date. For all we had been through and done together, this changed – something.

The fact he on suit pants, dress shoes and a collared shirt made him look different too. In a good way.

"Thanks. So do you."

"Just go already!" Taylor pushed me towards Cody as she walked past with a pizza and taking my hand, Cody yelled bye and we left.

Now I understood what Adam had been referring to about cleaning out the car. This was new, and I realized it must have been what was under the tarp in the bike shed. It was a sleek black car that was from a different era. Getting in the roar of the engine vibrated through every inch of me and as Cody sped down the driveway, I could tell he enjoyed driving it.

"This used to be my Dads. He spent my childhood working on it and I used to help him as I got older. I still do every now and then, make sure it keeps starting and take it out for a spin."

"It's really nice." I enthused, the smell of leather from the seats was inviting and as we made it to the town, I was sad for the ride to end. I had never been in a car like it before and the history behind it only made it more special.

Dinner was amazing and we fell into easy conversation about nothing and everything. It was the most perfect date I had ever been on, complete with champagne and red roses. All around us couples in love mimicked our actions, all of us blissfully unaware of each other as we lived in our own bubbles. There was a proposal in one corner and everyone erupted in applause as the woman said yes, and yet as dessert was placed in front of us, something changed.

I felt it first.

My wolf appeared instantly, searching around the restaurant for something we weren't sure about.

"What is it?" Cody turned serious, proving again how in tune he was to my moods. I only shook my head, not sure. I felt restless, my wolf agreeing with me that it was time to move.

"I don't know, but we need to go."

I stood without thinking, moving through the crowded restaurant every step was slow and cautious and as Cody paid the bill, I followed him out onto the street. Something was missing. The crowded windows of the restaurants and cafes around us offered no clues, just like the empty streets. It wasn't something to see, rather than feel.

Or maybe it was something to see.

"Cody, that's Max." I saw the man up the street, with a couple of others and it made sense now.

'Go home. He's here.'

"We need to get home, now."

Cody said nothing, he didn't need to. The look on his face told me everything I could ever want to know and we ran down to the car leaving the roses behind.

Instead of going home, we turned early and I realized this was Adam and Taylors old house. Kane and Brett ran out to meet us and Cody parked in the garage at the side of the house. We got out and met them half way.

"Have you heard from anyone at home?" Cody demanded.

"No, nothing. What's happening?" Kane asked.

"I don't know, come on."

We all shifted and sprinted across the paddocks until the lights of the house greeted us as we reached the top of a hill. Nothing seemed wrong, until the gunshot echoed through the night and we went on with even more urgency. Getting closer we all spread apart, and crouching low against the ground I let my wolf take over.

We circled the house and I realized it was Kane ahead of me. Distracted looking for Cody, I failed to see the light being waved in our direction and dropped down just as it passed me.

"There are others here now, get the ones from inside out." I didn't know the voice and my fur instantly bristled, no one threatened my family. I wasn't the girl I was before, now if they wanted to take us down – I was able to fight back. The work truck was parked close to the paddock and I quickly jumped the fence, reminding myself Cody could look after himself and to stop worrying. The gypsy's reminder that he was a distraction, hit me hard.

Did she see this?

Crawling under the vehicle, I managed to hold back the growl as everyone was dragged out at gunpoint. Connor, Ethan and Adam were already in wolf form, but they were outnumbered. There was about twelve shifters out here and then I saw the one I wanted.

Damon.

"Where is she?" He screamed at them. Taylor started to sob against Jay who stood definitely in front of my mate.

"Who?"

The second Damon's fist swung out to punch him, I saw the movement to my left and Kane came running out to stop him. It was too late and Jay was knocked down. Everyone turned on Kane, and Damon stepped back as his pack came forward. As chaos ruled, I kept hidden urging Taylor and Jay to shift.

As if they could hear me they took the distraction as their chance, shifting and running to where I was hidden with the others. Jumping out to join them, I wasn't missed by Damon.

"Get the white and grey!"

I took the lead, keenly aware that Cody had joined us and rather than taking off across the paddocks where we had come from, l lead them to the area I knew best; the forest.

With no set path to guide us, I knew exactly where to go. Taylor was whining as she ran, her fear infecting the rest of the group as we charged on. Glancing back, the sounds of being followed were clear and Cody was leading up the rear of the pack. Brett joined us soon after and the others were gaining ground. We needed to split up.

I shifted, pointing at Taylor, Adam and Jay.

"Keeping up to the ridge. When you reach the rocks, turn right and go to the water. Cross the river, the water will weaken your scent until you get the rocky outcrop on the hill. There are caves there to hide in."

They took off, doing as I said.

"Cody, take Connor and one you reach the clearing following it back down towards your property. Connor needs to let Caprice know whats happening here incase he has planned something for them too."

I didn't get to finish before he shifted.

"I'm not leaving you!"

"Its us they want, they will follow our scent. I know this area and all the places to hide. You need to look after your brother!" I growled, my wolf coming out. She didn't want to leave him either, but we had to keep them safe. This is what we wanted to avoid, what I didn't want to happen and now it was.

"No! Get Ethan to do it!" He wasn't going to back down.

"This is because of us, you've lost your family before and I won't let you suffer through that again. This is how it is meant to be!"

"And what about you? What if I lose you?"

"Then you still have them." I patted Connors head, kissing his nose before turning to shift. Seeing the direction I turned Ethan began to run and the sounds were only getting closer.

Instead Cody grabbed my arm and his eyes frantically searched mine.

"They need you, more than I do."

I pulled my arm out his grip and shifted, taking off after Ethan it hurt to say that. I needed him more than any other person on this planet and I hoped after tonight I could tell him that.

Ethan let me guide him and we headed away from the others. The other wolves kept coming and it wasn't long before Ethan began to slow. This was why I was always telling him to train, not just with fighting, but for fitness. Wolf and human both needed their own strengths and they were so close now I could hear each breath.

We'd have to fight.

Taking him up to higher ground, we moved amongst some rocks and as the first three appeared, he didn't hold back now to make a kill. They were even more exhausted than us and as their back up appeared, the sight of the dead shifters scared them more than anything.

They kept coming. For everyone we killed, two more appeared and nine shifters later my wolf was on an adrenaline rush from her kills. Blood stained her chest, muzzle and sides. The few wounds we had, not enough to slow us down and I realized they worked on a number basis. If you saw six wolves charge at you, you would flee. Fighting wasn't their strong point.

It was only as the sound of dirt bikes reached us that I urged Ethan to run again.

It wasn't just a number game with them, but a weapon one too.

The gun shots started to follow us, the whiz of bullets splintering the wood from trees and rebounding off rocks. Ethan's own adrenaline gave him the ability to keep up with me, yet his fear was only growing.

I had seen him get shot.

Twice.

He didn't know about the second time, he never knew about Esmeralda and I wondered if I should have told him.

'Not this way!'

My wolf was seeking control, trying to guide us not only through the forest, but from the bikes and wolves that seemed to be circling us and breaking out into the clearing we both saw our mistake and my fear for Ethan was possibly greater than his own.

Damon stood waiting with two men either side of him, and each way we turned there was a gun there to block us. The wolves were taken down easily enough, and as the last few who had shifted joined us, they went back to human form. Soon each man had a gun, and I couldn't stop the growls as my wolf paced around in a circled beside Ethan, this was a cowardly attack.

"Shift. Mate." Damon demanded. His face was unreadable yet the authority in his voice was obvious. Ethan cowered beside me, and I tried to keep a clear mind. My head dropped slightly, staring up at the one the fates decided for me. And then I saw what I was looking for.

Doubt.

Fear.

He was more scared of me than I was of him. It was as if he sensed his mistake, squaring off his shoulders as the feeling in the clearing only get worse the longer I disobeyed.

Cocking the gun he aimed it at Ethan, "Do it or your pack mate dies."

The vision had Ethan in human form, if he shifted – he was dead anyway. There had to be way out of this, I had just had to find it.

All I did in response was growl more, my lips curling to reveal blood stained saliva covering my canines and I snapped my jaws. Any dominant wolf would be struggling to take over right now. The more I challenged him, the more he knew it.

'Weak coward.'

Seems some opinions never change.

"Shift pup!" Damon tried it on Ethan, his fear outweighed any chance he had over refusing him too. Using the distraction of him changing, I jumped towards Damon, set on tearing him apart. Two wolves appeared from behind him and as one knocked me over, I grabbed hold of the other, making him fall with me. Bringing my back legs up, I aimed for the softer flesh under his ribs, curling my paws with the force of the push, my nails tore into his skin.

His yelp rang out through the clearing and as the other pinned me down, I managed to grab hold of his cheek. I didn't hold back as I rolled away, the flap of his lip ripping with me. He let go before his hold became deadly on my throat and wriggling free, I didn't make that mistake. I heard someone gasp, another was throwing up as their pack mate dropped to the dirt torn apart. Looking to Damon, he only smirked .

"I told you to shift."

The shot was fired and everything stopped as I turned to watch the bullet collide with Ethan. Different to the vision, he was shot in the chest and I hadn't shifted. Could this have been his fate all along? Could I have stopped this?

With these thoughts racing through my mind, I couldn't breathe. the frantic panting I was already subjected to making me choke up as he fell. Images of my father's final moments hit me as the wolves stopped their fight, then seeing Leanna dead on the grass.

I failed her.

I failed Ethan.

Whining I went to his side, my heart breaking as I knew he was dead. Shifting I put my hands over the wound, and my hands became covered in his blood. I couldn't hold back the sob that escaped me.

"I'm sorry Ethan, I'm so sorry." I mumbled over again and again as the wound stopped leaking and the color left his face. "I'm sorry."

My wolf gained control just as I felt the warm metal being pressed against my own forehead. Looking up the dark brown eyes of Damon met mine, frantically searching them for something.

"You coward. Why do you all follow such a weak excuse of a shifter?" The fear was only directed towards me. They had seen me take down two of their pack mates after doing the same to the others. "I mean it. What kind of Alpha hides behind a gun?"

I was pushing him to far, the way his hand was trembling told me his wolf was fighting to take over.

"Pathetic."

"Shut your mouth she-wolf!" He roared, and in the second he raised his fist I knew he was planning on hitting me with the gun. Ethan was dropped and seeing my opening, I lunged towards him. He easily stumbled back-wards and the gun fell from his hand.

"You should have killed me when you had the chance, mate." I growled, my fist colliding with his cheek before he could try to defend himself.

He didn't need to defend himself. He had his pack surrounding me to do that and as I got in my third blow and went to strangle him, two men pulled me off him. With my arms restricted I kicked out with my legs, acting like I had gone insane. In some ways I had.

Another helped him up and holding his jaw, his gaze was deadly.

I welcomed it.

Cody's howl met my ears and everyone froze. It was like playing with children and freeing my arm I swung around the man who had the other, knocking him under the chin.

What I didn't expect was the shot to my leg and as the pain ripped through my body, I stumbled to the dirt. Before I could focus and try to defend myself, the pain that filled my skull told me it was too late and everything disappeared.

Eighteen.

Damon watched as the housekeeper cleaned Bianca's wound. She didn't flinch in her unconscious state as the bullet was removed. Damon was completely enthralled by his sleeping mate. It was hard to imagine barely an hour ago he had witnessed her tear apart two of his pack and was also ten men down thanks to her. If he had not seen it himself, he never would have believed she had been capable of doing it.

Her dark hair was spread out on the pillows, surrounding her like a dark halo, and his eyes lingered for a second to long on her more than kissable mouth that so far had only spat venom at him.

It wasn't supposed to be like this.

Bianca looked completely innocent as she slept. The blood and dirt that had covered her skin had also been cleaned away and her arms looked more muscular than some of his guards. His wolf was just as hypnotized by her beauty as the human, the urge to guard her stronger than the one to kill her. In some ways Damon reasoned it was a good thing she had taken out his closest four. If he had learnt she was alive when they were, his own punishment for not completing his orders would have been just as severe.

"Anything else sir?" The older woman stood, and holding the bowl of bloodied cloth she was scared to leave the girl alone with him. A simple flick of his hand had her leaving and sliding the door closed behind her they were left alone.

If Bianca wasn't drugged to make sure she didn't wake after being knocked unconscious, Damon may have even feared her. Her beauty hid a nature as cruel as his own, he was certain of it and it only added to her mystique. She had no hesitation in killing his men, in going after him. The gypsy's prophecy weighed heavily on his mind and the woman had been more than eager to disclose her location during their last session. For someone who could see the future, even she didn't see that his mate was alive until he told her so.

"The girl from that night is not the same one you will meet now. She is older, stronger, wiser, but she cannot deny the bond you share. She just needs to believe in it."

He received no visions from her crystal ball, the darkness that came was due to the future being undecided. Damon couldn't believe his fate still dangled in the hands of the woman opposite him. Could he kill her again?

'You can't do it.'

His wolf was right. He hadn't been able to bring himself to end her life the first time, turning the task over to the others instead. Was he as weak as she said? There was no hesitation in her assault on him. Had she been given the chance, she would have succeeded in his demise and that was something he just couldn't let happen again.

Against his better judgment he sat beside her, daring to reach out and stroke her cheek; her hair. Yet the scent of another male was all over her, one he recognized from the ranch she had been living on. A new rage washed over him, one fueled by jealously. He was tempted to wake her now, demand to know who he was, but resources were limited in the air and he needed to get control of the situation before he could wake her.

He placed a gentle kiss on her forehead, breathing in her scent as he did so and she stirred slightly - moving away from him. The frown that appeared from the contact had him growling and he stormed out of the cabin. He needed time away from her think because around her that wasn't possible and he needed to work out what was going to happen once the plane landed.

--

Wake up!

Wake up!

Wake up!

The constant screaming in my head only added to the agony I was in, but it worked. I was awake. Reaching out for Cody, the other side of the bed was empty and cold causing me to open my eyes. That movement alone let the memories come flooding back and I sat up so quickly, the head spin that followed had me curling in the fetal position on the bed until it passed.

The last thing I remembered was fighting Damon, then something came from behind.

'Coward.'

His scent was everyone around me and taking a slower look around the room, I knew I was definitely not on the ranch anymore. My wolf was urging me to shift and obliged. Things didn't improve being in wolf form, but the tingling on my leg was fixing the bullet wound.

'We need to get out'

Obviously.

The room had no windows, and the light was built into the wall above the mirror. Didn't take a rocket scientist to know that it was double sided and with her limp disappearing my wolf laid down underneath it. Where the hell were we? Pressed against the wall, we tried to hear for any movement on the other side. It was either re-enforced, empty or they were very quiet as there no noise.

We stayed there for what felt like hours and finally we were able to make out some voices.

"She woke up about two hours ago, shifted and hasn't moved since."

"Feed her. See if that can lure her out."

Seconds later a tray appeared through the slot on the door with a bottle of water, an apple and a chunk of raw steak. My wolf licked her lips, but we managed to avoid the temptation it offered.

"Still no movement?"

"Maybe she passed out down there?"

"Wake her up then!"

The shrill beeping of an alarm echoed about the empty room, the sound bouncing off the walls like nails running down a blackboard and groaning my wolf put her paws over her head which was nowhere near as effective as hands over ears.

"Still nothing?"

"Wait and do it again."

For over an hour this went on, all because we didn't move from under their window. My wolf had healed me now, and while the food and water were tempting, we weren't moving.

"Well, let's just check on her in case she reacted to the drug or something." The room became silent and she quickly slipped under the bed, hiding in the dark as the door creaked open. Looking up from underneath, three sets of boots appeared their panic seeped through the room like the gust of fresh air.

"She isn't here. You said you were watching the whole time!" the one to the left growled.

"There is nowhere for her to get out!" The middle didn't hide his surprise.

The one of the left moved towards the mirror, banging on the wall and floor as if checking for a trap door. As he leant down to feel the ground, we awkwardly got up and before they could make a grab at us we ran past, knocking the red button outside the door. It shut quickly leaving them in there and so far our record of escaping confinement was in our favor.

Running down the corridor she used her shoulder to push against the green button and sure enough the wall in front of us slid open. I wasn't expecting to be running out into gardens, and glancing behind the building looked like your usual everyday shed.

Tilting her head up, the breeze that came by offered no clue as to where we were. There was nothing familiar other than the salty tang to the air and taking off towards the fence line, it was going to be easier to try and get out compared to standing around trying to work out where we were.

We didn't make it that far as four wolves appeared from over a hedge in front of us and turning two men with guns were coming down from the side of the shed. Again the odds were against me, and instantly I went into defense mode. One of the four stepped back, and he was the one I went for first. The female was quick to help him as I tore at his shoulder and with his flesh in my mouth; I spat it out as she went for my neck. Lowering myself, I grabbed her paw biting and shaking my head until she yelped and as the other sprang forward, I took off.

The sounds of the guns made me go faster and finding the fence line I looked for a break or a way to climb out, yet one of the others managed to tackle me down. He was a big wolf, more than double the size of mine and pinning us, we couldn't find a way out of his hold.

So I shifted.

Not expecting it, he stepped back, cocking his head to the side curiously. That changed as I punched him, throwing myself around his neck. He stumbled as I tried to climb him, but he was smart and dropped down. Rolling to the side, I felt him panic as I kept hold of his neck. He was too big for me to try and snap it and as he rolled on top of me, his weight was crushing to my human form and I was struggling to breath.

The two men with guns appeared as he moved off me I was left gasping for breath from where he had winded me. The duo grabbed me roughly by the arms to stand. The wolves all circled, snarling and snapping in my direction yet all them froze as Damon appeared walking down the path.

"So you're awake then?" He greeted severely, looking at the two wounded wolves and panting giant.

"We will take her back to the shed Sir." One of the guards muttered, and instead he shook his head.

"Why? She has already escaped once you morons." He grabbed my arm and pulled me closer, the look he sent them clear and they all backed down. "Come on."

"Go to hell." I spat on his face as I glared at him, not stupid enough to try anything else with two guns pointed at me. Disgusted he pulled a tissue from his jacket pocket and wiped his face, glaring right back. I braced myself for his attack, not expecting him to instead take off his jacket and hand it to me.

"Put it on."

"No."

"Do it." The giant wolf growled; stalking closer and rolling my eyes I did as he asked. "Inside."

Still dragging me along by the arm, we headed inside. This wasn't the LA mansion, so where the hell were we?

The same old shifter who had bought me water in the library met us at the door and he roughly shoved me in her direction.

"Clean her up." He ordered, before turning to me. "Try anything and everyone has a shoot to kill order if you step one foot outside this house."

He disappeared down the corridor and the woman smiled sadly at me. "Come on, this way."

While it wasn't the mansion from before, it was just as decadent. We went up a flight of stairs and with the curtains all closed I couldn't see outside and one at the end of the hall we went through a bedroom to the largest en suite I had ever seen. The bath was more like a swimming pool and I stood in the corner while she went about preparing it.

"I'll give you some privacy." She smiled so quickly it would be easy to miss and sure enough I was left alone in a bathroom that would rival the Presidents. The water was heaven, the soft aroma of the rose scented bubbles filled the space and just for a minute I forgot where I was and why I was there. Sitting back against the headrest, I found the button for the jets and my tired muscles welcomed the treat.

What are we going to do?

'Hide.'

We weren't allowed to step foot outside the house, but if we could disappear in it we could go from there. The towels were even more amazing than the bath. Soft and cuddly, it was like wrapping a teddy bear around my body and leaving the room, the bed was covered in a variety of clothing appropriate for the warmer climate. Choosing jeans, flats and simple singlet I dried off my hair and had a look around the room. Decorations were minimal and there wasn't even a coat hanger in the wardrobe to use as a weapon.

Peeking out the door, no one was around and leaving the room tried the others. All were locked and creeping down the hall, I found a living room. Going inside the TV would have the guys drooling and thinking of them hurt too much to do again. I didn't even know if they were OK, anything could have happened after I was knocked out.

It wasn't that simple, even with the help of my wolf trying to block off the emotions threatening to take over. The fact Ethan ended up being shot didn't help and rather than finding a hiding place, I curled up with a cushion in the corner and screamed into it before hysterically starting to sob.

It wasn't intentional, but I did end up hiding.

After my crying fit I managed to fall asleep and from where I laid down, the drapes had covered me slightly. Either way, you wouldn't have noticed me and with the shouting downstairs, no one had.

"Why are you fucking useless retards even here? Why?" Damon was screaming. If I had lost control before, he not only lost it but it had also flew across the country. It was the sound of someone else crying that lured me from my spot, more out of a morbid fascination with the world I had just been pushed into.

The maid from earlier sat on the top step against the wall holding her cheek and that was where the crying came from. I instantly felt guilty, not thinking of how my actions would impact others around here. Especially the innocent ones like her.

I swiftly moved to her side, and she shied away from my touch as I reached out to help her stand. I kept an ear out on the argument and helped her stand, frowning at the purple bruise that hadn't started to heal yet.

"I'm sorry." I whispered, leading her back into the bathroom. Getting a washcloth I put it under the cold water for a moment before wringing it out and folded it to press against her cheek. "I don't even know your name."

"I'm Hannah." She took over holding the cloth and the sounds of a door slamming had the windows rattling through out the building. "He thinks you escaped again."

"He can think what he wants. He's only going to kill me and I'm not going to make it easy for him."

"It's not easy for him Bianca. If anything, you doing this is probably helping."

"What?"

"He's mad, so when he does find you – it will be easy for him to end it before thinking it through." Clearly the innocent old lady act was just that, an act.

"This is my life we're talking about." I growled.

"I know, I'm sorry. I didn't mean it like that. It'll be easier for you too. He isn't known for being merciful. The things he put those Alphas through..." Her voice drifted as did her gaze and I knew she was talking about Caprice and Brian.

"I'll be sure to return the favor."

"An old Confucius saying goes, before you embark on a journey of revenge, dig two graves. I hope you know what you're doing." She took my hand and squeezed it gently.

"How's your cheek?" I changed the subject, not wanting to dwell on my death.

"I'll heal. I better get back to organizing dinner."

She had already started to heal; slowly. I wondered how she ended up here and just how often that happened and let her go. I shadowed her down the hall, listening out for any movement and downstairs was now empty.

I sat where I had found Hannah, completely lost as to what my plan was actually going to be. While no one was around, I should at least work out the layout of the house and started to walk around cautiously. The dining room was near the kitchen and from the sounds down there Hannah wasn't the only one here to do the cooking.

Most doors were locked and finding a library, another living room and games room, going into the study I ran for the phone.

The fact Cody answered had me biting my tongue to stop from crying, and closing my eyes fresh tears made their escape as I held my breath.

"Hello? Hello?"

"Are you all OK?"

"Bianca? Shit! Where are you?" He demanded.

"I don't know, but you're all OK?" I asked again desperate to know.

"We're fine, Ethan. He…"

"I was there, I got knocked out and when I woke up I was here. I can smell the ocean, but that's all." I realized I should have asked Hannah, but I'd already put Cody and his family in enough danger.

"I will find you, Connor is already working on it. I love you Bianca, I promise I will find you."

"You love me?"

"Think I only kept you around for your cooking abilities?" He teased, though even the humor was strained in his tone. I let out half a sob that was mixed with a laugh, only before I could find the ability to answer – Damon was back.

'Hide.'

I hung up, wiping my eyes and tried to focus. All I could hear was Cody telling me he loved me and rather than hide, I sat down at the desk. That was enough to wake me up and just like Caprice had said from the other house, a younger Bianca was smiling at me.

I picked up the frame, completely lost in the memory of the image. It had been just before my birthday, just Leanna taking stupid pictures like she always used to do. I hated her taking them, now I wished I'd been the one obsessed with taking photos or at least got her to pose in them with me.

I couldn't help but wonder how he got it. And if he had this, what else did he have?

"Make yourself at home." Damon strode into the room, and looking behind him I knew he was alone. It was the first time I could properly look at him, but I was still distracted.

He was calm; too calm.

"Well no one gave me the tour so I did my own." I put down the picture frame; thankful my hands weren't shaking like my insides.

"Find anything interesting?" He walked over to a cupboard and opening it, pulled out a couple of glasses and a bottle of something brown. Sitting on the opposite side of the desk, he filled both of them and pushed one towards me.

"Where did you get that?" I pointed at my picture and he raised his eyebrow curiously before sipping on the bourbon. Leaning back in the chair he was the one in control and my wolf wasn't impressed.

Everything he did was slow and deliberate. Our first meeting had him acting erratic and desperate, completely fighting the internal battle with his wolf. Clearly they had resolved their issues. His calm presence did nothing to calm me and his cocky arrogance was soon back in action.

Confidence radiated off him. He was well groomed and clearly put effort into keeping up appearances. Being so close to him now I understood why others feared him, and looking him in the eyes there was nothing there but darkness. If I thought Cody and I were broken, we were merely dented compared to him.

"I've gathered a few things along the years."

"Of course you have." I sat back in my own chair. Holding the glass I swirled the liquid around idly.

I could tell he was assessing me, as I was him. What memory I had off Damon from that night had the gaps filled in. The moonlight didn't help me see him clearly and in the times since then it wasn't like this. Not this close and not in person.

Now I could see the slight twitch under his eye when I challenged him, the curve of the lines around his mouth and that smirk that never quite turned into a smile. If he wasn't so sure of himself, it could have been appealing. He had that bad boy charm perfected, yet if you looked deeper – that was where danger lied. It didn't take much to trigger the monster; I wanted to see just how much that really was.

"You're not scared of me are you Bianca?"

"Don't flatter yourself."

I made sure to keep eye contact, within minutes he was already starting to fidget. Watching closely his free hand was balled into a fist, and the smirk was turning into more of a scowl.

"Something wrong Damon?"

"Not at all, do you not drink?" He pointed out my glass before sipping his own as if to make a point.

"No, I've never been able get a taste for it." I smiled, trying to appear as innocent as I could.

His eyes narrowed and standing, he towered over me from where I sat. Simple intimidation that wasn't going to work and again the slight twitch under his eye appeared as I looked at him expectantly. His anger was being contained, and I didn't understand how or why.

"Where are your guard dogs? I'm surprised you're able to come in here without hiding behind them." I continued to taunt him, and my wolf was waiting for her chance to be let out.

"You think I'm a coward." He growled.

'Yes'

"Didn't I tell you enough before? Oh right, you had someone attack me from behind unsuspecting or was that you? I didnt get a chance to see." I snapped, my own anger starting to rise as I thought of the weak attack.

To my disappointment, he still didn't bite.

"Dinner is at seven, I have something you might be interested in. Mate."

My wolf growled, the vibration in my chest clearly heard by Damon and for a second I thought that alone was enough to trigger him. I half smiled, trying to look just as cocky as he did and it didn't go unnoticed. Damon took a deep breath as I dragged out my response, playing with him how he intended to play with me.

"Wouldn't miss it for the world." I answered sarcastically, glaring at him as he walked out.

Seconds later the smashing of glass sounded out and finally smiling, I sat back in the chair and put my feet on the desk comfortably.

Lifting my own glass, I toasted the air. Now I just had to get through dinner.

Nineteen.

B eing seated to Damon's left, while he sat at the head of table annoyed my wolf and made it harder to stare at him directly. Arriving late should have been impossible to do considering I was barely a hundred meters away from the dining room, but at seven thirty, I made my grand entrance.

The large wolf from earlier, who I learned was called Dean, had been the one to retrieve me from the upstairs living room. Size didn't matter, unless you were being crushed underneath a larger opponent and my wolf loved the challenge he posed. We hadn't come across another shifter we couldn't take down, and she was eager to try again. He seemed able to sense it and I refused to show him any submission.

I never intended to go down there at all, so Dean's arrival only helped delay the inevitable. Our fight had been mostly word based, seeing who could scare the other. In the end he threatened to pick me up and carry me downstairs, so telling him I'd like to see him try is how I ended up at the table.

The fact I was starving didn't help my resolve not to eat and so I picked at the roast meat idly. It wasn't long before my stomach won and I'd cleared the plate. Guards were positioned outside the door and it was Hannah who came in to fill up glasses and clear plates. She had being invisible perfected and my wolf even missed her coming in a couple of times.

The silence between us only grew and remembering what he had said earlier, I decided to break it.

"So what do you have that I might be interested in?" I kept my tone neutral, when in fact I was slightly curious.

The only indication he gave of hearing my was a slight raise in his eyebrow and he chewed thoughtfully for a moment.

"Considering you were carried in here, I don't think you deserve it." He thought he was amusing, slyly smiling there was a glint of mischief in his eyes as he met my own.

"Considering I haven't killed you yet, I think I do." I snapped back.

He put down his fork and sat back in the chair, looking thoughtful once again.

"That's what you want isn't it? To kill me for what I did all those years ago?"

I closed my eyes for a second as the pain in my head shot through me. My wolf saw the challenge in his words and wanted to take him up on it.

"Why am I here? You could have killed me with Ethan or anytime since then. Instead we're having dinner?" I picked up the knife beside my plate, slowly dropping my hand from the table and rested it on my thigh.

"You're here because I want you to be." He yelled. It was like flipping a switch and his fist slammed down on the table. All the glassware clinked together and the platter of food trembled as the force shook the table. His eyes seemed to glaze over, and I held my breath as he stood to stand before me. The fight in his mind was obvious and I wondered if his anger was all his own or his wolf too. Something was holding him back, just, but it was there.

'Back down. Not now.'

Panic swirled in my stomach and I was almost scared to move in case that would be the trigger he needed. My hand was close to bending to the handle of the knife, and one move towards me would have it ripping through whatever part of him I could make contact with.

The tension between us was close to catastrophe levels and after a few moments, he coughed awkwardly. His hands ran down the lapel of his jacket and I saw how they were trembling. My wolf was telling me to stay still, wait for the threat to pass and sitting upright, barely breathing I couldn't help myself.

"What is wrong with you?"

Sweat beaded along his forehead and the scowl on his face made my skin crawl. Slipping underneath the table was tempting and as the silence was drawn out, I managed to swallow without choking.

"Do you think this has been easy for me?" He growled, stepping away from his position, I tried not to flinch as he pulled my chair away from the table. "Do you think I like smelling someone else on you?"

Any walls I had in place crumbled at the mention of Cody and even my wolf fell to the back of my mind leaving me on my own.

"This is all your fault." I reminded him, surprised I could actually talk.

"My fault? You're supposed to be dead."

"Then you should have done it yourself." I hissed through gritted teeth as he leant down closer, trapping me in my chair. I tensed my arm, ready to make my attack only I didn't get a chance to do anything as his lips touched mine. Shock shut down my brain. My wolf growled, not welcoming the contact. My eyes stayed open in surprise, awkwardly looking into his.

It wasn't like kissing Cody, yet it wasn't as horrible as I told myself something like this would be. My body was uncooperative and the urge to pull away was leaving me the longer I just sat there. His arms surrounded my head as he leant against the back of my chair, and his scent was filling my mind like a toxic gas. I could tell he was assessing my reaction, waiting for me to do something.

The fact I kissed him back didn't help.

The gypsy woman had it right. I did wonder. I thought about all of it like the one who got away, only it was more than a failed romance. He was my mate. Cody got to experience time with Jill, he would have slept beside her every night. He got to know the smell of her skin, the curve of her lips and the feel of her body against his.

For just a second, I felt that thread between Damon and I glowing. The promise of it all, the temptation to experience it for myself. Life with my mate, the one who loves, protects and cherishes you above all others. The one who was meant to die for you, not be the reason for your death. Cody had Jill; had – past tense. He even admitted that when I left it hurt him more than losing her. I had everything I was raised to believe mates to be with Cody and that was where I needed to be.

I closed my eyes, not willing to risk letting him see what was coming. My left hand slid along his arm, holding his shoulder to steady to his torso as I shifted my position slightly to give me room to move my right arm. With all the effort I could subtly muster, I rammed the steak knife into his abdomen.

'Run!'

I didn't need to be told twice.

Gasping he stepped backwards, instantly reaching to the handle and removed the knife. I knocked the chair to the side and scrambled up, running to the door and past Dean who hesitated in running after me as he turned to look into the dining room.

"STOP HER!"

The rage in his order has goose bumps breaking out all over my skin and I knew I should have listened to my wolf. Now wasn't the time for this, and I should've gone at least gone for his neck.

I shifted as I got out the front door, the driveway my path out of the complex and my wolf ran faster than I ever could. Dean was behind me before I had even got half way, the larger wolf snapping dangerously close to my tail. He went to lunge at me to knock me down, and expecting it my wolf managed to swerve to the side. She weaved her way towards the gate, making his next attempt just as pointless and as he tried one last time – he got us.

In a wrestling mass of fur and teeth, we rolled from the gravel to the lawn. My wolf was in a frenzy, blinded by rage which only grew for each bite or nip he placed on us and kicking up at his jaw, she managed to get herself free of his attack. We kept running, the gate was barely meters away and this time the grey and white wolf that knocked us over wasn't going to let us back up.

Damon.

Standing, my wolf mimicked his movements as we circled each other. His wound wasn't healing yet, but it didn't seem to slow him down. The scent of his blood had her thirsty for more and a part of me knew, this wasn't the fight we had been wanting. This wasn't a battle for life, rather one for dominance. He wanted us to give in to him, and fortunately my wolf and I agreed on this.

Never.

Minutes in I realized his intimidation wasn't for show. That cold and calculating manner of the human was reflected in the wolf, yet even though Damon wasn't in control his bites never pierced the skin, even when ours did. He was holding back. I saw it before my wolf. She was mad with anger and not thinking straight. I had never experienced her like this, not even when I'd lost control of her before.

Her mind was on her mate. Like Cody had attacked me, she was wanting to make him suffer for hurting her and he was letting it happen. I couldn't' see a peaceful reunion after this and had never fought so hard to get her to back down. It wasn't working, she was to powerful. When I could I tried to keep an eye on what was going on around us.

As expected he had his pack surrounding us, some in wolf form and others with their guns. Dean was pacing near two humans and out of all the wolves he was the only threat; well him and Damon.

If my wolf wasn't biting or attacking him, she was growling and snarling to the point she was foaming at the mouth like a rapid dog. Her exhaustion was only growing, so was his. He defense got slower. So did her attacks. I was proud of how well she kept her ground, despite that fact it would only take one signal from him and we'd be dead or have a pack of wolves set upon us.

Circling each other again, I couldn't see it lasting much longer. Both wolves were on shaking legs, panting heavily and neither a clear victor. The pack were all unsettled, unsure if they should have been assisting their Alpha and most were just enjoying the show. Slowly the wolves stopped moving and it was almost as if the two animals were having their own conversation as my wolf whined and he answered, raising his paw slightly to scratch at the ground I felt control come over me with the urge to shift.

To my surprise he did the same.

We were both bruised and bloodied, the wound from the knife still open and unhealed. It wasn't bleeding now though, but it hadn't sealed.

"Put her in the shed, if she escapes again you know what to do." He was sucking in breaths as if he had been running a marathon, then again so was I and my body felt like jelly as two men stepped forward to grab me. Damon stalked off towards the house, limping slightly I could tell he was trying not to show it.

The fact he hadn't killed me and that I was still standing had everyone in awe so as the guards came to grab me, I decided to use this to my advantage.

"Do not touch me. I am not going in there." I growled, finding my last scrap of energy to stand tall and proud. The fact the guards hesitated filled me with confidence and Damon stopped to turn. This was it.

If he gave in now, the power had shifted and this was how the victor would be decided upon.

"Fine." I looked over to him as he crossed his arms over his chest, not missing the way he shuddered at the movement. I realized then I made a mistake, the sense of victory was obvious. "Put her in my room."

"What?" The guard asked, not sure if he heard right. Neither was I and this felt more like a death sentence than anything else I'd experienced lately.

Damon didn't answer, disappearing inside. No one moved and finally Dean shifted, grabbing my arm. "You all heard him. Move it, now."

I was tempted to try and make him carry me again as the walk back to the house had every muscle in legs burning and getting to the door, he hesitated as much as I did. I looked at his hand that he had wrapped around my arm, his dark skin made my slight tan appear moon light white.

"You bought this on yourself." He warned, finally opening the door.

"What did you do?"

"Lost a fight, my pack. My dignity." He growled.

It made sense, he had all the characteristics of an alpha and now he was here working as a lap dog.

"Why not try again?" 'Right now, hit him while he's down.' I thought to myself. I had a feeling Damon would stoop that low so maybe he needed a taste of his own medicine.

"I have. Twice. You learn to choose your battles little she-wolf. Remember that."

We went past the lower living room and finding a stair case, he pushed me up the first couple and blocked the way out. We both knew I had no choice other than going up. I couldn't fight him now, and I had no idea how I was going to make it up the stairs. Holding onto the wall, I practically crawled and getting to the top it was a whole other level like the one I had first come across. Slowly I walked towards the open door, trying to muster as much poise as I could and entered.

He wasn't there.

Hannah appeared from the bathroom, frowning as she saw the state I was in.

"Come here." So I obliged, letting her lead me into another bath. I struggled to stay awake in the warmth of the water, the burning sensation lessening as my body finally relaxed and started to heal. Hannah washed my hair with the careful patience a mother would show a child, helping me wash away the blood and getting out my cuts had healed to pink scars and the bruises were changing from purple to green. Soft silky pajamas found the way onto me and as we went into the bedroom, she slipped right out. Damon sat on the bed, freshly showered and he didn't look up as I started to follow after Hannah.

"Come here."

It was a command, not a request and I turned slowly to look at him. He had a pair of sweatpants on, but no shirt. The knife would was still red and sore while his own bruises and cuts were like my own.

"I'm not going to bite."

Against my better judgment I moved closer to the bed, and he motioned to sit in front of him. Folding my legs underneath myself, we sat crossed legged opposite each other. I wanted to sleep, and after the bath, sitting on the comfortable bed wasn't helping stay awake.

"I was going to give this to you after dinner, so I'll do it now."

His hand was balled into a fist and I watched as he uncurled it. My hands flew to my mouth, trying to hide my gasp and my wolf offered no help in keeping my emotions in check as for the third time that day, I cried. The soft lamp light caught every corner of the diamond in his hand, the colors shining up from it like a piece of heaven. The silver snake chain was still perfectly new and my hands were shaking as I took it from him. Next to the clasp there was a tiny oval disc and the curling shape of the B my Mum had engraved on it hadn't aged a day since I lost it.

"May I?" He offered and I nodded, letting him take it to put it back where it belonged around my neck. He gently dropped my damp hair down against my back and clutching the diamond, I fell forward – away from him to cry some more. The irony of the fact Damon was then trying comfort me over something he did wasn't lost on me, but I was too tired to care.

Thankfully it didn't last long, and pushing him away I got up and locked myself in the bathroom. He made no effort to get me out and wedged between the wall and the counter, I fell asleep on a towel.

I woke up a couple of hours later, my wolf was more active as I needed her and we managed to open the door without any sound. Damon slept soundly where I left him in the middle of the bed and getting out of the bedroom, I headed for the study.

"Bianca?" Cody answered straight away and spying a clock, I had an idea on how we could work out where I was.

"What time is it where you are?"

"Ah, just on midnight. Why?"

"It's just gone two am here."

"Anything else? Connor can't find anything on Damon, no accounts have been touched, nothing. Are you OK?"

"I'm OK. Is Caprice OK?"

He sighed, and I instantly felt worried.

"Yeah, nothing has happened up there."

"And you are all OK?"

"We're as good as we can be with you being taken." He growled and my wolf was whining in my mind, wanting to go to him.

"I miss you, all of you. Even Adam."

Cody laughed, not his usual one but it was close enough.

"He misses you too."

"I love you Cody."

I hadn't said it before, I wasn't sure if I even knew what love was – saying it to him felt right.

"I love you too Bianca. How about we skip on Valentine's Day next year?"

My laugh was genuine and yet a stray tear managed to escape at the prospect of even having another Valentine's Day.

"I think that would be a great idea."

9 781787 991101